A Million Years in the Future

By Thomas P. Kelley

Cover art by Hannes Bok

ISBN 978-1-7334086-8-4
Cover layout by Michael Greylord

A Million Years in the Future originally appeared as a serial in the January, March, May, and July 1940 issues of *Weird Tales.*

ALSO AVAILABLE

Want to get an e-book for free? *The Infernal Bargain and Other Stories* is available exclusively for DMR Books mailing list subscribers. Go to www.DMRBooks.com and get your copy now!

ABOUT THE AUTHOR

Before Thomas P. Kelley (1905-1982) became the self-proclaimed "King of the Canadian pulp writers," he worked with his father's traveling medicine show, then had a brief career as a boxer. *Weird Tales* was the first pulp to publish his stories. During the late '30s and early '40s he regularly contributed to *Weird Tales, Uncanny Tales,* and other pulps. His best-known work is *The Black Donnellys,* a supposedly non-fiction account of a family of criminals who were murdered by an angry mob. Originally published in 1954, *The Black Donnellys* has sold hundreds of thousands of copies.

CONTENTS

Chapter I
Jan of the Purple City

This is a story of triumph and failure, a story of what happened when the Black Raiders came from the stars with their vapors of death; the strange tale that I, Jan, Prince of the Purple City and last man of my world, the planet Earth, tell of the year 1,001,940.

Nor will there ever be a sequel to this story. Never again will the ebon hordes bring terror from the skies. Never again will their spaceships come to bear our maids to the orgies of their temples, or carry fettered slaves and warriors to the sands of their arenas. No more will the eternal Tara flaunt her blinding beauty, or laugh while all around her are the cries and screams of the dying. The terrible Secret of the Bells was at last told to an Earthman, and mine are the hands that blew a world to a hundred trillion atoms.

And now I am alone, alone in the gathering dusk of my own planet to begin the writing of this strange narrative—Earth's last and final story. All around me are the dreary plains and moss-covered hills of what was once the bottom of a mighty ocean. Overhead the stars are growing brighter and more numerous. Soon they will appear in the great number that will encompass the heavens. Then will come the moons—those three tiny, jagged bodies— to brighten the bleak landscape with their weird and ghostly light.

And yet in the terrible silence of a lifeless world I write on and on, writing of a planet and a civilization that is no more, writing words that can never know the eyes of other than myself.

Why, then, should I continue this story, or insist on telling that which must forever remain a secret? Perhaps it is the memories of the wild adventures that were mine upon that distant world, Capara. Perhaps it is the thoughts of how I so well held my own against the swordsmen of the Eternal One, or the warriors of the Fire King who reigned on a distant sun; how I found the golden Ball of Life, beheld the great god, Time, or slew the Nine Terrible Sisters who

4

had known a million years!

But no. In these final hours I believe it is for another purpose—that I take a pride in telling of the bravery of my race, of that white-skinned, dark-haired people who are no more. For I am a Prince of the Bardonians, that proud and fearless race who were last to fall before the Migs when the terrible little brown men came to our world with their incalculable numbers, to raze our homes and steal our women.

That, of course, was eons ago. Since then our world has known many invasions from the sky—the yellow-skinned Trulls—the Saurian men of Sura—the weird, insect-like creatures with their wands of light, who came from the lost planetoid—the beautiful warrior-women from a star so distant as to be invisible to the naked eye.

And then at last the ones whose very name brought terror to our world, that shouting and barbaric horde who swept down all before them—the Black Raiders!

Through the ages, at irregular intervals the invasions had continued, while the inhabitants of our ravaged planet slowly dwindled in numbers, in power, in intellect itself. The elders of the twenty or more still remaining tribes who inhabited the ruined cities of the ancients were ever loud in telling of that fact, talking always of the great civilization and the billions our world had known as far back in the dawning as a million years ago.

And amid the crumbling grandeur of a once mighty metropolis that my people knew only as the Purple City, I, Jan, Prince of the Bardonians and the world's last man, was born a score and some four years before the death of my planet.

My father, Thargo the Just, had long been king and sole ruler of the thousand or more barbaric, almost naked people who were his subjects. It was this same monarch who had fought so bitterly against the black hordes, years ago, when last the Raiders came to loot and terrorize our world. It was this beloved ruler also, who for so long had been trying to bring about a semblance of peace between the still remaining tribes.

It is needless to mention those early years that passed so swiftly and pleasantly, while I was blissfully unaware of the wild life before me. Suffice it to say they were spent in learning the wisdom of the elders, and those who were my tutors; of the little known lands beyond our borders; of what would be expected of one of my royal lineage, as well as the strange history of the mighty ruins around me.

Nor was my physical welfare neglected. From the first it was evident nature had endowed me with an almost superhuman strength, and the sword-arm of a master. Not that powerful men were uncommon in our clean-limbed, six-foot race, but even in my teens I excelled in wrestling and all feats of endurance, and on entering into manhood found their stoutest warriors unable to withstand me in the sham duels and athletic contests that were the delight and diversion of the warrior-like Bardonian tribe.

Strength and a skilled sword-arm were ever quick to win applause with the populace of the Purple City, and to that little community I was not only their future king but an acclaimed hero as well. Even now I can recall the proud face of my sire at the shouting of my name; but far more vivid is the memory of that last night when I was summoned to his presence, where, alone amid the towering pillars of his great throne room, he spoke to me in a soft tone, for I was his only heir.

Thargo, my father, was a tall, powererful man, of almost my own height—and I am six feet four inches. Naked, except for the leather trappings and soft sandals that were the universal apparel of our planet, the terrible fate of the woman he loved, years before, had so embittered him as to make habitually stern the features of a once handsome face. And yet there was an approving light in his eyes as they met mine. He looked at me before he spoke.

"You are fortunate in more ways than one, my boy," he began, "fortunate in being endowed not only with a royal lineage, but the muscles of a Titan as well. That in itself is good. Used wisely, strength becomes a blessing, and an aid to those around you.

"But there is another side that must be considered," he added in warning, "a dangerous side as well, Jan. Used wrongly, it becomes a curse, and brands you a tyrant. Remember always those words when that brawn is called upon."

His strong fingers gripped my shoulder in a half-caress. "But I have little fear that your actions will ever bring me other than honor.

"There are only too few of us left, Jan. We cannot afford to war with the tribes that still remain. At best, our planet holds no more than fifty thousand humans, who inhabit the ruins of the once great cities that dot its dreary, war-scarred surface. Ah, but the many invasions from the other worlds have indeed taken their frightful toll, have reduced to a mockery of a once great number, a wild and war-like people—an almost naked and comparatively primitive people, when one thinks of the great spaceships and terrible weapons of the Black Raiders."

"The Black Raiders," I echoed, uttering the three most terrifying words in our universe—words young mothers frequently used to silence an unruly child.

My father nodded.

"You have never seen them, Jan. It is my prayer you never will. When last they came I was but a young man, scarcely much older than yourself. I had your lovely mother then. You were a tiny baby. I had my life before me. For thirty years no alien foot had touched our planet, and we were beginning to hope that at last the great curse had lifted, and our ravaged little universe had been forgotten by its terrible conquerors.

"And then one day they came again. Out from the great void that lies between us and their distant planet came the Black Raiders, and once more our world ran red with blood. Oh, the memories of those awful hours! Battles by day—fires by night—death and pillage all the time. Why they did not seek our total extinction is strange, for it was well within their power. It was as though they but used us for sport, and permitted the survival of a few thousand for further invasions.

"For two long weeks stark terror reigned, and when at last the ebon hordes departed in their great spaceships, sated with blood and weary of slaughter, they took our greatest treasures with them—our hardiest warriors for the sands of their arenas, our fairest daughters for the harems of their nobles. Yes; they indeed took our loved ones, and—among them was—"

Here his voice trailed off to silence, but no words were needed to complete that sentence. Well I knew what had happened. When the Black Raiders finally left they had taken the loveliest maids of the Purple City with them, among them was the beautiful girl who was the Queen herself—my mother!

There was nothing I could say, and so in silence I followed my sire to the tiny alcove at the far end of the room that led to a lofty gallery and a starlit summer night. Below us lay the crumbling grandeur of the Purple City, wrapped in slumber, for the hour was late. A night wind whistled in the ivy-covered ruins, while high overhead a million stars flashed green, blue and bright crimson.

The Bardonian King pointed to a distant, brilliant star, somewhat apart from the others, whose silvery light shone cold and unblinking.

"That is Capara—the home of the Black Raiders. That is the terrible world to which your unhappy mother was taken, long years ago. That is the awful star from which she may be looking down upon us at this very moment—sad-eyed, longing, hoping.

"So remember what I have told you this night, Jan," he concluded. "Remember that a wise king seeks not war, but peace; that a good ruler will go to any length to protect the welfare of his peo-

8

ple. But should the Black Raiders ever again come to our world, remember what was stolen from both you and me when last they were upon us."

𝕴 had, of course, expected many other nights in the company of my royal sire, but fate, which even then was spinning the impenetrable webs of the future, ordained I should see him no more, nor was I ever again to know the plains and valleys of my homeland.

Early the following morning I and four Bardonian warriors rode far to the north, and toward the distant mountains that marked the boundary of our country, in the annual inspection of its long unguarded borders. It was a barbaric-looking picture we presented in that early light. The leather trappings and soft sandals were our only raiment, while strapped to the waist of each of us was a longsword, a shortsword, a keen slender dagger—weapons whose use we had been acquainted with since childhood. The weird, fleet-footed kangs we rode but helped to complete that picture.

It was these speedy, timid beasts, kangs, which were the universal mounts of our world; and while their exact origin was not known for a certainty, it was generally supposed they had descended from a small herd the Black Raiders had brought with them on their first invasions to our planet, fourteen centuries earlier. Though possessed of an almost unbelievable speed—a kang in flight has been known to clear a twelve-foot-high obstacle with a rider on its back—their tiny pink eyes, black fur-like hair and slender legs, together with the long, solitary horn protruding from the center of the head, tended to substantiate this hypothesis and render them most unearthly in appearance.

High noon found us within a few miles of the mountain range that was our objective. We were rapidly nearing its rocky base when one of the warriors suddenly called my attention to a thin column of smoke rising upward, directly ahead. Almost at the same instant shrill cries reached us, and a moment later we were pulling up beside a little scene both grim and tragic.

There crawling slowly toward us was a grimy, blood-covered figure. Only when I had dismounted did recognition come. In our little community of some ten hundred people there was scarcely a face that was not at least slightly familiar, and the gray-haired old woman before me I knew as one who, with her son, eked out an existence in the raising and selling of young kangs which they brought to the markets of the Purple City at regular intervals. Nearby the smoldering ruins of a tiny hut were black and desolate.

The glazing eyes went wide as I knelt beside her.

"Prince Jan!" she gasped. "It—it is you?"

"Yes, mother, it is I," I nodded. "But tell me, what has happened? Who has dared to do this to you?"

I bent low to catch her words, for I could see the end was near.

"They came yesterday—the Thovians," she answered. "There were three of them. They rushed in on us and slew my son as we sat at our morning meal. Their bearded leader buried his knife in my body. Then with terrible shouts and curses they set fire to our hut, and drove off with our little herd of kangs. I was only half conscious, but dared not move, for they thought me dead and would have surely killed me had I made a sound. I waited and—and—"

She gave a little sob as she spoke, then sank back into my arms.

The Thovians! Ah, but I might have known it! That cowardly, treacherous, thieving tribe, whose crumbling city lay a hundred miles or so beyond our mountainous borders. For years we had attempted to live in concord with this neighboring people—my father willing to overlook their petty thefts and misdemeanors. This, however, was more than thievery. They had not only dared to enter our country, but had murdered its subjects as well!

My blood boiled as I wheeled to my followers.

"Look after this woman," I ordered two of them. "Give her every possible aid, and if she rallies, try taking her back to the Purple City."

"And you, Prince Jan?" asked one, a grizzled old warrior I had known since childhood.

"I am going to find the men responsible for this," I answered, vaulting to the back of my mount. "I am going to follow them to the Thovian capital if need be, and drag them back to the Hall of Justice for trial."

"But you dare not!" he cried. "No; you dare not. It's the command of your father to avoid bloodshed. He would be furious, O Prince. We must use tact and—"

"Too late for that," I shouted, motioning the two others to follow me. "This is beyond tact. This is murder. If we allow those men to go unpunished, they will be entering the Purple City next, and slitting our throats while we sleep. Tell my father I will either return with those murderers or renounce my lineage!"

The next instant my charger had sprung forward, and behind me came the others.

I could still hear the shouts of the old warrior in protest, but I took no notice of them or did other than to urge my kang on faster. I heard his shouts long after I lost sight of him, but on we went at a mad gallop, and a few minutes later were beyond the border of our own land and into a strange country where I never before had been.

Just at dusk we came to a vast and desolate landscape, a dreary, moss-covered waste that stretched away to the sky, which I knew was once the bottom of a mighty ocean.

Our ancients tell us that far back in the fogs of antiquity our planet knew many great seas; that as the ages passed they had slowly dried and vanished, till there remained but the few shallow lakes and streams we now know—adding that in a not distant day even these would evaporate, to leave an arid, waterless world.

But at the moment there was more of immediate importance than prophecies. Somewhere out on that desolate waste three murderers were hurrying with their loot to the Thovian capital. As Prince and Protector of my people, it was a duty I owed them to bring that trio to justice, and so, despite the protests of the others, I could but motion them on, and resume our tiring journey.

All that night we continued as fast as our jaded mounts would go. The stars came out and the three jagged moons sailed slowly across the sky, but still we pursued our weary way. Our age-old legends tell us that eons past those three small moons were one great satellite; that when the Migs first came to our planet, five hundred thousand years ago, there were mighty cities and millions of Earth folk living on the vast plains of its interior.

The legends have it also, that these same people refused to pay tribute to the little brown men, and that in their rage the Migs turned their terrible rays of light upon the moon—bringing instant death to its inhabitants, and rending it to the three tiny bodies we now know.

Through the night we rode. The first streaks of gray were paling the eastern sky, and it was evident the waning strength of our kangs would soon force a halt, when on topping a small hill I saw that which brought an exclamation from my lips, and sent a thrill surging through me.

There, directly below us in a little valley, was a tiny campfire; and stretched around its flickering flames, their weapons glittering in the firelight, three Thovian warriors lay in slumber.

Chapter II
Thovian Pursuit

There could be no doubt as to their identity. They were indeed the three we sought. Even from the hilltop I could make out the powerful frame and bearded features of one of them—features that readily tallied with the old woman's description of her attacker. The evil faces of the others were those of habitual thieves and murderers.

And if additional proof were needed, it was quickly given in the dozen or more black forms huddled together just beyond the firelight—fettered kangs, each of whose left front and hind legs were strapped together to prevent them from wandering away in the dark.

It was this that gave cause for an immediate worry. Kangs are notoriously timid creatures, and when frightened give the piercing little barks so familiar to our world. It was these I feared. Their sharp ears were sure to hear the slightest tread, and this would result in the shrill barks that could easily awaken the sleepers. Caution, then, was all-important. I had dismounted, and now motioned the others to do likewise and approach me.

"We will divide here," I said in a whisper. "It is our best plan. You two can encircle them from the left, while I close in from the right. Stay just beyond the firelight until you hear my signal, then draw your weapons and rush them."

"If they resist us, Prince?" came the answering whisper of one. "If they should show fight?"

"Then show fight also and—and—" But I suddenly remembered the many warnings of my father to avoid bloodshed. I could almost feel his presence, as if he were beside me awaiting my words.

"Well, try taking them alive, of course," I continued. "But remember you are to guard yourselves at all times, and be sure you take them. Be careful also, for the love of your ancestors. The slightest sound or misstep is sure to awaken the kangs, and that will mean discovery."

I waited till they had crept into the gloom, then turned to the task before me. A silent descent of the little hill was not hard. The soft, moss-like vegetation that covered the entire surface of this vast, once submerged land, made stealth an easy matter. It was not till I had come within a dozen paces of the sleepers that there was cause for alarm. Numerous dry twigs and small pieces of firewood had been strewn around, that could easily result in a loud crackling sound, were I to step upon them.

Softly I drew nearer. I could hear the rhythmical breathing of the trio, which tended to lessen the sound of my approach. I had already singled out the bearded man for my first victim. Could I gag and bind him, the capture of the others would be in order. I was within two paces of him now. Another minute and the soft stripping I carried would be thrust into his half-opened mouth and stifle any cry.

On tiptoe I came beside him and was sinking to my knees, when the man, as though warned by some subtle sense, suddenly opened his eyes and sat up!

For an instant we both stared at each other, the bearded face showing an amazement almost comical. So great was his surprise that for a second he forgot to cry out, and then it was too late. My hands flew to his throat even as his mouth opened, and the next instant I sprang upward, giving the powerful jerk that shot the startled Thovian up to and upon his feet as though he were a child.

There was but a single mishap, and yet it was enough. As the man flew upward his legs swung in the wide circle that sent them crashing against a heavy cooking-pot. In an instant it had awakened the others, who sprang to their feet, and then, simultaneously, several things happened. The bearded one sought to grapple with me. My right fist shot to his jaw with a force that dropped him, unconscious, in his tracks. Another sprang toward me with an uplift-ed knife. An instant later and he too was on the ground, disarmed and screaming from a broken wrist.

Even at the first sounds of the struggle several barks had risen from the nearby kangs—barks that were quickly taken up by the entire herd as the nervous creatures woke from their slumbers. And now these, together with the cries of the man at my feet, rose up in a frightful din to split that ghostly pre-dawn light.

As the remaining warrior saw the last of his comrades go down his hand flew to his sword, and I whipped out my own weapon. For a moment he stood thus, as though uncertain whether to engage with me or not, then, with a little cry, wheeled and dashed away at the same instant that my two companions appeared in the firelight.

"After him!" I shouted to them. "Don't let him get away!" In the cold spectral light, I could see their hurrying forms for a moment, and just ahead of them the running Thovian. Then the whiteness enveloped the three of them.

I turned to the two men at my feet. The one with the broken wrist was still groaning, but it was his companion with whom I wished to speak. Presently the bearded one came to himself, and at a word from me rose slowly to his feet, a hand nursing his swollen jaw.

"You are a Thovian?" I began.

He glared at me defiantly.

"Answer me!" I snapped.

"I am a Thovian." His reply was in a surly tone. "A Thovian and an honest man, as is my companion here. We have done nothing. Why did you attack us?"

"Who owns those kangs?" I went on, ignoring his question as I pointed to the little herd that had gradually quieted and were now watching our every move.

"I do," he retorted, "and what of it? I was taking them to the markets at the Thovian capital, and we camped here for the night.

Nothing wrong in that, is there?"

"Not if they're yours. But entering another country and killing to get them throws a different light on the matter."

$\mathfrak{J}$ had expected a vigorous denial, but his answering words were both incriminating and a surprise.

"Well," he growled with a shrug, "I cannot see what you are going to do about it, even if I did. If the Bardonians are fools enough to leave their borders unguarded, and are unable to protect what is theirs, they must expect such things. But enough of that. What I want to know is who are you, and what do you intend doing with us?"

"I am taking you back to the Purple City for trial," I told him. "You will be given a fair one, I promise you—much fairer than a Bardonian could hope for, were he on trial for a similar offense in your own capital.

"But I can also promise you will be under a close scrutiny," I added, for the eyes of the two men had met in a quick glance, "and that at the first attempt to escape I will complete the beating I have so well begun. Remember," I concluded, "that I am just waiting for some excuse."

As I spoke, my two companions appeared, breathing heavily. There was no sign of the third.

"He escaped us, Prince," cried one. "The fellow had the speed of a young kang. He dashed away as though a hundred devils were at his heels, and is doubtlessly making for the nearby Thovian capital at this very minute, to bring the help that will release his comrades and capture us."

Plainly there was not a minute to be lost. The tales we had heard of Thovian torture were enough to make us realize what to expect, were we to be taken by them. Tying the prisoners, we lashed them securely to the backs of two of the kangs, and transferred our own riding equipment to fresh mounts. A meager meal was then hastily swallowed, the fetters of the kangs untied, and we had begun that ill-fated journey homeward.

All that day we pushed on as fast as the herding of the young kangs would allow. The nervous, wiry creatures seemed to go in every direction but the right one, and the constant riding back and forth, made necessary to head them off, was not only tiring to the mounts we rode, but to ourselves as well.

Night found us still several miles from the borders of our own country, and almost ready to drop from fatigue; so it was a tired little party that finally went into camp—a hungry little party as well, for by this time our scanty supplies had been consumed. I volunteered to remain on guard, and a few minutes later the others were in a deep slumber.

The hours passed slowly; then along toward dawn one of the warriors arose to relieve me while I sought a few precious moments of sleep. It was a rest I had long looked forward to, as many hours had passed since I had known slumber, but even then it was to be denied me. It seemed I had scarcely closed my eyes before I felt the hand of the warrior on my shoulder, and heard his voice in my ear.

"Arise, Prince Jan," he was saying. "A great party of mounted men are in the distance, and riding swiftly toward us."

I sprang to my feet. It was early morning, and in that clear light the moss-covered waste was visible for miles. Ahead of us rose the great mountain range we sought to reach—our borders. A two-hour journey should see us in our own country once more. But far away on the horizon behind was that which at once centered my attention, a great company of mounted men whose identity needed no two guesses: Thovian warriors seeking to aid their comrades and capture us!

There was but one course, and I took it.

"Release the kangs and ride!" I shouted. "We must try to reach the mountains before they are upon us. It is our only chance. Once there we can find a hundred hiding-places among the hills that lie

17

within the cliffs."

"If you can reach them, Bardonian," taunted the bearded captive from where he lay, for already he had seen the distant warriors, and guessed their meaning. "If you can reach them. And I'll wager my life against a dead kang's hoof that high noon finds our positions changed, with you the prisoner and me the captor."

He turned to the other. "It means rescue, comrade! It means our rescue!" he cried.

"Perhaps," I answered, raising the bound man to his feet, and lifting him to the back of his mount. "But I promise it will be one you will never live to know."

Another moment and we were all in our saddles. Then with the little herd galloping before us we set off toward the mountain range which, could we reach it in time, might prove to be our haven. Of course we could not hope to equal the speed of our pursuers, handicapped as we were with the herding of the young kangs, but the pace we set was certainly a fast one, and at the end of an hour's time we rode out of that great waste to the dusty, boulder-strewn ground that was the last stretch between us and our goal.

Away on the horizon to the south was a far-flung mass of crumbling grandeur that had been a mighty city, thousands upon thousands of years ago—a city similar to the countless other ruins that dotted the invasion-scarred surface of our ravaged world. It was these that told of the many millions, and the wonderful civilizations our planet had once known; these and the hoary legends of the ancients that gave us our only knowledge of the past; though later, on a distant world, I was to see the history of my planet slowly unfolded on a glittering, magical mirror, while beside me the glorious Queen of the Stars interpreted the various scenes.

All this while the Thovian horde had been steadily gaining, till at length we could plainly hear the clanking of their weapons and equipment. The many hours of travel were beginning to show on the beasts we rode, and now as their speed continued to lessen and the warriors came nearer, a roar of triumph arose from the ranks behind as they realized our mounts were weakening.

By this time I had given up all hope of finding safety in the mountains ahead. Even if we were able to reach them, there would be no time to hide ourselves and our little herd before the Thovians would be upon us. Another ten minutes was all they needed. That this was realized by the two who rode beside me was evident by their continuous glances backward, and their half-unsheathed weapons.

For my own part I had decided not to go into the hereafter alone. I would at least see how many of those shouting fiends I could take with me. I knew that my end would be a blow to my royal sire, but I felt that his grief would be somewhat tinged with pride upon learning of how I had attempted to avenge his subjects.

And so, as that howling horde came closer and the drumming hoof-beats told the nearness of death, I hardened my heart, and drawing my longsword, set myself for the supreme struggle. For an instant it had come to me that by holding the bearded one at my sword's end I might force the Thovians to at least a temporary halt.

But this was just as quickly abandoned as I realized that my captive was of no special importance, and that it was our herd, our mounts and our own lives that the warriors sought, rather than the succor of their comrades.

And then occurred that startling interruption. The leading Thovians were within twenty yards of us when there came the thunderous roar that caused the very air to tremble and sent a dozen kangs and riders tumbling to the earth, while the survivors of that sudden onslaught forgot all else as their eyes shot skyward, to seek its terrible meaning.

There, floating lightly in the cloudless blue, a hundred feet or so above us, was a gigantic, black, cylindrical mass of metal that I knew to be a spaceship, though I never before had seen one. Behind it came another, and then another—some seven in all. There was no visible sign of life on either the foremost ship or any of the others, yet I felt that at that very instant, from the metal depths of each of those mighty monsters, thousands of unseen, cruel eyes were glaring down upon us.

There was no time for a closer observation. Even as we watched, another roar of flame and smoke burst from the leading ship, to bring swift and terrible death to that barbaric horde below, and sent me reeling, bleeding and unconscious, backward from my mount.

Yet in that fleeting instant I had guessed the identity of the newcomers, had realized who it was that manned those mighty metal monsters. And even as I sank to earth and all grew dim and hazy, I knew that once again the Black Raiders had returned to our planet!

And then a pain shot through my head, the world spun crazily around, and I sank to a dark oblivion.

Chapter III
The Black Raiders

𝕵t was the heat of the noonday sun upon my upturned face that aroused me some three hours later. At first I was conscious of only the throbbing pain in my head that temporarily obliterated all else, but presently became aware of the heavy form across my legs—the luckless kang that had been my mount when the Raiders fired upon us.

Gingerly my hand went to my head. The wound it felt proved to be but a slight, though painful gash that had furrowed the flesh across the temple. It had stopped bleeding, but the dried and clotted blood smeared my hands and face to present the gory appearance that doubtlessly convinced the Raiders I had been killed outright if, indeed, the ebon ones had bothered to land and inspect their victims.

Pushing the dead kang from me, I rose slowly to my feet, hardly knowing where I was or what I should do next. All around me the ground was strewn with the lifeless forms of men and kangs in every conceivable position, the first of the many thousands who were so soon destined to know death. Nearby lay the two Bardonian warriors who had been my companions, slain along with the others before they could as much as strike a blow in their defense.

For a while I searched among the bodies in the hope that there might be others who still lived, but it was evident I had been the lone survivor. So terrible had been that deadly fusillade that many of its victims were mutilated beyond recognition.

But what of those who had caused their destruction? Doubtlessly they were repeating the slaughter on a much larger scale at this very moment. It was that which aroused me to immediate action. I had no mount, of course, nor any means of transportation other than my own two legs, and it was a journey that would require many hours on foot. But there seemed to be no other way and every minute counted; so tightening my sword-belt and securing my weapons around me, I set off at a rapid trot towards the now nearby mountains.

Would I be in time to aid my people? I hoped against hope. The primitive arms of the Bardonians, as well as those of the other tribes of our planet, could hardly be expected to cope with the terrible weapons of the Black Raiders that spat fire and death from a distance, nor would the inhabitants of the Purple City be prepared for any such attack. At least I would be in time to avenge them, and in my rage it seemed I was equal to the task of slaying a hundred of the invaders.

Finally, after what seemed endless ages, I topped the mountain, and at a fast run began to descend the long, lumpy slope on its farther side, toward the distant bushes that arose at its base. My sandals of skin gave a firm foothold everywhere, and at length I had reached the bushes and was about to break through their thick growth, when my eyes suddenly caught that which brought me to a sharp halt and caused me to bless the leafy screen that stood between.

There, lying on the dusty, boulder-strewn ground not a hundred yards from the mountain's base, was one of the great spaceships I had seen earlier that morning. Even at that first glimpse I had been amazed by their huge size, but it was not till now that I realized their almost unbelievable magnitude.

Although at that moment it was all a mystery to me, I was later to become familiar enough with these mighty rocket-ships to learn they were equipped with wings, propellers, a tail skid, landing-wheels and other conventional parts. In space these same parts were so designed as to disappear into the ship, while instead of being driven by the propellers, the great metal monster was shot along at a terrible velocity by jets of gasses streaming from the numerous nozzles in its tail.

But standing before the great spaceship was that which was of even more immediate interest—four Black Raiders laughing and talking in a carefree manner. Their closely cropped hair and beardless faces made it easy to distinguish their strong, aquiline features.

Though I loathed the very name of them, I must admit that almost without exception they were perfect physical specimens of manhood. Standing well over six feet, each wore the gold-encrusted leather trappings that barely concealed their sleek ebon hides beneath, shimmering with a blackness almost blue. Around the waist of each was strapped a longsword, a shortsword, as well as a slender, glittering implement, the like of which I never before had seen; while their proud, intelligent faces and defiant, haughty bearing showed they realized their importance, and what, in truth, they really were—conquerors of planets and of space!

As I stood watching them, two of the Raiders began to saunter toward the nearby mountain, and in my direction, in the slow aimless manner of idle men who have no definite goal. Presently they were within earshot. Of course, I was well able to understand them, as their language is now ours. When the Black Raiders first came to our world, ages ago, they had compelled the conquered Earth folk to adopt their own speech, till in time it supplanted the mother tongues, and we present descendants knew no other.

The taller of the two was speaking:

"This is supposed to be our last stop between here and home. Let us hope so. An uninterrupted flight and we should arrive in time for the Great Games."

The other gave a laugh. "Only the Games?" he asked. "How about the three captive girls that will be yours on our arrival? Surely they are of as much interest as the Great Games?"

The taller one smiled, then gazed around him. "It's a dreary little world, this one," he commented, "so unlike the warm fields and valleys of our own beloved planet."

"What else could you expect of these primitive Earth folk?"

23

asked the other. "An uncouth, fast-dwindling race of barbarians, fighting constantly among themselves, who have not even a written language of their own. And yet I suppose we are as much to blame as any of the other worlds who invaded it in the past," he went on, "for our history shows that Earth once boasted a mighty civilization, and was well able to hold its own with any planet in warfare."

"Yes, yes," admitted the other impatiently. "I know all that, but it was ages ago. Surely they would have made some progress since then, had they not sunk to the mental level of the beasts they ride. No; I have no patience with them, nor are they numerous enough to give us an interesting fight. The sooner we release the Vapors of Vengeance and kill the lot of them, the better."

"Till then let us hope no wandering tribe comes this way," added his companion. "The fleet may not return for several hours, and there are only the four of us to guard the ship. In the meantime, perhaps it would be just as well if—"

That was all I wanted to know. For a time at least but four men guarded the ship, and at that very moment that same force was divided. Now was my chance. I had decided to gain an entrance to the spaceship, that I might behold the many wonders within, nor did I particularly relish the terms applied to my world by the Black Raiders. And so it was that the words of the speaker had scarcely left his lips before I whipped out both my longsword and shortsword, and leaping through the leafy vines shot out into the open and before them.

For an instant they both stared at me; then their hands flew to their weapons. But mine was the advantage of a surprise attack, and before the taller of the pair could set himself to meet me, my shortsword had been plunged into his throat to the hilt. In a flash I wheeled upon the other before he could escape, though to do him justice, he made no effort to flee. The man paused only to shout an alarm to the others, and then with an oath sprang fearlessly toward me.

The fellow was a splendid swordsman, and seemed to know every thrust and parry. But he was soon to find that there was still the occasional Earthman who had an even greater knowledge of the blade, for scarcely had our swords crossed before I nicked him, and a moment later he was being forced steadily backward—wide-eyed in fear, fighting desperately for his life, and wholly on the defensive.

From the tail of my eye I could see the others hurrying to his aid. It was this that spurred me to greater efforts. If I did not finish him within the next few seconds, it would indeed go hard with me, and I leaped forward to send the shower of cuts and stabs that terminated in the lightning-like thrust which found his heart, just as the other two flung themselves upon me.

And yet their mad rush was to prove more helpful than dangerous, for one of the Raiders ran full upon my sword at the first onset. Now we were even. The remaining warrior fought with all the bravery of despair, and our clashing blades rang out loudly. But I met his every thrust and stab with a faster parry and return. Then suddenly feinting the downward stroke that lowered his guard for a fleeting instant, I whirled my blade in the vicious backhand slash that decapitated the unfortunate black, and toppled him backward in a grotesque heap.

From the beginning of the encounter till the last of the Raiders fell lifeless before me, I doubt if three full minutes had elapsed.

Pausing only to sheathe my swords, I hurried toward the great spaceship, whose five open doorways were set at regular intervals in its thick metallic side. The words of the warriors had been enough to show their own uncertainty as to when the fleet would return, and at any moment those massive black ships might be appearing in the sky.

The huge bow of the space-flyer was toward me, and a dozen paces beyond it an open doorway led to a low-ceilinged chamber of innumerable glittering levers and instruments, of which I knew nothing, encircled by a score or more of tiny glass windows of an amazing thickness. This was the all-important pilot-room, and though I was later to become familiar enough with its many devices for a more detailed description, for a time at least it all was but a wonderful mystery to me.

Through this I passed at length, to come upon a room of such enormous size and weird construction as almost to defy description. At that first glimpse its great interior seemingly consisted of nothing but countless shelves, so designed as to rise in tiers from the floor to the ceiling, and running in numerous rows along its broad expanse. It was not till I drew nearer that I realized each was a narrow sleeping-cot. And then the next instant I had made the discovery that sent my hand flying to my sword-hilt, and snapped my eyes wide in surprise.

A thousand Black Raiders were slumbering on the little cots around me!

Yes, at least a third of the berths were occupied, and every sleeper lay in that same strange, death-like position, with arms enfolded on his chest. But what could it mean? Running from one side of the cots to the other, a stout strap securely held each occupant in place, and his ready weapons hung from the little ceiling a foot above him, that was the bottom of the berth overhead. Yet no one challenged my none too silent entry, nor did a single warrior arouse himself from slumber.

Then as I continued to stare at them, I became conscious of another inexplicable fact. No sound of breathing arose from the hundreds around me, nor was there the slightest noise to break that almost tomb-like silence.

A minute passed, another followed while I stood there, uncertain as to whether I should retreat or continue. Was it possible they were all dead? Gingerly I stepped closer to one of the sleepers.

There was no sign of any wound or violence on his person; yet on the other hand those ebon features were as devoid of life as the metallic floor I trod, nor did the tapping of my fingers above his head bring about the slightest change.

But at length curiosity overcame good judgment, and with drawn shortsword I began a soft advance to the far end of the room, though to tell the truth my stealth could be attributed to amazement rather than caution. On past the rows of slumbering blacks I continued, and through a second hall of sleepers equally as large as the first, then past the tiny storeroom that seemed so wofully inadequate to supplying the sleeping thousands, and through numerous other, larger rooms of various purposes, till at last I came to the little red door at the far end of the ship.

There I paused for a moment. What lay beyond I could not guess, and yet it was that wish to know the unknown that urged me on. Placing my ear against the frail barrier, I listened for some sound that might warn of the presence of others. But no noise came from beyond its panels, so taking courage and with ready shortsword, I gave the door the sudden kick that sent it flying backward, and sprang into the room before me.

It was a low-ceilinged chamber, at one end of which an open doorway let in the warmth and sunlight without. In the center of the room were a dozen or more metallic slabs that rose some three feet from the floor. And lying across the surface of several of these were five human forms, clothed in the flowing white robes that barely revealed their yellow-hued features.

But directly before me, seated at a table strewn with flasks and vials, was that which at once centered my attention—a thick-set little black dwarf, scarcely four feet in height, with a head so large as to be a deformity. His jewel-encrusted trappings clearly revealed the tiny arms and legs, while his full, repulsively ugly face was seared and marked by low passions and vices.

At my sudden appearance he half rose, then sat down again, his mouth open and his hand on the back of his chair.

"A hundred devils!" he kept on repeating. "A hundred devils!"

Then before I could answer him:

"The guards!" he shouted, leaping to his tiny feet. "Where are the guards? Where are the guards?"

The next instant he had broken into a mad dash for the doorway, his short legs striving frantically for speed. But a leap put me between him and the opening, and he ended his rush with a suddenness that equaled its beginning, halting but a pace or two before me.

"It is useless to call the guards," I told him quietly. "They are dead. I have killed them."

His eyes went wide. "All of them?" he gasped.

I nodded an affirmation.

"But what—what do you want?" he went on. "What are you going to do to me?"

"Nothing," I answered, "but you can do something for me. You can tell me where the fleet has gone and whom it will attack."

"I don't know," he replied promptly, and there was a truthful ring in his voice. "The fleet has no set destination. It will cruise around for a time, killing the barbarians and shelling their ruined cities; then presently it will return with the captives we will take with us to our own world."

"And what becomes of the captives then?" I asked him.

He looked at me for a moment before he spoke.

"It is hard to say," he answered at last, adding almost immediately: "But about yourself. Who are you who single-handed kills four of our best swordsmen, then boldly enters where none other than my own people have dared—"

"But the warriors," I interrupted. "The warriors in the other rooms, and these strange people here"—I motioned to the five figures on the nearby slabs—"they are all dead."

The little black man had been watching me as I spoke, as though still uncertain as to my intentions. Now, however, at my answering words, a faint smile appeared at the corners of his mouth.

"Dead?" he repeated, then he laughed. "No," he answered; "they are not dead. They have lain thus for days, and some of them for years, but they are not dead!"

Chapter IV
Vapors of Vengeance

"Not dead, yet some of them have lain thus for years!"

As the tiny black spoke those words, my features must have shown incredulity and surprise.

"They are not dead?"

"By no means," he went on softly. "Why should they be? These five here—yellow people—were kings and queens on a world of ice. We captured them some months back when we destroyed their distant star, but we did not kill them. That would have been stupid. Instead, they will be taken to our own mighty planet and forced to grace the great triumphal procession, along with the other royal captives we have captured on the many stars, in the march that will mark the return of the fleet—to be later sold as slaves and to serve the nobles of our world; though now, heavily drugged, they are unmindful of that future.

"And so it is with the warriors you saw in the other rooms—they too are but sleeping. It would take enormous quantities of food to feed the thousands of hardy fighters each spaceship carries. But what is far more important is the prevention of the enforced idleness to so many warriors during the months of flight from planet to planet. It might lead to terrible things. To safeguard against this, they are each injected with a serum that whisks them into a trance-like state till we arrive at our destination and they are needed. A counteracting serum then immediately awakens them to life once more.

"The same applies on our return journey. They are aroused when we arrive at Capara. Those you saw in the other rooms were not needed to subdue this primitive little world; so to awaken them would be useless. Indeed, often expeditions requiring from three to five years carry thousands of warriors who are never used, and remain in a death-like slumber till the fleet returns to its own planet.

"We of this expedition have already been gone two years from the mother world," he added as an afterthought.

"But who are you?" I asked. "How does it come that you are so familiar with all this?"

"I am Vaxarus," he answered solemnly. "Vaxarus the phrenologist, stunted in growth, but mighty in intellect, physician to the royal captives and the warriors whose privilege it is to fight and die for her wondrous Majesty, Tara the Glorious, Queen of the Stars, Goddess of Goddesses, Ruler of Capara, of space and of planets!"

He pointed to a jewel-encrusted pendant hanging around his neck.

"This priceless gem," he went on, "denotes my high station—physician and phrenologist. It is I who guard the welfare of the Princesses and the other royal maidens, who, if they can meet with the high standards of beauty and intellect demanded, and be virgins and unsullied, are selected for that greatest of honors—to serve, in her palace of glittering gold, the blinding beauty who is our Queen—our white Queen!

"And surely it is only right that all others should serve us. Ours, the greatest of all the planets, was old when your own tiny world, as well as a hundred million others, was but a bubbling, molten mass. It is said that time itself began with the birth of the glorious Tara, and that that same great God—Time—mated with the coldness of outer space to produce the divine pair who were the parents of our race.

"This, then, was the beginning of the holy lineage that today is the heritage of every human of our noble race, whose supremacy is maintained, and can only be lasting, in the conquest and submission of such creatures as yourself, and the continuous victories over the many worlds around us.

"Not always, however, did we demand the submission of others. Once in the dawn of time my people were a loving, peaceful race, who dressed in flowing white robes, and thronged the great temples of prayer with smiling faces and happy hearts; gentle people who lived on a lovely world of sky-blue lakes and deep valleys, of irrigated, picturesque fields, of marble halls and cool green meadows and fragrant, waving orchards. It was a golden age of simplicity and contentment, one, perhaps, that neither our world nor any other will ever know again.

"But as the ages passed they brought great spaceships and strange, savage people from the other planets, seeking our destruction and death, till at last in righteous anger, Queen Tara ordered our billions to arm themselves and repel the invasions, and our learned ones to devise weapons of such terrible power that nothing could withstand them.

"With these the Black Raiders at first sought only to protect themselves and what was theirs. But with their many victories arose their avarice, and with the passing generations their dissipations and degeneracy as well. Then, encouraged by their weapons, their spaceships and great numbers, they began sending out expeditions to the other worlds, to wrest whatever gold or riches the many planets might have, and bring their captured people to slave and serve our pleasures.

"From the first the invasions were successful, and swiftly won by our hardy warriors, who swept down all before them. Then as they continued, the many raids rewarded us with such an unbelievable wealth and power, that today ours is the mighty world that rules ten thousand planets; ours the ever-conquering world that brings such terror to the stars, and though with the passing centuries we have become drunk with power and careless, our victories but continue, and our riches and strength increase."

While the words of the little phrenologist held me in an almost breathless interest, I could not but wonder why he was taking such pains to explain all this to me—me, an almost naked barbarian whom his own kind looked upon with such contempt and scorn. It was the faintest wandering of his eyes that warned me. Those tiny orbs had suddenly left my own to flash a glimpse through the doorway behind me, and as I wheeled at that ominous signal I beheld the sight which brought an involuntary gasp from my lips—a great spaceship settling quietly to the ground not a hundred yards away, from whose numerous doorways a thousand ebon warriors were streaming toward us!

In a flash I realized the ruse with which the wily Black had tricked me. For long he had expected the return of the fleet, and cunningly managed to hold my attention till its arrival. And now with that awaited succor hurrying toward him, the short limbs of the phrenologist shot him into prompt and vigorous action.

Only for an instant did I stand there, staring at the oncoming Blacks. But it was time enough. The stunted Vaxarus had sprung for the table even as I wheeled away from him. And now as my hand flew to my sword, and I sought to reach and bar the door to the charging warriors without, it was to hear him scream a command to halt, then enforce it in both a swift and painful manner.

The phrenologist had secured a slender, glittering, wand-like device, similar to those I had seen hanging from the belts of the four warriors earlier in the day, and was pointing it at me. The next instant, with a soft, whirring sound, a beam of green light shot toward me, and I felt that every muscle in my body was being rent asunder as I was brought to the sharp, agonizing halt, stopped in my tracks, unable to flick a finger.

"Don't touch him! Don't touch him!" Vaxarus was crying the words to the warriors pouring through the doorway. "The paralyzing ray is upon him, and to come in contact with his person is to share his agony. Bring fetters to secure the barbarian when I release him from the power of the green beam."

Each instant was adding to the number of Blacks within the room, as well as increasing my terrible torture; yet strive as I would

33

I could not move, nor bring my muscles to obey my will. It was as though I had been suddenly turned into stone—my hand halfway to my sword-hilt, my left foot raised slightly in a statue-like rigidity—the same posture that had been mine when the green ray first fell upon me.

From all around came the laughs and taunts of the blacks, jeers that told they knew and enjoyed my agony. Half crazed with pain, through hazy eyes I could see several of them hurrying forward with lengths of rope and other fetters; though why they should wish to bind me in my present helpless condition I could not understand. Yet even as I wondered, there came the shouts of Vaxarus to take me alive. Then came the sudden snap that vanished the green ray and returned me to normal once more. The next instant a wave of warriors sprang upon me, and I was borne backward to the hard floor of the spaceship.

And so it was that I became a captive of the Black Raiders, though lashing out in a savage fury, I sent the lusty, smashing blows that brought a crimson trickle to the chin of more than one ebon warrior, and caused several others to howl in pain. But though the account I gave of myself was surely a most worthy one, there were always fresh hands to take the place of those I fought off, and at last they overcame me by the mere weight of their numbers. Then they bound me—my hands behind my back and my feet trussed up to meet them.

Presently they raised me from the floor, and half dragging, half pushing, hurried me from the ship and into the open, and the wild din and confusion that prevailed there. All around us the spaceships had landed, and from their great interiors thousands of Black Raiders and their bound white-skinned captives—Earth folk!—were streaming into the open.

Pushing and shoving, wild-eyed and disheveled, they were hurried along. Only the youthful, the healthy and strong had been chosen by the invaders. The whips of the Blacks were constantly falling on the backs of their prisoners, and the screams of young girls and women arose with the shouts of the conquerors.

Among the captives were hundreds of fettered warriors and chieftains—some from tribes so distant that their trappings were unknown to me. It was evident that even during the ten or more hours since they had landed, the blacks had been raiding and ravaging in the four corners of our planet. Many of the captives, grimy and bleeding, gave mute evidence to the fury of their resistance, but nowhere could I see a Bardonian, or the trappings of my own people.

Nearby the tiny Vaxarus was talking excitedly to a trio of Black Raiders whose jewel-encrusted trappings and proud features plainly stamped their importance. At a gesture from the dwarf my captors hurried me toward them.

"This is he. This is he," the little phrenologist was saying. "He came to the ship and slew the four guards as though they were paper men. His mind was as an open book to me, and the impression of the struggle easily read."

The eyes of the three Raiders turned toward me.

"By the Beauty of Tara!" exclaimed one. "He is indeed a powerful fellow. And a great swordsman as well, you say? Then he should make rare sport for us at the Great Games. Who knows?" he added, turning to the others; "perhaps we have at last found a match for the mighty Metak himself."

"Another victim, you mean," said the second. "And it's an ill-will you must bear this poor barbarian to suggest such a match. Why, the Commander would butcher him with the same ease as you conquer a captive maid."

"We might try putting him in the arena with a wild taggot," said the third, "or even a hairy man of Manator for that matter. But against our champion—ah, it would be a pity to kill one so young."

They all laughed.

"He is a prince, as well," went on Vaxarus, "a prince of some wild tribe known as the Bardonians. I read it all quite plainly. But we will wait till the Commander returns before deciding his fate. In the meantime," he said to the guards who held me, "confine him to the Ship of the Condemned till his presence is needed."

That was all. The fetters that bound my legs were then untied, and with my arms still lashed behind me I was ordered to follow my guards, who led the way through the thousands assembled within the great circle that the landing spaceships had formed.

Around us were scenes that appeared as the wild creations of a nightmare. Amid shouts and curses the Black Raiders were forcing their terrorized captives into long lines, for the purpose of inspection, with a brutality that was horrifying. Up and down the ranks black officers were scrutinizing the prisoners with a speed and skill that told of long practice, pausing occasionally to throw a taunt at some warrior, or a gloating, meaning glance at an unusually comely maid.

Night was falling. Numerous torches had been lit, and the flashing weapons and jewel-encrusted trappings of the invaders, glittering in the torchlight, together with the long golden rays shooting from the many windows of the surrounding spaceships in the backgrounds, but further tended to add a weird, unearthly aspect to the wild din and confusion, occasionally punctuated by feminine shrieks and terrible laughter.

Somewhat apart from the others was a tiny, black spaceship that seemed hardly capable of holding more than a score of people. Through its solitary doorway I was taken, handed over to the black warrior within, and the lock sprung behind me. The only light came from a slender glass-encased beam that ran the entire length of the low ceiling, to show six or more tiny cots similar to those I had seen in the great spaceship, as well as a narrow doorway leading to a room on the right.

At sword's point the warrior forced me before him to the far end of the room, where several iron rings protruded from the wall. One of these was snapped around the bonds that held my arms; then the Black sheathed his blade and sat down on a cot nearby.

"And what ill fate brings you to the Ship of the Condemned?" he asked presently. "Usually it is only our own warriors who know its interior."

"What kind fate will get me out of it is more important," I answered from where I stood, secured to the wall, "though my capture can be attributed to my own lack of vigilance, as well as the smooth tongue of Vaxarus."

The Black gave a laugh. "Ah, he's a cunning little runt, the royal phrenologist. And it is that same slyness, perhaps, which has raised him high in the favor of Queen Tara, and made him one of the richest and most powerful men of our great world, as well as the owner of a harem of a hundred chosen beauties.

"As to your own future, I can at least tell you some of it. You will be held here till the return of Metak, our Commander, which should not be very long. It is he who will decide your fate, which, judging from your size and what the guards have told me, will doubtless mean being sent to the arena for the Great Games. But again, one can never be certain of the Commander, and he might order your immediate death."

"His word is, I take it, your sole law," I put in.

"On our expeditions from planet to planet, yes—for he is our greatest general, as well as our mightiest swordsman, and stands high in the Queen's council. It is Metak who, on rare occasions, even enters the arena to meet some hardy warrior who has distinguished himself, whom he soon dispatches with his invincible swordplay and skill.

"And it is the sure way to win the plaudits of our world— physical strength and bravery. Indeed it is that same lust to fight which causes us to lay aside our great rays and other weapons of destruction, and meet the warriors of the other worlds on the fields of battle, armed with only swords and daggers like our foes. The paralysis-wand we each carry is used only when we are hopelessly outnumbered, or in the gravest danger. It is considered an act of cowardice for one of our race to use it otherwise."

I looked around the interior of the spaceship. The door at its far end, I reasoned, led to the pilot-room. Strapped to two of the cots were the silent forms of two Black Raiders.

"But this ship," I asked after a pause. "Why is it so small? It cannot possibly hold more than a score of captives."

"It is not meant to hold captives," informed the guard. "This, the Ship of the Condemned, is the dread of every warrior of our race. I am its pilot. A similar ship goes with every expedition that leaves Capara. In the months they spend on the different worlds away from home, any warrior found guilty of cowardice in battle, or some other grave offense, is sentenced to the Ship of the Condemned. That means he is never to know his homeland again, for when the fleet finally heads for the mother planet, the Ship of the Condemned makes for the moon of Capara, the tiny prison satellite but some fifty thousand miles from the homeland, which is known as the Moon of Lost Souls.

"There the poor unfortunates are compelled to toil on the great prison farms. There they are forced to labor in the dry, dusty fields as beasts of burden, till a merciful fate comes at last to release them from their sufferings.

"These two here"—he pointed to the two silent figures—"some months ago on a distant star they were found guilty of conduct unbecoming a Black Raider, once for cowardice in battle; the other time for treason. We have drugged them till the ship arrives at the prison colony, where they will begin their life of exile. Only the cowards and the traitors are sent to the Moon of Lost Souls; those and the most hardened of slaves who have become too unmanageable on Capara. They too are sent to toil on that Satellite of the Damned, till their spirits have been broken and they cry aloud for

38

death.

"So no matter what sentence the great Metak passes upon you, barbarian," he concluded, "remember that the arena, or even immediate death, is a thousand times better than a sentence to the tortures on the Moon of Lost Souls."

As the Black ceased speaking a roar of voices suddenly sounded above the din without. To the right a window of thick glass revealed the numerous fires and torchlights of the nearby encampment. The next moment the cause of the shouting was evident. Descending from the blackness overhead was a glittering outline of lights, which I knew to be some great spaceship.

The Black, whose gaze had followed mine, recognized it at once.

"It's the *Vastus!*" he exclaimed. "It's the flagship bearing our Commander. Let us hope it is laden with prisoners and plunder. At best Metak is none too patient, and doubly quick to find fault with anything if a trip has proven fruitless.

"You should soon know your fate, barbarian," he added, turning toward me.

But the statement was to prove untrue, for hour after hour dragged slowly along with no sound other than the gradually subsiding din without. It must have been well past midnight when footsteps suddenly sounded, and the next moment Vaxarus, followed by four others, entered the doorway.

"To your station, pilot, to your station," he ordered. "You are to put off immediately for the Moon of Lost Souls."

The half-dozing pilot sprang to his feet.

"At once, Worthy One," he answered promptly, and then: "But the fleet," he asked, "does it leave with us also?"

"At dawn," came the answer, while the others, hurrying to and fro, began making preparations for the departure. "This primitive world holds nothing of further value to us, nor is it worth any more of our time. Metak has ordered it destroyed. At dawn, then, the fleet will encircle it before turning homeward, releasing the Vapors of Vengeance as it does so; turning loose the poisonous red gasses that will penetrate to all corners of the planet, bringing a slow and agonizing death to every living thing upon it."

As he spoke, two of the Raiders had released me from the wall, and with arms still lashed behind me, carried and secured me to one of the cots with the strong straps encircling it. The black pilot noticed this.

"But the barbarian?" he asked. "Surely he is not going with us. I thought he would be sent to the Arena."

"So did I," answered Vaxarus, "and looked forward to seeing him in battle. The Commander, too, at first approved of it, but when I mentioned that he was a prince of some wild tribe known as the Bardonians, for some reason Metak's attitude suddenly changed, and he ordered his immediate exile to the Moon of Lost Souls.

"So that is to be your fate, Earthman," went on Vaxarus with a mocking smile, walking slowly toward me as his hands produced a glittering instrument with a needle-like point. "An exile for life on the prison farms. Say a farewell then to your own world, for in another thirty hours it will be as devoid of life as a burnt-out sun, and when next you open your eyes it will be upon the tiny Moon of Lost Souls, many hundred million miles away!"

Behind him the small crew of the Ship of the Condemned was watching us intently. With a wild surge I sought to break the bonds and straps that held me, but they were strong, and the next instant I felt a sharp twinge in my forearm, like the bite of a small insect.

That is all I can clearly remember. Almost instantly everything around me grew hazy. As in a dream, I heard Vaxarus laugh: "Farewell, Prince Jan of the Bardonians!" And then I knew no more.

Chapter V
The Prison Farms of Capara

It was, as I afterward learned, the equivalent of a hundred and fifty days of Earthly time, when I came to myself on the Moon of Lost Souls, that terrible satellite of sorrow, hundreds of million miles away from the bright green star that was my own beloved planet.

During the many hours the serum of Vaxarus held me in a death-like coma, I had been as unmindful of my surroundings as one in a deep slumber, unmindful that every living thing had passed away upon the Earth, and that the green star was now as devoid of life as it had been at its creation. Nor did I realize that while I lay there the tiny ship that was my prison had been plunging through the awful void with the speed of a falling meteor.

I opened my eyes to gaze into the features of a burly Black who held a flashing instrument with a needle-like point, similar to the one I had seen in the hands of Vaxarus. Behind him were two others. As I came to myself the Black gave a grunt of satisfaction, then motioned the others toward me. These in turn slipped past him, and lifting me to my feet—for the straps that held me to the cot had been removed, though my arms were still secured—hurried me out of the ship and into the open and the amazing world around me.

As far as the eye could see, on all sides, was naught but a great plain that stretched away to the sky, a dry and dusty plain on which thousands of humans toiled and strained under the flicking whips and watching eyes of black soldiery. Huge dust-clouds, constantly rising, marked the labors of the nearby toilers, as well as those on the far horizon, who appeared as tiny dots against the blueness of the sky. Later I was to find that almost the entire surface of the Moon of Lost Souls, with the exception of two great seas, was one vast unbroken plain, studded by the small white huts and barracks that housed the overseers and guards of this satellite of exile.

Even as we emerged into the sunlight I became aware of the winged forms shooting to and fro in the blueness overhead. At that first glimpse I thought they were huge birds, though a moment later I knew them for what they really were—winged, flying humans! These were the Tors, a timid, browbeaten race of bird-like men from a far-off planet, who served as both mounts and messengers to their captors, the Black Raiders.

The two Blacks who held me directed their steps toward a near-by white structure, with solid pillars on either side and an inscription across the lintel. This was the house of the Kamma, or Great Guard, the only voluntary exile on the Moon of Lost Souls. The Black overseers and guards, as well as the thousands of prisoners, were all exiles from Capara, though the Black officials took care that those of their own race were made guards and the superiors over the unfortunates who toiled in the fields.

As we neared the doorway, a stout Black with an air of authority appeared in the opening, frowning at our approach.

"Who is this one, who is this one?" he broke out in an irate tone. "Gods of my ancestors, will they never cease coming?"

"An Earthman, O Kamma," explained one of my captors as we halted before him. "The last of the three the great Metak sent us from his expedition. The other two, fellow countrymen, have been put in the ranks with the other guards who watch the slaves beyond the Sea of Tears. This one here—"

"Oh yes," interrupted the other. "I remember now; I read the report. He killed four guards, then threatened the royal phrenologist himself." The Kamma turned an angry glare upon me. "Well, I can promise you will never kill another. We have a way here of taking care of just such as you, and I intend to make use of it. What I cannot understand is why the Commander did not have you dispatched immediately upon your capture."

"Metak has recommended hard labor," put in the guard.

"The words of Metak shall be obeyed to the fullest," went on the Kamma, his voice rising slightly, for all this time I had been meeting his glare with an unwavering gaze. "To the plows with him then—Calabar's plow—and you may tell the Terrible One that it is the order of his Kamma to use his whip often on this fellow, and to lay on with a will!"

That was all. With the guards clutching me on either side I was hustled out onto the hot, dusty plains, where a million prisoners from a thousand planets lived and died and labored, humans of every conceivable shape and color who were to be my associates in the following days; sturdy, thick-set little men of a standard thirty inches, who were the dwarfs of Panthra; frail and timid twenty-foot giants from an unnamed world of mist; the dog-men of Zaxona, whose speech consisted of various gestures, barks and whines; the beast-men of Yat; the skull people of Canaxis; weird and serpent-like men from a distant star who hissed and wiggled their rapid ways up and down the fields; all those and a thousand others, some so grotesque that even a description would be revolting.

Hanging in the heavens but some fifty thousand miles away was the gigantic mother planet, Capara, whose great size made it appear so near one felt he should be able to hear the thunderous din of the ten billion power-crazed inhabitants, who laughed and debauched on its broad expanse. Despite the intervening void, the black outlines of mighty continents stood out upon the lighter hues that were its vast lakes and oceans. A second tiny satellite—it had two—and again as far from Capara as the Moon of Lost Souls, showed little better than a small black dot against the blueness of the sky.

Everywhere strange shapes and forms were pursuing their arduous labors under the eyes of brutal guards. Indeed, the entire Moon of Lost Souls was but one gigantic farm that supplied the mother planet, and countless air transports and freighters were constantly coming to and from Capara, whose own fair fields had been deemed too lovely for toil and agriculture. Many fields therefore on the Moon of Lost Souls knew the harvester, while a thousand miles away others were knowing the plow; and it was to slave with a crew that was one of the many that drew those heavy implements that destiny had chosen as my lot.

Presently five almost naked humans, begrimed and straining, came slowly toward us, struggling against the leashes attached to a heavy plow, on whose seat a huge Black forced them on with loud oaths and a long-lashed whip. This was Calabar, the Terrible One—a burly brute of a man, whose cruelties had distinguished him, even among that heartless clique who were the guards on the Moon of Lost Souls.

As he came abreast of the guards who held me, he roared a halt to the poor devils he drove, and as the exhausted men dropped to the ground, glad of a brief respite, turned two inquiring eyes upon us.

"Another one for you, Calabar," called out the guard. "A big powerful fellow this time, and the Kamma says you need not spare the whip."

The gaze of the huge Black went to mine. "I can use him," he answered in a deep voice. "My front slave, a yellow man, gave out on me this morning. Put this one in the foremost place, then, and I will soon teach him the rest," and he tossed a thick leather collar toward us.

Before leaving the Ship of the Condemned my trappings and sandals had been taken from me, and I was given a scanty loincloth to hide my nakedness—the apparel of the slaves who worked the farms. The five before me were chained neck to neck on a long slave-chain secured to the heavy plow. A few more links were now pulled through the ring of each collar, the end of the chain attached to the one around my own throat, and the ancient padlock sprung shut. The bonds that held my arms were then untied, and with the huge Black shouting at us the plowing was resumed once more, and I had begun my sentence on the Moon of Lost Souls.

All that long day I and the five who were my companions in toil pulled the great plow through the hard, dusty soil that stretched away to the far horizon. All that day we endured the heat and the grime of the field, as well as the falling lash of our driver, with neither food nor drink.

Several times Calabar left his seat the better to punish one he fancied was not giving his best to his work, and once he approached me with uplifted whip. But there was something in my eyes that kept it from falling, and so in silence and misery the little plow crew toiled on with the many others who worked the seemingly endless fields of that terrible satellite.

At dusk Calabar roared a halt and swung from his seat. I looked around me in the gathering twilight. As far as the eye could see, the thousands of toilers had ceased their work and were lying on the hard ground, while the Black overseers were gathering together in little groups, laughing and talking; nor was it much later till a hundred of the flying men—Tors—came winging overhead, and dividing into pairs, brought the evening meal to the hungry wretched awaiting them.

The two that alighted and came forward to serve us were typical specimens of their race. Dressed in the leather trappings of the Black Raiders, their dull, lemon-colored skins, their frail arms and legs and hairless heads, together with their trembling, high-pitched voices, presented an outstanding contrast to their burly, domineering captors. The huge, membranous, bat-like wings gave the weird, bird-like appearance, made but the more pronounced by their sharp aquiline features.

Each carried the two pails that contained our food and water—the former a thick, stew-like substance, not unpleasant to the taste—while from their waists hung numerous copper bowls.

As we were being served, one of the winged men whispered to me: "You are the Earthman?" he asked in a low tone, looking fearfully toward the nearby Calabar who was talking with the others.

I nodded from where I sat, looking up into the large eyes that were watching me with the frightened, puzzled stare of a trapped animal.

"Yes," I began. "But how does—"

"Sh—" he cautioned, making a pretense at refilling my bowl. "We must be silent till Calabar leaves."

Just what he meant by that I was not certain, but presently the huge Black gave the sharp whistle that sent the second bird-man winging toward him, while from all around a score of others began flying toward the guards. A moment later Calabar had climbed upon the back of the Tor, while the guards mounted the others; then with their huge wings flapping loudly, the bird-men rose into the air, and toward the distant barracks that were the quarters of the guards.

As they disappeared a murmur ran through the men behind me, and their eyes turned to the remaining bird-man.

"Refill the bowls, Tor!" growled one. "Refill the bowls!" In an instant the words were taken up by the others, while the timid bird-man, coming forward, worked feverishly to meet their demands.

"He will be punished for this, perhaps, but we must eat," explained the one behind me. "The Tors are expected to use but a certain amount of food for each feeding, and he can only explain the shortage by saying he fell and spilled our rations. It will doubtless mean five lashes for him, but better that than a broken neck at the hands of the prisoners."

Presently the bird-man reached me.

"You wish your bowls refilled, Prince Jan?" he asked.

I stared at him.

"How is it you know my name?" I answered.

"Do not be angry with me, Prince Jan," he went on; though I had neither raised my voice nor given the slightest indication of anger, "but I was arranging the reports in the office of the Kamma a sun's width ago, and read the one that was sent in by Vaxarus. It mentioned you, and said you had killed four of the Raiders."

"And by that I have earned your hatred?" I asked.

"By that you have earned my respect, Prince Jan. You have done what I wished a thousand times that I could do. But we are not a race of fighters, we Tors. Ours was a planet of peace and kindness, whose people lived only to help each other, and to whom war was but a hideous, terrible word. So when the Black Raiders came to our world it was easily subdued, our cities burned, and most of my people taken to Capara, to serve as the mounts and slaves of our conquerors, while I and a hundred more were sent here. So is it no wonder that the heart of Abel is bitter against the Black Raiders, and that he rejoices when any ill befalls them?

"But the bowls," he went on after a pause; "you will want them filled, Prince Jan?"

"No," I smiled. "No, Abel; I do not want you to be punished on my account. But why is it you have not escaped? You are not chained, and you have your great wings."

"Where could I hope to go, Prince Jan? The entire moon is but one great farm that supplies the mother planet, and Black guards are everywhere. That is why the prisoners are not watched at night. There would be no place they could flee to if they did try an escape, and they could only hope to gain some terrible torture for such an act.

"Why, if the Blacks thought I ever contemplated flight, they would have my wings severed."

"Quite right, Tor," said one of the men who had been an attentive listener. "And you had better banish all thoughts of escape, Earthman. Neither here nor on any other world can one

47

be safe from the Black Raiders."

"Except the Moon of Madness," put in another.

"The Moon of Madness?" I asked.

"Capara's second satellite," explained Abel, pointing to a tiny moon in the void overhead, for night had now fallen. "For some strange reason the Black Raiders fear that moon and will not go near it, though they have conquered all the nearby stars, and worlds five hundred million miles beyond it. Why, I do not know, but it must be something ghostly and terrible, for though indifferent to danger, and even death itself, the Black Raiders tremble when the name, the Moon of Madness, is mentioned."

"I can tell more," put in one of the others, for by now the little plow crew had gathered close, "something that is known to only a few, other than our captors. It is said that many years ago a spaceship of the Black Raiders was caught in a terrible space-storm, and forced to land upon the Moon of Madness. Years passed, during which it was all but forgotten. Then one day one of the Black fleets came upon it again, far out in the trackless void—a lonely drifting derelict. But the Commander of the fleet ordered its destruction, and the great ray-guns turned upon it, for it is an ancient law of the Black Raiders that any ship or person that has known the Moon of Madness be immediately destroyed.

"But it was not destroyed before three brave young officers swung the flyer they commanded alongside the spaceship, and entered it through a small door in its bow, while without, the others waited. Then suddenly, amid terrible screams, the three staggered back through the doorway and into their own ship, wild-eyed, mouths contorted, and gibbering like idiots. Whatever terrible horror they had seen, they were never able to tell, for it had robbed them of their reason."

His voice sank to a whisper.

"The story has it also that from within the ship there came chuckling laughter and a terrible tapping sound, like the tread of one who was neither man nor beast!"

"Do—do you believe it?" asked one after a pause.

The other shrugged. "I hardly know, but it is said to be a true story, and whatever evil thing it was, it could have been spawned nowhere else but upon the Moon of Madness."

Soon after that Abel gathered up the bowls and empty food-pails and fled toward the great kitchens that were also the quarters of the Tors, while the little plow crew stretched themselves upon the ground and sought slumber; for there were no huts or sleeping-quarters for the prisoners who worked the farms on the Moon of Lost Souls, only the great fields in which they labored through the long hours of light, that knew them also in the darkness that accompanied their slumber-tossed dreams.

Nor was it much later till the poor exhausted devils were all in a deep sleep, and for a time at least unmindful of their sufferings. But sleep did not come so easily to me, nor did I court it. For hours I lay there, with the rhythmical breathing of the others around me, looking upward at a million stars, and the nearby giant mother planet, Capara, that covered half the heavens—already planning escape and vengeance on the conquering Black hordes.

And despite the awful odds against it, an escape from the Moon of Lost Souls was soon to be mine. Yet I dare say, that could I have foreseen the wild future before me, I would have considered the prison farms of the Black Raiders as naught other than a safe and friendly paradise.

Chapter VI
A Break for Liberty

At dawn the Tors came flying into the fields with the morning meal, nor was it much later till the guards themselves appeared. With them came Calabar, who ordered us to our feet. Again we rose to throw ourselves against the sturdy leashes, and with the huge Black shouting at us the plowing was resumed, and that inhuman labor taken up once more.

For ten days I toiled in the great fields on the Moon of Lost Souls. For ten days, along with a million captives from a thousand planets, I endured the heat and horror of that terrible prison satellite. I could tell of the many grotesque creatures the Black Raiders had captured on the various stars and forced into a life of slavery. I could tell of the many brutalities of the guards in general, and of Calabar in particular, that transformed brave and spirited men into weak and whimpering cowards—but enough! Even now they come in dreams to haunt me.

At nights I would lie in my chains on the great fields of exile, hearing the groans and the troubled dreams of those around me.

Again and again I asked myself that seemingly inexplicable question: Why had the Commander of the fleet, Metak, ordered me sentenced to the Moon of Lost Souls, rather than to the Great Games and the arenas of Capara? There could have been no personal enmity, as the Black leader had never even seen me; nor did it seem possible that my existence before my capture could have been known to him.

But for that matter, why to a score of other questions? Why should any of us be here at all? Why had it been decreed that the Black Raiders should conquer a thousand planets? Why should that gigantic world, hanging so close above us as to obliterate half the heavens, be the unchallenged master of all others? Ever since my arrival on the Moon of Lost Souls, in the forbidden whispers of the prisoners and loud banter of the guards, I had heard of nothing but the wonders of the great mother planet, Capara; of the luxuries and pleasures to be had upon its broad expanse, and of the glorious Queen who was its supreme ruler.

While I could not be certain as to the truth of all the tales I heard, they were enough to confirm that it was indeed a planet of uncensored vice and pleasure—the Eden for the debauchee. A world of ten billion people, drunk with power, with wine and riches given over to a life of continuous dissipations, and ruled by a white Queen who reigned in a palace of glittering gold! A Queen of such indescribable blinding beauty, as to be almost terrifying! A Queen who was said to have been present at the birth of time itself!

And then one dusk there occurred that which changed everything. It was the evening of the tenth day, after long hours at the plow, when there happened the first of a series of incidents that were to lead to such a startling climax.

All this time, despite its apparent hopelessness, I had not relinquished any thoughts of escape, and I was sure that others could be relied upon at the first opportune moment. The five who worked with me—yellow men from a distant world of ice—were all seasoned warriors and powerful fellows, as indeed they had to be, to stand the hardships of those who drew the plow of Calabar.

I might add here that all prisoners on the Moon of Lost Souls spoke the language of the Black Raiders. When the ebon ones conquered a world it was their custom to compel the inhabitants to adopt their tongue, as they had done to my own planet ages ago; so that while some of the captives were from stars so distant as to be invisible to the naked eye, their speech was readily understood.

And then on the evening of the tenth day, as Calabar passed me on his way to a waiting Tor and the distant barracks, chance sent the key that unlocked our slave collars tumbling from his belt and directly before me. The Black continued on, unaware of the loss, nor did any of the others notice the incident. The next moment the key had been concealed within my loincloth.

During our hours of steady plowing we covered a considerable area that took us to the various sections of the different fields, and when we halted that evening it could not have been more than half a mile from one of the great barns that dotted the Moon of Lost Souls. It was in these massive storehouses that the harvests of the field were baled and kept, awaiting transportation to Capara. It was before them also that the huge space-freighters landed to take on the mighty cargoes they would carry to the mother planet.

I had noticed that most of the ships, especially those arriving late in the afternoon (one had recently landed, and its crew were busily loading its huge interior in the waning sun rays) would invariably delay their departure till the following dawn, and it was this that prompted me to the course I had been planning for several days.

Twilight had been hurried into darkness by the appearance of black clouds. There, together with the gradually rising wind, the angry rumbling and occasional flashes in the void overhead, told of an oncoming storm, but I felt that it could be to our advantage.

I made no immediate mention of the key, but shortly after, as Abel served the nightly rations, I beckoned him and the five others around me. The guards had departed to the barracks, and only the prisoners remained in the fields—they and a few of the Tors who were busy gathering up the bowls, preparatory to leaving—but I spoke in a low tone, for several other plow crews were nearby, among whom might well be one eager to hurry to the guards with any information.

"Another of the freighters," I began, pointing to the outline of lights in the distance. "It has been loaded, but will doubtless remain till dawn, while its crew drink and revel with the guards in the barracks. That means the ship will be ill guarded this night. What is to stop us from taking it over?"

There were a few gasps and a brief pause, then: "The guards, for one thing," said one.

"These, for another," said a second, pointing to the collars that held us to the slave-chain.

"But suppose you were freed from them?" I went on. "Suppose I could promise to unlock your collars? How many of you would follow me to the ship? How many of you, if you had the chance, would bear arms against the guards; would cut down those who watch the ship, and attempt that which has yet to be accomplished—an escape from the Moon of Lost Souls?"

And I withdrew the key I had secreted in my loincloth, and held it up before them.

As my voice died away, a death-like stillness settled over those around me, for the thing I suggested was almost unheard of. True, several times in the past daring captives had attempted to escape from the Moon of Lost Souls, but they had always been speedily captured and their punishment was so terrible that by now even a mention of the word, flight, brought a shudder from the prisoners.

The five yellow men sat as though turned to stone, the eyes of each roving from one to another. Despite the many tales of torture, however, there was no sign of fear among them; I was quick to realize that. A moment passed. They were but waiting for one of their number to take the initiative. It was the one beside me who spoke first; a grim and grizzled old warrior I felt I could rely upon.

"You can count on me, Earthman," came his low tone. "You can count on me to the last. They will probably get us before we have gone a mile, and it is more than likely that we shall never even see the inside of the ship. But at least we can try, and anything is better than the slow living death here."

It was enough. The next minute, all of them, together with Abel, the bird-man, were voicing their willingness to follow me and share in the rash venture—raising such a clamor, in fact, that I half feared the sudden din would attract the other inmates of the field.

"But how do you propose to go about it, Earthman?" one of them was asking presently.

"In a way that will require the help of every one of you," I answered, then turned to the bird-man beside me. I knew that the others weren't over-pleased that he was to be one of us, for the Tors are a notoriously timid race, and in truth we had need for only fighting-men. But I could not find it in my heart to leave poor Abel, no matter how much of a burden he might prove to be.

"You have said that you Tors are allowed to come and go from your quarters whenever you please," I asked him, "and also that when a freighter puts in for the night most of the crew spend the hours in drinking at the barracks with the guards?"

The other nodded.

"You should not find it hard then, to slip from your quarters and let us know when they are well filled, and vigilance is lax."

"I can do it, Prince Jan, I can do it!" cried Abel, eager and thrilled that his services were needed. "I can wait till they have become fuddled with wine, then hurry to you. It will not be hard."

"Good," I answered. "Once we are sure of the guards, it will be a simple matter to free ourselves."

It was then agreed to wait till we had heard from Abel, and with a few parting instructions to him, we watched the bird-man rise into the night and fly toward the glittering lights in the distance. Once he returned to tell us all was well, it was my plan to make for the great freighter, and with a sudden rush surprise and overpower its guards, then piloting the ship ourselves (two of the yellow men had said they could handle her), put off for any destination that would place many miles between us and the Moon of Lost Souls.

An hour passed—a second, then a third. The wind that had been gradually rising was now whistling wildly over the fields, while the poor toil-worn wretches below huddled together, some for

54

warmth, others in terror, for volleys of thunder were constantly rumbling, with lightning flashes splitting the sky, and to many of the prisoners a storm of such violence was almost unknown.

Then came the rain, loud, sweeping gusts, a veritable deluge, bent on drowning all before it, and obliterating vision with the fury of its downpour.

But it was neither the rain, the lightning nor the wind that was foremost in my mind that night. Why did not Abel return as he had promised? I had the utmost faith in the loyalty of the bird-man, and was certain that his absence was no fault of his own. At length, after another hour had dragged its course, I could stand it no longer, and turned to the wet and dripping men beside me.

"Something has happened. Something has gone wrong," I told them, shouting so that my words could be heard above the fury of the storm. "The Tor should have been here an hour ago."

"He might have become frightened," cried one of them, shielding his eyes and blinking at me through the rain. "He might have decided the risk was too great, and left us to get along without him."

I shook my head. "No," I answered, "it is not that; it is something else. He would be here if he could."

"But what about us? What had we better do?" asked the other.

I unlocked the collar that held me to the slave-chain, then handed the key to the speaker.

"Stay here," I told him. "The guards may be aware of the plan and waiting for us. If so, there is no need why you should all suffer. I will go and see what has happened to the bird-man. If I do not return within an hour, you will know I have been taken, and the venture best dismissed as useless."

Then before a protest could be voiced, I had wheeled and was off.

At a fast trot I started toward my goal, my bare feet sinking ankle-deep into the ooze of the storm-swept field at nearly every step, my almost naked body a target for the wind and rain. The greatest danger, of course, lay in the unknown darkness that might send me running into some waiting guards, or toppling over another plow crew, whose outcries could easily mean discovery. Several times I heard the rattling chains of some crew nearby, and once, faintly, a sound of voices to the left. But no shout or challenge came to halt me, and I gradually drew nearer to the great structure ahead.

At length a golden twinkle shone through the rain, and a moment later I was halting beside the huge storehouse that held the products of the fields, its massive outlines occasionally illuminated by flashes of lightning. The constant thunder and whistling winds deadened any sound of my approach, nor did it seem probable that a sentry would be abroad on such a night.

Pausing to regain my breath, I rested, then continued on to round the corner of the building, and stepped directly into the path of an oncoming Black guard—Calabar!

It is a question which was the most surprised. For a moment we stared at each other; then: "Blood of a Thousand Beasts!" he roared. "—You?"

The next instant his hand went to his sword-hilt, while his mouth flew open to shout an alarm.

It was never uttered. My hands shot out and were around his throat even as he attempted it. Together we fell to the ground. Calabar was a huge and powerful man, but my own strength had long been the boast of my people. Wildly he sought to free himself from my death-grip. Stubbornly I clung to it. The Black fought furiously but futilely. My fingers tightened. Swiftly and silently the life was choked from him. His dark eyes bulged, his tongue protruded to dislodge me, and a moment later there came a convulsive tremor of his stiffening muscles, and the Terrible One lay quite still.

Quickly I looked around, but none had witnessed that little tragedy. Raising the dead Calabar, I threw his limp form upon my shoulder, then hurried into the doorway of the great storehouse. Among the bales of its dark interior I had soon stripped the body and donned the handsome leather trappings and sandals, after first discarding the filthy loincloth that had been my only apparel. Then with the longsword and shortsword of my victim buckled around my waist, I crept toward the doorway to resume my search for the bird-man.

Directly ahead was that which claimed my attention—the freighter I had seen loading earlier in the day. A faint glow glittered from its open doorway, but there was no sound to betray any occupancy, and I was on the verge of leaving my shelter and gliding toward it, when my gaze suddenly raised to behold that which snapped my eyes wide in surprise and sent me leaping back into the darkness of the storehouse.

Shooting downward from the blackness overhead was a gigantic spaceship, its massive outlines agleam with lights, cutting swiftly through the storm with a well-armed crew of thousands, and preparing to land upon the ground not twenty paces from me!

Chapter VII
Vonna

𝕴 doubt if twenty seconds could have passed from the time I first saw the ship until the great space-flyer had landed—halting its mad rush at the last minute, to right itself, then settle noiselessly upon the storm-swept ground.

But that fleeting interval had not found me idle. Despite the blackness within the storehouse it was not hard to find my way. The whole interior was piled high with huge bales running in rows the entire length of the vast structure, between which were numerous narrow passageways. Into the nearest of these I hurried, and with the wall on one side of me continued on for a dozen paces or so, to halt before a slight chink in the wood that gave an unobstructed view to the night without, and the new landed spaceship.

It was evident the descent of the latter had not gone unnoticed. Even as I halted, several shouts sounded from the barracks, and forms came hurrying through the rain. The next instant the doors of the spaceship were flung open to send long vistas of light streaming into the darkness, and dislodge a thousand black warriors who came swarming into the open. Loud laughs and greetings passed between them and the guards.

And there I stood, wondering what I had best do next and how I could find Abel, while scarcely twenty paces from me hundreds of guards and warriors were streaming past. It was all-important that I see the bird-man, and yet I could not show my nose without being taken prisoner. It came to me also, that Abel might not have been discovered, but was unable to leave the barracks, and that any mistake on my part would not only cost me my life, but his own as well.

Yet I must do something. Crouched in the shadow of a grain bale, I made a thousand plans, each more dangerous than the last, and was balancing one against the other when a hurrying of footsteps sounded above the din without. In an instant I was at the chink to behold the warriors stiffening to attention. A tall figure whose glittering, jewel-encrusted trappings and proud features stamped his importance, appeared in the open doorway of the ship and looked frowningly into the storm.

A guard came running through the rain to halt, panting, and with an arm held out before him in salute.

"The Kamma sends a thousand welcomes, noble Magog, and asks that the son of Metak follow me to his quarters, where the questioning of a Tor detains him—"

The other nodded. "I come, I come," he broke in. He turned and flung a few unintelligible words over his shoulder, then at a fast run followed the guard through the rain toward the Kamma's quarters, while behind him the rest of the ship's crew hurried into the open, making for the barracks.

A thrill shot through me at the words of the guard. I felt certain that the Tor he mentioned was Abel, nor had the identity of the ship's Commander been uninteresting. This then was the son of Metak—Metak who alone was responsible for my being on the Moon of Lost Souls—Metak the cruel, and champion swordsman of the Black Raiders. And now the son of the man who had caused the death of every living human upon my planet, as well as my own exile, was scarcely a hundred paces away. My hand crept to my sword and toyed with its heavy hilt.

The many lights streaming from the spaceship prevented my leaving the front of the storehouse, but the rear of the great structure seemed temporarily deserted and every minute counted; so turning into a passageway I hurried through its sinister gloom, and a few minutes later found myself at the far end of the building, directly before a small door secured by wooden bars upon the side of my approach. I opened it and stepped out into the storm.

As I had expected, the back of the storehouse was deserted, but directly ahead was an outline of lights, surrounded by a low wall that I knew to be the office and quarters of the Kamma; while on its far side, and some distance beyond, rose a much larger structure that was the barracks itself. In a half-crouch I hurried forward, and a moment later found myself beside the white wall that encircled the building—a barrier some seven feet in height.

This, however, was no great obstacle. With a running leap I sprang upward and grasped a secured hold on its top; then, observing no one in the surrounding darkness, I dropped lightly to the ground within.

Once within the walls there was no immediate danger of discovery, yet to remain hiding among the bushes into which I had landed would gain me nothing. Still holding my shortsword, I sped across the wet terrace toward the rear of the building before me, wondering how I could gain an entrance, as all its doors were certain to be either barred or guarded. My eyes fell upon a balcony above me, beside which grew a slender tree. It was the work of but a few minutes till I stood on that deserted little gallery. It led to a dim-lit hallway.

Down this I made a silent advance. In the distance a slender glass-encased beam of light glowed in the niche of an intersecting passage, a somewhat wider hallway from which came the murmur of voices. Here a small circular balcony was mounted by a railing, while at the far end of the passage a stairway led downward. A quick scrutiny showed the hall to be deserted, so on tiptoe I advanced to the railing and looked down into the room below.

It was a good-sized chamber, well lit and well furnished. At the tables in its center sat two men—one the Kamma I had first seen on my arrival on the Moon of Lost Souls. The other was a tall and much younger man of about my own age, whose well-chiseled features might have been handsome were it not for the too thin lips and close-set eyes. But what was far more noticeable was the lightness of his skin—an outstanding contrast to the blue-black hue of his companion. Plainly there was a strong dash of white blood in him. His jewel-encrusted weapons and trappings flashed and sparkled. This then was Magog, son of Metak.

Seated on a chair in a far corner of the room, gagged and bound and looking at the others with frightened eyes, was he for whom I had been searching—Abel the bird-man.

The Kamma was speaking:

"But what you ask is madness, Worthy One," he was saying. "Stealing is one thing, but to murder a royal captive—and one expected by the Queen at that—"

"Don't be a fool," broke in Magog. "It is neck or nothing now. My father's influence put me in command of one of the ships that collect the ransom and tributes demanded of the various worlds our armies have conquered, but even he would be unable to save me were the Queen to ever learn the truth; that four times during the past year I have landed here and left as many ransoms in your care, then proceeded on to Capara with the report that certain worlds were unable to meet our demands."

"This Princess you speak of?" asked the Kamma.

"Vonna of Penelope," went on the other. "It is her world for one whose ransom we have taken. Twice within the past year I have been sent to the tiny blue star to collect its semi-annual tribute. On both occasions I have brought the treasure to you, then returned and reported the failure of the Penelopians to pay. I expected nothing to arise over it, for Penelope is a tiny little world containing nothing of any great value, and its payments ridiculously small compared to the huge tributes of some of the larger planets. But for some reason my report displeased the Queen, and she ordered one of her fleets to return with me, to release the Vapors of Vengeance on Penelope and destroy it; also for me to bring the Princess of Penelope to her. That means discovery, for the Princess Vonna is certain to tell that the ransoms have been paid."

The Kamma gave a gasp, half rose from his chair, then sat down again.

"I knew it. I knew that we would be found out sooner or later," he sobbed. "But I am not the one to blame. It was you. It was you who—"

Magog's laugh was short and harsh. "Too late for that. You are in it with me up to the neck, and if discovered I will not go tumbling into the Pit of Blackness alone. Any time mine or any other ransom ship returns to Capara it is officially searched, and its contents taken to the royal treasury. But when your own small flyer lands it is never inspected, for how could one possibly be bringing gold and jewels from the Moon of Lost Souls?

"What if I were to tell that every time you landed for those innocent, overnight visits, your ship contained a king's ransom? That you and I have later met and divided four treasures which rightfully belong to Queen Tara?"

"But this girl—this Princess Vonna?" asked the other. "If we murder her they are bound to suspect us and wonder why. It will only mean discovery."

"Not with me running things," answered Magog, and it was only by straining my ears that I could hear him at all, for continuous thunder volleys were crashing across the heavens, and a furious downpour splashing against the windows. "Luckily a storm has arisen—good. I can say it forced me to land here for the night. I have given orders for the crew to stay in the barracks with your guards. That means the ship is unguarded at this moment save for the pilot, a stout fellow in my service, and one we can trust. The Princess Vonna is tied in the entrance cabin. Fortune has further favored us by the timely misbehavior of this Tor."

His eyes signaled to the bound Abel. "By the way," he asked, "what did he do, anyhow?"

"He?" said the Kamma absently. "Oh, he was caught by one of the guards sneaking out of the barracks tonight, acting in a suspicious manner, and he refused to tell where he was going. I was questioning him when you arrived. But—but how can he be of any use to us?" demanded the Kamma.

"By relieving us of any suspicion that might arise over the murder of the Princess Vonna," answered Magog. Then as the other looked quizzical:

"Let us take this Tor to the ship with us at once. No one is without, and we shall not be seen. There we can release him and dispatch him, along with the Princess Vonna, then raise the cry that the Tor escaped us and ran to the ship; that he murdered the Princess, then attempted to put off into space; that we arrived in time to prevent his escape, and though too late to save the royal captive, we were at least able to avenge her."

I waited to hear no more. The words of Magog made clear his intentions. I now knew the ship was unguarded. Could I rescue Abel and reach it, there might still be a chance for us both. And so, before any of them dreamed of the nearness of my presence, I had vaulted over the low railing, and with drawn shortsword dropped lightly to the floor ten feet below me, and directly before the seated pair.

What a surprise! The Kamma and Abel both knew my identity, of course, but to the startled eyes of Magog I must have appeared as the figment of a dream. There was a moment's silence; then: "Blood of my Ancestors!" gasped the son of Metak. "Who are you and where did you come from?"

I motioned them to remain in their seats, my glittering blade waving from the breast of one to the other.

"Don't move," I told them quietly. "It just so happens that at this minute an Earthman has the upper hand."

With my left arm I made the gesture that brought Abel from his chair and beside me, for though his arms were bound, his legs were free. Then without taking my eyes off the seated pair, I had soon released the bird-man, whose thongs dropped to his feet. This done, I ordered him to disarm both men, then gag and bind the Kamma to his chair. The latter was loud in his protest of this, but a painful jab of my sword-point quickly silenced him, and a moment later he was but a mute and helpless witness to what was to follow.

I turned to Magog. All this while he had risen and was watching me with a surprised, puzzled expression that was gradually changing to one of fear.

"What do you want?" he whispered as our eyes met. "What are you going to do?"

"Witness the end of a Black Raider," I answered him. "I want to see if the son of Metak can meet death as readily as his sire sentenced my own world to it."

He looked wildly about him. "But I am unarmed!" he cried. "You would not kill a defenseless man!"

"Why not?" I answered grimly. "Surely that's what your own kind have been doing for centuries. Turning those terrible Vapors of Vengeance upon a thousand worlds, and killing untold billions without giving them the slightest chance for their lives. It would be no more than fair were I to run you through where you stand. But I am no Black Raider, nor will I kill a defenseless man. Here—I give you the chance your own would not give mine," and I tossed his unsheathed longsword to him, the handle of which he deftly caught.

"On guard, Caparian," I warned, and fell into position.

His reply was a quick thrust at my heart which I side-stepped and the next instant our blades clashed together as they met in a fast exchange of thrusts and parries.

I had no fear of the noise attracting the warriors in the barracks. The great building was scarcely a stone's throw away it is true, but it was a strongly built structure that deadened vibration, and again the wild din of the storm obliterated all else. Our two sole witnesses were the excited Abel, and the bound and gagged Kamma—the eyes of the latter glaring hate and horror—the dark orbs of the bird-man wide and gleaming.

Not that there was any great doubt as to the outcome. From the first it was evident that the duel would be of short duration.

A fast counter-thrust had laid bare the cheekbone of Magog at the first onset, and a moment later he was in a steady retreat—stepping between and around the various pieces of furniture with an accuracy that showed a thorough knowledge of the room, while I pressed ever forward, as I realized the possibility of a chance entrance of some guard.

At length a sudden maneuver backed him into a corner from which there was no escape. That Magog realized the end was near was evident as, wide-eyed and desperate, he frantically sought to parry the thrusts of the dazzling blade before him. His mouth half opened as though to appeal for mercy, but shut again as he realized its futility. That merciless steel whirred ever closer. Then, doomed, crazed with fear, the doors of death opening to claim him, the Black Raider did that which branded him as the lowest of cowards, even among his own.

In desperation he lashed out with a wicked slash that halted me for an instant. Then as the cut was met and parried, his free hand brought up the paralysis-wand from his belt. But before its green rays could be turned upon me, an upward sweep of my blade sent it flying from his hand. The next instant three feet of steel went tearing through his heart.

With a groan half bestial the son of Metak sank lifeless to the floor.

Pausing only to wipe my blade on a hanging I motioned for Abel to follow me. Then in a deathly silence we hurried from the room and out into the raging night, where numerous lightning flashes showed a narrow, stone-flagged walk that led through an open gateway, above which hung a huge alarm gong. The rain-drenched courtyard between us and the ship was deserted, but I now felt that the moments till discovery were rapidly drawing to a close, for already the first evidence of dawn was stealing across the thundering sky. Soon would come the light of day, and then the awakened warriors from the barracks.

The open doorway of the ship was soon before us, and with a nod to the bird-man I crept forward, hearing his faint tread as he followed.

The interior of the huge ship was brilliantly lighted. A narrow passageway stretched through several large rooms to terminate in the exit chamber at its far end. But there was no need for further exploration, for there on a chair, her shapely arms bound behind her, was a lovely young golden-haired girl of my own color that I intuitively knew to be Vonna, the captured Princess of Penelope.

Chapter VIII
The Moon of Madness

It was a lovely vision she presented even in captivity. Her scanty jewel-encrusted trappings revealed rather than concealed her lithe, delicately rounded body. A brilliant red feather protruded from the back of the slender band encircling her shapely head. But despite the glittering, barbaric apparel, it could not hide the royal beauty of those exquisitely chiseled features; of those long-lashed, blue eyes, and slightly parted, perfect lips, that showed a row of pearly teeth—a beauty enhanced a hundredfold by the tumbling mass of wavy golden hair that fell to her white shoulders in a lovely disorder.

On a cot nearby a huge Black lay in slumber.

As we appeared in the doorway the girl saw us. That she realized we were friends was evident, for as I raised a finger to my lips her eyes signaled warningly toward the Black. On tiptoe I approached and knelt beside her, laying down my longsword and reaching for her bonds.

"Sh!" I cautioned in a whisper. "We are friends. We have come to help you."

"Who are you?" came her answering whisper. "How did you learn of me? You are my color, yet are not of my world."

"I am an Earthman; Jan of the Bardonian tribe," I told her. "I come from a distant world that was conquered and destroyed by the Black Raiders. I was sentenced to this Moon of Exile, and have just now managed to escape from my chains. This here"—I nodded to the bird-man behind me—"is Abel the Tor. He too seeks his freedom."

She nodded, her blue eyes wide with excitement.

"We are going to arouse this Black," I went on. "We will force him to fly the ship and take us somewhere, anywhere so long as it is away from here. I heard Magog tell that he is the ship's pilot."

"You know Magog?" she asked.

"We have met," I answered.

As I spoke, the thongs dropped from her arms and together we rose, her golden head just topping my shoulders.

"Vonna thanks the gods of her ancestors for sending you," came her soft voice. "My own world has been destroyed by the terrible Vapors of Vengeance, and I, its sole survivor, was destined to a life of slavery. But Magog," she added thoughtfully; "will he not follow us?"

"Neither us nor any other," I answered. "He is dead."

"Dead?" The slightest of frowns showed her bewilderment.

"Yes; Prince Jan killed him," put in Abel, speaking for the first time in his high shrill voice. "Prince Jan can kill anybody. Prince Jan saved me from the Kamma, then killed Magog. They were both planning to murder you and—"

We had been speaking in whispers as we talked, so as not to awaken the Black. Now as a running of footsteps suddenly reached us, we froze to rigidity and listened. The next moment a wild crash roared out through the night; a loud metallic boom that sent a chill to the hearts of the three of us, and brought the sleeping barrack's guards leaping to their feet—the alarm gong!

Twice more it thundered out above the din of the storm, and then a loud voice cried:

"Out, guards! Out, all warriors! An Earthman has killed your Commander and fled to the ship! After him! After him! Tear him asunder! Avenge the noble Magog!"

Together we wheeled toward the open doorway. There running across the courtyard was the Kamma, who had somehow managed to free himself from his bonds.

His right hand held a longsword, his left a paralysis-wand. Nor had the alarm gong or his wild cries gone unnoticed. The great barracks, a moment before so dark and silent, was suddenly ablaze

68

with lights as its awakened inmates sprang to life. Its huge doors were flung back with a bang, as a hundred half-dressed guards and warriors came streaming into the open toward us with angry shouts and glittering weapons.

A startled gasp and a rustling sounded behind. Evidently the good fortune that had been with us was waning, and yet we must do something to meet this unexpected turn of fate.

"Close and bar the door," I called to Abel, then turned to meet the awakened Black, who was scrambling to his feet. The man's hands flew for his weapons, but before he could draw them my longsword was at his throat, and he was forced to raise his arms while his eyes glared their anger.

Outside, the shouts and running footsteps came nearer. I could hear Abel's frenzied efforts as he sought to reach the door and bar it against the guards. Another ten seconds and they would be upon us, yet I dared not turn to help him or take my eyes off the Black before me. There came the sound of a mad scraping, then a frantic call from the bird-man.

"The bar, Prince Jan! The bar!" he screamed. "It will not go into place—it is stuck!"

The leading guards were scarcely five paces off, running madly.

"Raise it a bit to release it from the catch—it has caught!" I cried.

There came the sound of a last wild effort from Abel, a loud shout from without. And then the bar shot into place just as the first guard flung himself against the door—late by a fraction of a second!

At sword's point I forced the Black before me to the front of the ship, whose metallic wall was studded with glittering levers and instruments, in the center of which was the thick-glassed lookout window.

"Get us out of here!" I ordered. I knew that if we did not soon get aloft we never could, for a continuous rain of blows was now being sent against the door. Despite its thickness it could not withstand that furious onslaught more than a few minutes.

The Black sought respite in a parley. "But what you ask is impossible," he began. "I know nothing of the handling of—"

"Don't lie!" I broke in, and made the gesture that threatened to send my blade plunging through his throat. "Do you take this ship aloft, or remain here to wallow in your own blood?"

It was enough. His comrades were scarcely a longsword's length away, but the thick door that stood between gave me ample time to butcher him before they could come to his aid. With a shrug he turned to the control gears, his hand reaching for an oval-shaped instrument just above his head.

"Hurry, and no tricks," I warned, emphasizing the words with a sharp prod of my sword. The next moment there came a soft whirring sound that vibrated through the entire length of the great space-flyer, and the huge ship was rising into the void, while the shouts of the guards grew fainter, then died away.

Well, we were off. It did not mean we had made good our escape, of course, but at least there was no danger of an immediate capture. All the other ships on the Moon of Lost Souls were freighters, which could not hope to compete with us in flight. It would be hours before a fleet could be sent to find us, and by then we should be well out into space, with a million worlds and planets to choose from as a hiding place. Higher and higher we rose.

The Black pilot had clicked on the switch that sent a huge beam of light shooting into the rain ahead. He paused to look at a small, compass-like instrument, before he turned to me.

"I have obeyed you and we are aloft, Earthman, but not for long," he said, and there was a triumphant ring in his voice. "The fuel tank was nearly exhausted when we arrived, but we did not stop to have it replenished, for nearby Capara was our next stop. I doubt if we can keep going more than an hour. You have no alternative other than the mother planet or a return to the prison farms—unless you prefer to drift around in space till you are over-taken by the fleet that will be sent to find you."

Could not keep going for more than an hour! This was a surprise. The eyes of Vonna and Abel went to mine. I had given no thought to any definite destination—it was enough that we were leaving the Moon of Lost Souls. Any world could be reached by the Black Raiders, and they were sure to follow. It might have been that a return to my own planet was behind it all, but now the words of the Black pilot doomed that, for it was a journey that would require some hundreds of days, while we had but fuel enough to keep us going an hour.

Then as I stood there, bewildered and uncertain, there came that sudden flash of light that showed my only course—the words of my fellow captives the first night I had spent in the fields: "The Moon of Madness," they had said. "Capara's second satellite." "The only place in all space the Black Raiders will not go." "It must be something ghostly and terrible, for the Black Raiders tremble when the name, the Moon of Madness, is mentioned."

Directly ahead was that tiny satellite itself, scarcely a hundred miles in circumference, and looming larger every minute. Vonna and Abel were looking at me expectantly, for whatever my decision, they would abide by it. Then, as I continued to stare ahead:

"Where will we go. Prince Jan?" asked Abel.

"The one place no Black Raider will go, the only place where they will not follow," I answered him; then turning to the pilot, I pointed to the tiny world that showed through the thick glass of the lookout window.

"That is our destination, straight ahead—that unknown little satellite your own people call the Moon of Madness!"

For an hour the great spaceship plunged steadily ahead, while all the time that tiny world loomed up ever closer.

The Black pilot had put up a loud protest when I named our destination, and it required more than one jab of my sword, as well as several threats of immediate death, before he would continue our flight. Evidently it meant eternal banishment from his own land, as well as a life of torture in the hereafter; for he said he would be unable to return to Capara, even if that remote chance ever did present itself, once he had set foot on the Moon of Madness, as it was the law of the Black Raiders to slay any and all who returned from that terrible satellite—a law, he added, that had been made by the glorious Queen Tara so many thousands of years ago there was no record of its origin.

Presently I heard Vonna call to me from another compartment. The girl had been exploring the ship, for we had given it but a brief scrutiny and the back rooms might contain anything. Handing my shortsword to Abel with the words that he was to use it at the first sign of treachery from the Black pilot, I hurried through two large rooms, was soon beside the Penelopian Princess and knew the cause of her excitement.

It was a good-sized room in which she stood—the sleeping-quarters with its thousand or more tiny cots rising in tiers from the floor to the ceiling, and running along the broad expanse of the room in rows. And half of them were occupied. At least five hundred Black Raiders were lying on their backs, strapped to the cots with hands folded on their breasts in that drugged, death-like coma, from which the counteracting serum alone could awaken them.

At first I could not understand their presence, for this was a ship used only in conveying the ransoms and tributes of the various worlds to the mother planet. It was Vonna who enlightened me.

"These warriors are used solely to impress the various worlds and kingdoms the ransom ship visits," she said. "Always, when they landed in the courtyard of my father's castle, the warriors would march behind Magog, stern and silent, as he received the payments demanded by Queen Tara—grim reminders of their power and what could be expected were we to be backward or hesitant in its delivery.

"And did they not also demand ransom of your world?" she asked.

"No," I admitted, "but the reason for that is plain. My world had been robbed of its treasures thousands of years before the Black Raiders landed upon it. Our legends tell us that first there were the Migs, who came and conquered the Earth five hundred thousand years ago, and that their descendants remained for many generations.

"When they finally left they took with them nearly everything of value my planet had to offer. Centuries passed; then came the Saurian men, who either seized or despoiled what was left. When the Black Raiders finally came they found only a ravaged, treasure-less world, and a primitive, war-like people, divided into numerous small tribes and constantly fighting among themselves.

"So no matter how barren the Moon of Madness proves to be, or how war-like its inhabitants, if indeed it is inhabited, it will be only the hardy life to which I am accustomed. It is for you, Princess Vonna, that I fear, as in all likelihood we are doomed to spend our lives on that bleak little satellite. Perhaps I should have had the pilot return to Capara as he suggested, or—"

"No," she broke in hastily. "No; you have done right, exactly as I would have wished. All who were dear to me are now dead, and only my freedom is left. I would not want the Blacks to claim that also. No, Jan—er—Prince Jan." She stopped for an instant and smiled. "It is Prince Jan, isn't it? I heard the bird-man call you that."

I nodded, looking intently at the redness of her lips, the waving loveliness of her golden hair, the beauty of her youthful face. And perhaps the approval of my gaze was noticed by the slender princess, for her eyes dropped shyly to the floor and a crimson flush mounted her cheeks. She was very, very beautiful.

resently we heard Abel call. We returned to the pilot room. It was now dawn, the storm had passed, and directly ahead in that clear morning light, rushing swiftly toward us, was the weird and tiny world that was our destination—a small, bleak and desolate satellite, whose ugly, age-blackened surface appeared as one great boulder countless millions of years had seared and broken into jagged plains and peaks and valleys, studded occasionally with the gaping mouths of long-extinguished volcanoes.

The bird-man stood behind the pilot with ready sword. "He says we should not land, Prince Jan," said Abel. "He says it would be better for us all if he were to stop the ship and let us die out here in space. I told him you would kill him if he did."

The Black turned, fear showing in his eyes.

"You do not know the danger, Earthman," he cried. "You cannot understand. It is beyond the conception of one of your primitive race."

"Suppose you try enlightening me," I suggested.

"It is the oldest world in space—the birthplace of Time!" he answered in an awed whisper. "Yes; somewhere on that bleak little satellite the great god, Time, once came into being. Can you not realize the enormity of it? Can you not understand what is certain to happen if we invade the sanctuary of a god? A hideous fate, perhaps a drawn-out existence filled with torture, that will last down through the ages. Let us stay aloft out here in space where death will at least be normal, for once we have landed, our exhausted tanks will not permit us to rise again.

"And perhaps there is a chance we may not die," he went on earnestly. "Perhaps if we remain out here, the fleet will come upon us sooner or later and we shall all be saved."

But I had little faith in tire guard, and less that the arrival of the fleet would better the fortunes of either Vonna, Abel or myself—a life of slavery for the Penelopian Princess, and torture and death for the bird-man and me, would be the probable outcome. With a shake of my head I motioned the Black to continue his course and there must have been a finality in the gesture, for he gave a half-sob, then turned to the control gears once more.

But now that tiny world ahead was almost upon us. Soon we had plunged into its thin atmosphere, and shooting downward at terrific speed had a brief glimpse of black plains and towering peaks that flashed across the lookout window, weird and dream-like, and several times the gaping mouths of huge volcanoes; but no life or habitation showed on its desolate landscape, and presently the great ship came to rest, halting its mad rush at the last moment to right itself, then settle lightly in the center of a small valley.

There was a moment's silence on our part following the landing, for we were now upon that unknown world of a thousand ghostly legends, the only world on which the fearless Black Raiders themselves refused to land. What perils or horrors it might contain we could not even guess, but that human urge to know the unknown was strong within the breasts of all of us; and presently I had unbarred the door, flung it back and was stepping into the tomb-like stillness without, while behind me in wide-eyed awe and silence came the others.

It was a weird little valley in which we had landed, a valley entirely surrounded by towering peaks of jagged and fantastic formations, that glowed in the rising sun with a lustrous black hue. And the surface of that little valley was seared and gashed with a million cracks. Everything around us bore an uncanny, ghostly aspect, a hoary age almost terrifying. It was as though this tiny world had known a hundred billion years before any other came into being. And then as we continued to stand and stare I suddenly realized the significance of the smooth blackness of everything.

It was a petrified world on which we stood, a tiny jagged world of black stone, covered with the smooth ebon film of petrification!

Evidently the others realized it also, for presently Abel said in a dull, apathetic tone:

"It's—it's all stone. Prince Jan. Everything is black stone."

"It's the birthplace of Time," was the awed whisper of the pilot, and his voice seemed to come from a million miles away.

"It's a world of stone, at any rate," I answered. "An ancient, ancient, age-blackened world. A world of such a hoary, unthinkable antiquity that—"

And then I stopped as though an unseen hand had been clapped over my mouth. From over the jagged peaks ahead a sound had suddenly reached us. Breathlessly we listened while it grew louder. Now we could hear it plainly, a steady, rapid *boom-boom-boom,* that might have come from miles away, for in the death-like stillness of that world of stone the vibration's din was almost limitless. Occasionally it would pause for a moment, only to resume that grim foreboding *boom-boom-boom,* whose origin we instantly knew—drums!

We were not alone on the Moon of Madness!

Chapter IX
Blood-Stained Altars

There could be no doubt about it.

From beyond the jagged heights encircling that tiny valley unseen humans, or at least unseen things, were beating a steady cadence for some unknown reason.

It would be difficult to pen the individual effect it had on those around me, but they were one in keeping rigidity and a wide-eyed, breathless silence. Nor was it to be wondered at. There was something uncanny, something terrible in the rhythmical beating coming to us through that tomb-like stillness, for it represented life where there should be no life—and somehow life seemed out of place on that age-old world of stone.

It was Vonna who spoke first. "Drums," came her soft voice. "Signal drums, perhaps? Can it be possible a strange race of people live here; that they saw the ship descending and are gathering their numbers before coming to investigate?"

"It is hard to say," I answered, hardly conscious of my words as I scanned the surrounding peaks. "I saw no sign of life as we descended, but then our speed was so great I could have missed it."

"No," came the rising voice of the Black pilot, and it was evident the strain was beginning to tell upon his nerves. "No; you did not miss it, for it was not there. It is the drums of the dead we hear, the drums of the long-dead who guard the birthplace of Time. They are assembling; then they will come forward and claim us." He broke down and commenced to weep.

"Nonsense," I answered. "Those drums are beaten by beings as much alive as you and I. The fact that they wait to gather their numbers before coming here tells they're not over-courageous beings at that. Yes, they are real enough, and unless I am very much mistaken we shall soon have proof of that reality."

The Black, unconvinced, stood in the doorway as though uncertain whether he should leave it or seek a hiding-place within the ship. And then, quite unexpectedly, there occurred that which decided the question without the necessity for further thought. Out from the silence of the peaks behind us there suddenly rolled another, faster, louder and much nearer *boom-boom-boom* of a drum, and with a scream the Black pilot turned and fled down the passageway to the far end of the ship.

"Let us all get inside," I said to the others. "It is evident we are being surrounded, and until we learn what manner of humans they are, and their intentions, it will be safe within the ship."

The day passed slowly. With eyes strained on the lookout window we awaited the appearance of the inhabitants of that tiny world, and made plans for the future. Upon his promise of loyalty I armed the Black pilot with longsword and shortsword. It was not difficult to obtain such a pledge, for the man had been in an almost speechless funk since our landing and realized that any attempt at treachery could at best but reduce an already tiny party, and hasten his own end.

But despite our long and vigilant watch we saw nothing, though several times we heard the beating of distant drums, and once a drawn-out scream so far and faint we could not be certain whether it was man or beast. At dusk I stepped from the ship for a few minutes and watched the sun's last rays grow fainter on the black peaks around us—a sun, incidentally, much larger than the one I had known on my own planet, for we were now three hundred million miles beyond the green star, and its own distance as well from its sun.

With the coming of night the tension increased, for we felt its blackness heralded an attack of some kind. All that day we had the feeling that unseen eyes were upon us. There was nothing tangible the eye could spot, only an eery perception that we were being watched, and that those same watchers were but waiting for the darkness to make their presence known. An air of impending disaster hung over the entire valley.

It was at last decided that we three men stand turn at keeping an all-night guard. Mine was the first watch. Vonna then retired to a nearby chamber, while Abel and the Black threw themselves upon the small cots they had dragged into the pilot room and were soon asleep. The hours passed slowly; then along about midnight I awakened them, and with their promise of a wary vigilance, sought slumber for the first time in many hours.

It was broad daylight when I opened my eyes. The sun had long risen and its warm rays were streaming through the open doorway. But what surprised me most was the solitude. There was no sign of my companions, or the slightest sound to betray their presence. Springing to my feet I ran swiftly from room to room, calling loudly as I traversed the entire length of the great ship, then returned again to the pilot room before I fully realized that awful truth—Vonna, Abel and the Black had vanished!

In the name of sanity what had happened? Where had they gone? If they had been captured and carried away, they would have at least put up a struggle enough to awaken me. And why had I not also been seized?

Half dazed by the suddenness of it all I ran out into the opening, looking hurriedly around and seeing only that bleak valley and the jagged peaks around it. I was about to return to the ship when a twinkle of steel caught my eye. In a moment I was beside it, picking it up—the shortsword I had given to the Black pilot the night before!

It was then I discovered the pass that led through the cliffs—a narrow cleft, twenty inches wide, directly before me—so narrow, in fact, that till now I had not seen it. Into this I hurried, my shoulders turned sideways that I might enter. It wound and twisted in a serpentine manner, several times narrowing to such a width as to be almost impenetrable, then suddenly at a sharp angle debouched upon a dreary plain and the strange, strange world beyond.

It was a black and desolate sweep of stone that stretched away to the far horizon and a distant outline of gigantic peaks, of such towering heights and fantastic formations as to appear as the creations of a nightmare. Fully a score of miles away arose those colossal barriers, but what at once caught my eye was that massive evidence of mankind; for far away on the uttermost tip of the highest of those great peaks was the outline of a mighty castle, its lofty turrets, spires and towers rising upward to disappear in the clouds.

Nearby—a mile or so away—were three small hills.

I did not hesitate. I did not even give a thought as to what I could hope to accomplish single-handed. With that unthinking, characteristic rashness that has so often brought me to the brink of death, I started off at a rapid trot I could keep up for hours, toward that distant castle in the sky as I somehow felt it was there I would find the three I sought.

So swift had been my impulse, and so quickly had I acted upon it, that I had gone some distance before I realized I was unarmed save for the shortsword I had found and now held in my hand. But to retrace my steps to the ship and back would take many minutes, and might prove a fatal delay to those I sought to aid. And yet there seemed no other way. The three small hills were now before me, as was the black mouth of a large cave in the heart of the center one, in front of which rose a small stone dais. I was in the very act of halting my advance when the frantic cry of my name sent my gaze sweeping skyward.

"Prince Jan! Prince Jan!"

There a score of feet above my head and winging madly toward me, was the familiar figure of Abel the bird-man. He carried Vonna in his arms. The eyes of both of them were rude in horror as they cast continuous glances backward, and it was evident that Abel was nearly exhausted. The next instant I knew the cause. Close behind

80

and gaining rapidly came a huge, serpent-like thing, fully twenty feet long, whose great wings and dull, brown body stamped it as both terrorizing and repulsive.

It was evident that grim race was swiftly drawing to a close. Another moment and the horrible thing would be upon them. Indeed, how they had managed to stay away from it this long was a mystery. The wings of both the pursued and pursuer were churning the air with a loud flapping.

Vonna looked down, forgetful of her own danger. "Run, Jan!" she screamed. "Run! Run for your life!"

How all this had come about I did not know, though I was certain of its outcome were not drastic steps immediately taken. There was but one chance for them—if only I could gain the attention of the awful thing that followed. Yet even as I thought this, I was running forward, shouting for Abel to fly toward me. Just before the cave I halted, and even in the excitement of that wild moment was conscious of footsteps within—some other terrible beast, perhaps. But I dared not divert my gaze from the grim tableau before me. Then several things happened almost simultaneously.

There came a frantic flurry of wings—Abel sank, panting and helpless, beside me—I heard Vonna come to her feet with a little cry of terror as gruff voices sounded from the cave—and then that snake-like thing shot straight toward me with the speed of a spaceship, its great mouth open and hissing loudly.

Straight into those onrushing jaws I plunged my shortsword to the hilt. The impact flung me against the side of the hill, which rose upright for a dozen feet, then sloped toward the top, but it also brought a hiss of pain and anger from the snake-thing. In a flash its tail whipped around and toward me, missing my head by a dozen inches in the awful blow that would have broken every bone in my body had it landed.

Before it could recover I leaped forward, and with every ounce of my strength sent my sword plunging once, twice, three times, into the scaly, armor-like skin of its neck. A long, fork-like tongue shot out toward me, but a backhand slash of my blade severed it close to the root. With a loud, bloody bubbling, the snake-thing rose into the air, streaming a crimson, fetid froth.

But it was evident it had no intention of relinquishing the struggle. With huge wings flapping dismally it circled slowly around as though waiting for some opening, then suddenly dove once more toward me. Again my blade plunged into those open jaws; again that tail whipped once, but this time I was only partly successful in evading it, for it half caught me with the terrible blow that threw me to my knees, and sent my shortsword flying from my hand.

In a flash that huge mouth shot toward me, and defenseless as I was, I was nearer to death that instant than ever before in my life. It was a nearby boulder that saved me. In falling, my hand had come upon a heavy stone the size of a fist, and without waiting to rise I let drive at that hideous head with the vicious throw that smashed my jagged stone into a lidless eye, and closed that wicked little orb as its owner shied away.

Half dazed I rose to my feet, weaponless. Once more the snake-thing rose high into the air, then gathering its waning strength for a final charge, dove suddenly toward me in a mad, blind rush.

What happened was so fantastic as to seem almost incredible; and it must have been that the god of luck was with me; for as that giant body plunged down to mine, and Vonna's scream came to me, I gave the sudden side-step that sent it shooting past me, to smash against that hill of stone with a loud crash that could be heard for miles!

Picking up my shortsword I sprang upon the dazed and dying snake-thing. With two strong strokes its head was severed and a rivulet of thick blood gushed forth, to turn the blackened ground a dirty crimson; though it was some moments before life had fully left its scaly body, and that huge tail ceased its thrashing. But it would never battle or pursue another, and presently its long thick bulk lay still.

𝕴 turned to gaze upon a weird assembly. From the nearby cave, watching me intently, a hundred or more beast-like men had issued—short, stocky, white-skinned men some five feet in height, with great beards that covered their faces and fell upon their hairy breasts and bodies. Their little eyes were blood-shot and close-set. Their crooked legs were short and heavy, their arms long and muscular. Their thick brown hair grew low on their receding brows, and hung down their shoulders and backs. About their loins were faded skins of animals from which the fur had long since worn away, and some were even minus this primitive apparel. Each carried a heavy, knotted bludgeon.

Vonna and Abel, who had managed to put distance between them and the newcomers during the struggle, now glided beside me. And perhaps my own appearance was as unique to the little men as theirs to me, for I was disheveled and grimy, my leather trappings torn, and covered with the thick blood of the snake-thing.

We stood staring at each other; then I spoke. "What do you want?" I asked.

They looked at me in a dull, brute-like wonderment.

"Who are you, strange warrior?" said one. "Who are you who single-handed kills a trok, and speaks the language of the Nine Terrible Sisters?"

"A stranger to your world," I answered. "I come from a distant star, as do my companions."

They came forward, but more in curiosity than menace. They muttered among themselves for a few minutes; then:

"What are you doing here?" asked the spokesman, who appeared to be one of authority among them.

"Searching your world for such as you," I answered. "We want to be friends," Again they conferred; then the spokesman said:

"Come, we will be friends. I am Shebak, Chief of the tribe of Shebak, and these are my people."

In another minute they were all around us, curious, feeling our trappings, and asking questions. Several of them gathered around the dead snake-thing—a trok, they called it. From what I could gather they seldom ever saw one, for it was supposed to inhabit some strange world within their own, and only on rare occasions flew to the surface through some long-extinct volcano. They looked at me in awe, for they said killing one single-handed was unheard of.

Plainly these primitive people were but a step above the beast. They spoke in muffled tones, and in halting, short phrases, as though it were only with the greatest effort the words would come forth at all. The questions they asked were few and simple.

Presently, at a word from Shebak, they drew up in a long line, and totally ignoring us, raised their heads solemnly to the sun, and with arms extended above them murmured a weird chant. Several of their number, who carried odd-shaped, primitive drums, now began a steady thumping, low at first, then gradually rising till at last it drowned out the prayer of the others. These, then, were the drums we had heard on our arrival, and it was evident their owners were some strange sect of sun-worshippers.

It was now that I began to take stock of my surroundings. A time-worn pathway led into the blackened mouth of the cave, and through the gloom beyond. But before it rose that which was far more sinister—a stone, altar-like dais, from whose holed side protruded heavy stakes, to which a bound victim could be tied and laid across its hard surface. The altar itself was caked with dull, brownish stains, as was its immediate vicinity.

The rites concluded, Shebak came forward as though to lead us into the cave. But I wished to be more certain as to his intentions. Vonna and Abel had also noticed those sinister-looking stains, and gathered close to me. I pointed to the altar.

"For what purpose do you use the dais, Shebak?" I asked.

The stocky little man pointed to Capara, hanging massive and majestic in the sky.

"It is the altar of the Sisters," he answered. "Once every fifty dusks the Nine Terrible Sisters fly out from their Castle in the Clouds, and carry one of us off to their lofty fortress, so that they may drink red blood and prolong their age-old existence."

"They drink blood?" I asked.

"Of course," he answered. "It is what they live on. They are Vampire-Women. They fear only the sun we worship, for if its warm rays strike them they will crumble to the dust that should have claimed them millions of years ago."

"How long have they been here?" I went on.

"Since time began," he informed briefly.

"Where are they now?" I continued.

He pointed to that far-away fortress in the sky, whose frowning portals showed dark and ugly against the surrounding blue.

"Lying in their moldy graves, deep in the dungeons of their terrible castle, awaiting nightfall when they may come to life once more. Queen Tara left them there to guard the great god, Time, and the secret of the Black Tower, countless ages ago.

"It is there they hold the great god prisoner. It is there they guard some great secret, which were it known, would bring destruction to the mother planet, Capara.

"But they will come at dusk," he went on. "Yes, at dusk they will be here, for it is tonight they come to carry one of us off to the castle to sate their terrible thirsts."

He nodded to Vonna.

"It will probably be the golden woman they will take with them, for she is young and tender, and her blood sure to be sweet. Yes; it will surely be her they will take with them to their terrible castle this night."

Chapter X
The Thing that Came in the Night

There was an apathetic tone of resignation in the voice of Shebak as he spoke, a finality that told of the many years, of the many generations, his kind had known only an unquestioned submission. The others, too, were staring in a dull, beast-like stolidity. It was as though it never occurred to them that they might question the authority of the Vampire-Women. Evidently they accepted their commands and perpetrations as being as inevitable as death, or night and morning.

"Suppose she refuses to go with them?" I said after a pause. "Suppose your own people would refuse to go with them?"

"Would they not take them anyhow?" he demanded.

"Not if you stopped them," I answered.

"How could we do that?" he asked.

"Kill them," I replied.

He looked at me in a dull wonderment for a moment. What his thoughts were I did not know, but presently he said: "Come, I will take you to our huts, where we can eat," and with that the matter was temporarily dismissed.

Holding Vonna's hand, I followed Shebak into the cave, while close behind us came Abel and the stocky men, the latter with their bludgeons on their shoulders and trooping along wordlessly on their short, crooked legs. Our way led down a cold, smooth decline, worn hollow by the countless bare feet that had traversed it for ages.

But what at once caught my eye was the construction of the passage—it was evident that at some remote date this broad decline had been hewn by human hands, a theory strengthened by the many grotesque carvings on the surrounding walls. Gladly would I have tarried, but Shebak continued on without the pause that would permit a closer inspection, and presently the trail debouched up the strange village, and the stranger, buried country of the tribe Shebak—the world of eternal twilight.

The first impression was that we had come upon a great subterranean chamber, though I was to learn later that it was indeed a tiny, man-made world, that stretched away for several miles into the surrounding gloom on all sides of us. The only means of light and ventilation came from the numerous holes, twenty inches in circumference, which had been bored into the jagged roof some twenty feet overhead at regular intervals, and penetrated on through to the petrified surface of the black world forty feet above us.

There were thousands of them—thousands of those rounded holes from which streamed the light of the world above in pale and ghostly beams. This alone told of a labor and workmanship far beyond that of the primitive people who lived here—relics, perhaps, of a distant civilized race that had long since passed into oblivion. Like weird haloes streamed those thin pale glows of light, to cast their eery reflections upon the forty or more tiny, clay-built, cone-shape huts that now rose up before us.

The surface of this dank world was a hard, damp clay, patted smooth by the countless naked feet that had trod it for ages. From nearby came the noisy gurgling of a swift-moving, underground river.

Toward this primitive village we were led, and to the hut of Shebak, where we were well fed on hot wheat loaves and boiled tiny fish from the nearby river, a narrow stream in whose cold, shallow waters I was able to bathe and remove the blood and grime of my recent battle. The dead trok had been brought along by several of the men, cut into great pieces and consigned to the boiling-pots. From what I could make out, it was considered a rare delicacy, as the tribe seldom, if ever, captured one, and they could not understand why we three newcomers refused to partake of such a treat.

All in all the little community numbered, perhaps, three hundred humans. My six feet four inches of height, short black curly hair and beardless face were a source of wonderment to them, as were the bald pate and skinny arms and legs of the bird-man. They could hardly take their eyes from Vonna, whose golden beauty they regarded as something unreal and fragile.

Immediately following their meal the men curled up in sleep, while the slovenly, stupid-looking women, who wore only the skins of animals around their waists, and whose mentality, if anything, was inferior to that of their lords, returned to their clay fields and resumed the primitive agriculture that grew their simple needs; for it seemed that feminine labor alone prevailed in this strange world, even to supplying food and clothes. The men did nothing—absolutely nothing—even their bludgeons being carried for show, the women later using them to slay small animals that abounded in the two underworld forests.

It was now that I first learned how Vonna and Abel had been captured, as well as the fate of the missing Black pilot.

"It was shortly before dawn, Prince Jan," the bird-man explained. "The Black had stepped outside the ship for a bit, when suddenly I heard a slight noise like that of a struggle. The Princess Vonna, who had awakened and returned to the pilot room, followed me to investigate, as we did not wish to awaken you unless it was necessary. Hardly had we stepped without before a great claw seized each of us, and we were borne up into the blackness.

"For a time we could hear only a flapping of wings, and could not be sure what manner of creature had seized us. Dawn showed the terrible snake-thing, as well as the one ahead which carried the struggling Black pilot. Presently they came to ground in a small hollow between two hills. I whispered for the Princess Vonna to feign death, and I did likewise. The terrible beasts then killed and ate the pilot before our eyes, and fell into a slumber. When I was sure they were asleep, I whispered to the Princess, and gathering her in my arms, rose up and flew in the direction of the ship. But one of the snake-things must have awakened and started in pursuit. We were rapidly being overtaken when fate sent you toward us. The rest you know."

Soon after this one of the women, Shebak's mate, came to us to say that her lord had ordered we be shown their buried, man-made world. For several hours we followed her through a maze of wonders, seeing the tiny, subterranean fields of wheat and vegetables, and the two small forests in which roamed a number of small, harmless animals that supplied the tribe of Shebak with both meat and skins—forests whose twenty-foot trees brushed the jagged roof overhead.

As to the origin of this world our guide was hazy, though we gathered it had been hewn many thousands of years ago by the inhabitants of that little planet above us, during the long ages the surface of their small moon had been gradually changing from earth to stone. There had been thousands of them then, and they had managed to dig a world some twenty miles square. But the many sacrifices demanded by the Vampire-Women down through the centuries had gradually reduced them to their present small number, and the woman added that another hundred years would doubtless see them extinct.

By the time we returned to the village, Shebak and his men had awakened and were sitting in a circle around a small fire, discussing some topic obviously important by their manner and gesticulations. At our approach they stopped, to gaze at us with their narrow, blood-shot eyes. Shebak motioned us to come forward and be seated; then he spoke.

"We have been talking among ourselves, strange warrior—talking of what you said," he began. "Never before have we dared to think such things, let alone speak them, but always do our numbers grow less, and we are desperate. If we do not do something soon, there will be none of us left to do anything. But how," he asked, "may we save ourselves?"

"What of the course I suggested?" I answered.

"But we cannot do that," said one. "They would be immune to our weapons and any normal death. Our legends tell us that once, ages ago, a bold chief of our tribe attempted to defy the Nine Terrible Sisters, but that the Vampire-Women called the Wolves of Worra—the black, cloven-hoofed wolves from the inner world—to aid them, and that a thousand of our people were devoured, and the chief subjected to such fiendish tortures that the echoes of his terrible shrieks can often be heard in the dead of night, even to this day."

"The rays of the sun alone will crumble them," said another, leaning forward as his little eyes found mine.

"Why not hold them till the coming of daylight, then?" I suggested. "As to their invulnerability, it is my belief that a well-placed sword-thrust or bludgeon blow will prove the contrary.

"Not that you should fall upon them without warning," I went on. "First tell them that they must never again harm any of your people, or return to this country."

"But they will refuse," said Shebak. "I know they will. They will be angry and probably sacrifice many of us on the stone altar as a punishment for such rashness."

"Then slay them," I answered. "After all, there are only nine of them, and you number more than a hundred warriors."

"Suppose they call upon the wolves to aid them?"

"Then slay the wolves also," I replied.

They conferred among themselves for some minutes. At last Shebak turned to me.

"Will you lead us if we defy the Vampire-Women, strange warrior?" he asked. "Will you speak to them tonight, and if they seek battle, will you lead us?"

"If you wish it, yes," I answered.

"We do," said Shebak. "We do, we accept you." Then the others echoed after him in unison: "We do. We accept you."

The women, who had come forward and squatted about the edge of the circle, now began a low beating of the drums and clapping of their hands. This seemed to be an awaited signal, for one by one the men rose to their feet, and screwing their faces into the most hideous grimaces and contortions, commenced a slow dance around the fire, chanting in time to their steps:

"We accept him. He shall lead us. We accept him. He shall lead us."

With the gradual rising of the drums, excitement and abandon waxed. Faster, faster became the dancing, louder, louder the yells of the dancers. The women rose and fell in unison, shrieking at the top of their voices. The men swung their bludgeons savagely at imaginary foes, with many boasts of the strength and the valor that was theirs. The din was deafening, but blood-quickening as well, and it was some minutes before the tribe of Shebak had run the gamut of their emotions, and lay back on the hard-packed clay, panting and exhausted.

But as the pale light streaming through the holes grew paler in the dimness that announced the coming of dusk, their bravado was replaced by silence and nervous glances toward the pass that led to the cave above. As the dusk deepened, numerous torches were lit and stuck in the age-old niches.

It had been agreed that with the coming of darkness Shebak and a dozen of his sturdiest warriors, together with myself, would meet the Vampire-Women at the mouth of the cave and order them away. But it required considerable encouragement and urging before they would follow me. At last, however, they agreed, and with several of their number holding flaming torches we again traversed the tomb-like blackness of the shaft, and a few minutes later emerged into a glorious night and a million glittering stars.

Out here all was clear and calm—the combined light of a huge moon and the mellow glow of gigantic Capara, brightening the bleak surface of the tiny world we trod with a soft, silvery radiance. Miles away rose the towering outlines of the mighty peaks and the ugly blotch on the highest of them that we knew was the Castle in the Clouds.

Scarcely had we taken our station, when: "Look!" exclaimed Shebak, pointing. "Lights! Lights in the castle!" and sure enough, out from that eery, far-away blotch, a little golden twinkle had suddenly shone forth; then, in rapid succession, another and another.

"The Vampire-Women!" gasped one in a frightened whisper. "Again the Nine Terrible Sisters have arisen from their coffins, and walk once more through their great halls of death!"

"Soon one of their number will come to claim one of us," added another after a pause. "Oh, we are fools to even try to thwart them!"

It had a strange effect on those stocky men around me, that lighted castle in the sky, and it required considerable effort on my part to prevent a wild retreat into their buried world once more. At length they agreed to remain with me, though it was evident the watch was not a popular one.

An hour passed; then suddenly a flapping of wings sounded in the blackness overhead, and the next moment a human form dropped lightly to the ground before us.

Up till now I had little faith in the stories I had heard of the Vampire-Women but the sudden appearance of the weird thing before us seemed wholly to justify them. It was a tall feminine figure; a slender, shapely black woman, devoid of even the slightest wearing-apparel, whose long straight hair hung down her back with a blackness almost blue, clasped with a golden ring at the back of her head. The face was that of a black granite statue, a terrible hardness that depicted every conceivable evil, cruelty and lust. The thin, slightly parted lips showed a row of beast-like white teeth, and the glittering, agate-like nails protruding from her tapering fingers, flashed and sparkled like diamonds in the torchlight.

From each of her shoulders protruded a huge, membranous, bat-like wing.

At the sudden appearance of that nude, black body, a frightened gasp arose from the warriors behind me; then with horrified cries, half of their number turned and fled down the age-old shaft, leaving Shebak, five others and myself to face the newcomer. The Vampire-Woman wasted no time in salutation.

"Out, out, all of you!" came her high, strong voice. "Bring forth your women-folk and your young that I may choose one to—" and then her eyes fell upon me and went wide.

"Golden Blood of Tara!" she exclaimed. "Who is this one?"

"A stranger, Great Sister," ventured Shebak. "A stranger. He comes from a distant star and—"

"A lie!" snapped the Vampire-Woman. "None dares come to this world. It is the command of Tara herself!

"But can he not speak? Has he no tongue?" she demanded.

"Yes; he has a tongue and—"

"Then find it!" she cried, wheeling to me, "or must I find it with the plucking-tongs?"

"What is it you wish to know?" I asked.

"Oh, so you can talk, eh?" The Vampire-Woman stepped back where she could better see my face, her lips curled in a sneer, her hands on her hips, wholly unmindful of her nudity, and wicked and barbaric in the torchlight.

I nodded in a manner that did not decrease her wrath.

"Then explain your presence here, and quickly," she went on. "Who are you? Who is your tribe, and where is their hiding-place?"

I looked directly into the black eyes before me.

"My identity and that of my tribe is of no immediate importance," I answered, "though the message I have for you is. Neither you nor any of those other black fiends who dwell in yon castle must ever harm or come near these people again, or so much as set foot within a mile of this cave and their buried world."

"What!"

"The words were plain and you understood them. Return now to your kind and tell them that the tribe of Shebak will destroy them if they ever come here again. Haste! Not for long can I hold my itching sword-hand, or that desire to plunge cold steel into your putrid heart!"

At the mention of plunging steel into her heart, a wild terror sprang to the eyes of the Vampire-Woman, who up till now had been glaring only maniacal rage and hatred. She stepped back fearfully—incredulous, amazed.

Shebak and the others had noticed that sudden fear and were heartened by it. Now they came forward with raised bludgeons and muttering:

"Go, Vampire-Woman! Go or we will kill you!"

She glared wildly around her, then raised a faltering arm. "Stop, tribe of Shebak! Stop!" she screamed. "Have you gone mad? Has this man bewitched your minds?"

But the stocky little men came closer, growling angrily:

"Go! Go or we will kill you!"

She must have realized that they were indeed past her authority, for she continued to retreat as she spoke.

"I go, I go." She spoke hurriedly, for it was evident that in another minute the fast-mounting rage of the little men would hurl them upon her. "I go to tell the Sisters your answer, but remember what happened ages ago when a chief of your tribe sought to defy us. Again we will send the black wolf to the inner world to summon his cloven-footed brethren. Again they will come from the volcano in the great number that will sweep all before them. And tomorrow at sundown I and my sisters will wing from the castle, and lead them straight here to devour you all.

"Then we will see if this man can save you!" she cried. "Then we will see if the defiance he now flaunts can protect the tribe of She-bak from the dripping maws and rending teeth of the cruel Wolves of Worra!"

And with a wild scream that ended in a high, terrible laugh, the Vampire-Woman leaped into the air, and flapped dismally away into the night.

Chapter XI
Wolves of Worra

There was little sleep in the underground village of Shebak that night. Though the words of the Vampire-Woman had told that we need expect no immediate attack, excitement ran high, and it was quite late before the tribe settled down to sleep.

At dawn they were all up and about, making ready for the coming battle. Knives were sharpened, bludgeons inspected, and the long hair of the men pulled tightly to the back of their heads and secured in a knob, so as not to obstruct vision. Huge quantities of fish and game were boiled and tied to their persons, for the coming battle might last for hours, during which the warriors would have but brief intervals to eat.

All the while these hurried preparations were going on—since dawn in fact—a score of the older women had kept up a continuous beating of the drums, and chanting of age-old songs whose very origin had been lost centuries upon centuries ago.

By mustering every able-bodied man I was able to gather a fighting force of some hundred and forty warriors. Most of them were past their best years, but such seemed the general case with the populace of this strange world; most of the victims demanded by the Vampire-Women being between the ages of fifteen and forty, that left an inhabitance chiefly composed of children and elders.

It was decided we would meet the Wolves of Worra upon the plain just before the cave, and not allow them the advantage of gaining the shaft leading to the village. The women and children would remain in the huts with a guard of ten old warriors. Watchful sentries had been posted on the plains with instructions to warn us at the first approach of danger.

From what I could gather, the wolves were expected to come from the great volcano whose gaping mouth showed black and ugly on the plain some two miles away. The warriors said that a giant spiral runway led around its massive interior to the inner world, three miles below. None of them had ever been there, or even seen the Wolves of Worra, but they were certain they existed and would shortly be upon us.

Shebak had offered Vonna the protection of his own hut, along with his wife and child. All that morning the girl had been assisting the women in the preparations with a skill and swiftness that belied her royal heritage, and raised her high in the esteem of the tribe. She asked my opinion as to the outcome of the impending battle.

"There may not even be one," I answered with a smile. "Those Vampire-Women, or creatures, or whatever they are, have terrorized these people for years. Consequently, many stories are told of them about their supernatural powers. However, even if that is the case, I fail to see what we have to fear from a few hundred wolves. The warriors are armed with sharp knives and heavy bludgeons, and each should be a match for a dozen such animals."

Shebak, who had been listening, was certain of the struggle, but it was the Vampire-Women more than the wolves, that frightened him.

"They are the terrible ones, the Vampire-Women," he said, "for how may we kill creatures that die at dawn and awaken at dusk?—creatures who sleep the slumber of death in the hours of light but arise at sundown? Legend tells us that sharp steel alone must be buried in their hearts to bring eternal death."

Shortly before noon one of the sentries came tearing down the shaft and into the village, to report that moving forms could be seen emerging from the great volcano two miles away. In an instant all was confusion. The women made the air hideous with their screams, while the warriors hurried into their huts for knives and bludgeons.

With Shebak and several others I hurried up the shaft to the mouth of the cave, where several excited sentries beckoned our glances into the distance before us. Two miles away the open mouth of the volcano lay close to the earth, and rising from it were black, running forms, while nearby were numerous others.

Shebak shaded his eyes, then spoke: "It's they," he said with finality; "it's the first of the thousands of the cloven-footed wolves that will shortly be lining up on the plain. Doubtless the great spiral trail within the volcano is packed with them at this moment, all hurrying to answer the call of the Nine Terrible Sisters.

"But they will not attack till sundown," he went on, turning to me. "They will mass before the volcano in their great numbers, but they will wait for the Vampire-Women to fly from the castle and lead them against us. That is what they did, ages ago, when they nearly killed us all."

All that afternoon the Wolves of Worra continued to stream from the volcano in a seemingly endless black swarm, and join the great number already there. As the shadows began to lengthen and the sun to sink lower, there must have been five thousand of them assembled on the plain before us. They made no effort to attack or come nearer, but now as the waning light told the end of day, many of the great brutes squatted upon their haunches, and throwing back their heads to the dying sun howled out the long, blood-chilling wails that came floating over the desolate plain toward us.

I had drawn up my warriors in a triangular shape before the cave, placing the strongest in various positions of importance. With Shebak and his stoutest warrior on either side of me, it was my plan that we three would form the tip of the triangle and meet the brunt of the expected charge.

Not that we attempted to delude ourselves as to the outcome. In the face of those terrible odds there could be but one outcome, and we all knew it. They had but to give the one wild charge that would sweep all before them. The men of Shebak had resigned themselves to the inevitable, though with a surprising bravery, for they resolved to go down fighting. The women, who had come from the cave, were mingling among the warriors for a last farewell. Realizing the nearness of an attack, Shebak now ordered them below.

Vonna and I had been talking together, a little apart from the others.

"I suppose this means good-bye, Jan," she said, as the women began to move into the cave and back toward the village; and though the voice of the Penelopian Princess was steady, there was a suspicious moisture in her eyes. "My one regret is that I was unable to repay you for saving me from the Raiders."

"You will have ample time later. It should not take long to finish off those brutes," and I tried to smile as I lied.

But the girl knew better.

"No, Jan. Do not try to deceive me. You know as well as I do that it is the end."

"If we only had more warriors," I answered bitterly, looking around at that little group of primitive soldiery so soon to meet the onrush of thousands. "Or larger, well-armed men. Or for five hundred good blades! Why, we could sweep—"

"Jan!"

The eyes of Vonna went wide, and her little hand dug into my arm in excitement. "Jan!" she screamed. "The Raiders! The five hundred Black Raiders!"

"The wha—"

"The five hundred Raiders, Jan! The drugged warriors back in the ship! Arouse them! Awaken them and they will help us!"

In a flash I understood and realized what she expected of me. A mile away were five hundred seasoned fighters. If I could awaken and return with them in time we might yet be saved.

I wheeled to Shebak.

"Hold every man in place!" I cried. "Fight with a vengeance, and keep courage till my return! The tribe of Shebak may yet be saved!"

He did not answer, but nodded as the eyes of all of them flew to mine. The next moment I was beside the surprised Abel, and climbing on his back ordered him to fly swiftly to the ship. The Tor spread his great wings, and with me clinging tightly to him rose upward, then shot straight toward the tiny valley, cutting through the air with the speed of an arrow, and the wind screamed in our ears.

All this time the howls of the pack on the plain had been increasing. It was evident that the beasts were rapidly becoming impatient at the long delay. I strained a swift look backward at the distant Castle in the Clouds, fearful of the twinkling lights that would announce the Nine Terrible Sisters had again arisen from their coffins, but as yet no light gleamed through the gathering dusk.

Presently we topped the peaks surrounding the valley and a moment later came to the ground before the open door with a soft thud.

"This way, Prince Jan, follow me!" cried Abel, for I had whispered my plans to him in flight, and his years of confinement on the Moon of Lost Souls had familiarized him with the ships and habits of the Blacks. "They keep the awakening serum and the needles they use with it in the cabinets at the far end of the ship."

"Haste, for the love of your Ancestors!" I answered. "Even now the Sisters may be winging from the castle!"

Through the door and down the passageway we dashed to the cabinets at its far end, passing the five hundred drugged Raiders, our hurrying footsteps resounding loudly in the death-like stillness of the spaceship. Abel instructed me in the use of the needles and vials of thick, brown-colored fluid, and a moment later I was beside one of the cots, sinking my needle into the arm of its occupant, while the bird-man did likewise to the sleeper on another.

The two Raiders came to themselves, then sat up, wide-eyed in wonder. I thrust a needle and a small vial into the hands of each of them.

"Here! Help arouse the others!" I ordered. "Quickly, and ask no questions! It's a matter of life or death!"

They looked their surprise but spoke no words, and as I hurried on to the others I heard them come to their feet and follow my example. A minute later and six more were awakened. These were given the same brief orders, as were those whom they in turn restored to consciousness. From first till last it could not have been more than twenty minutes before the Raiders were aroused, and the entire five hundred of them, each with a longsword and shortsword strapped around his person, were pouring from the ship into the little valley where I addressed them.

Their ranks were buzzing with a thousand questions, but as I buckled a longsword and a shortsword around me I yelled above the din:

"Hear me, soldiers of Capara, hear me!" I cried. "Hear me before your throats have been ripped by terrible teeth! How all this came about and where you are is secondary, and can be explained later. Your lives depend on your immediate actions. A mile away five thousand wolves are preparing to attack a little party of a hundred and forty warriors. After that they will come here and fling themselves upon us!"

I paused, and the wild wailing of the wolves echoed to us.

"One course alone is open to you!" I shouted. "The ship's fuel tanks are exhausted, nor can you hope to leave this world. Unite yourselves then with the warriors on the plains. Together, with our combined strength, we may yet beat off that terrible pack. You are all armed. Hurry, then, and follow me. It's your only chance!"

Without waiting for an answer I turned and ran for the pass, shouting for Abel to fly ahead and tell Shebak we were coming.

Close behind me came the others, and as I hurried through the rocky defile I heard the steps of the following Raiders, and the scraping of their weapons against its narrow sides.

A grand assurance, that sound of arms, and increased by the knowledge that doughty swordsmen carried them. But as I came out from the defile to the moonlit plain beyond I beheld the sight which told I would need every one of them, for far away through the silvery gloom and towering high above us, the mighty outline of the Castle in the Clouds was a golden blaze of lights.

Just above us gigantic Capara covered half the heavens. The tiny silvery sphere that lay between was the prison satellite, the Moon of Lost Souls. Even now if they chanced to glance upward the warriors might realize where they were, and becoming terrorized, refuse to follow. But luckily the excitement of impending battle made them oblivious to all else, and if a few did guess their whereabouts, they made no mention of it.

But now the Black Raiders were streaming from the pass in wild disorder, some shouting, some laughing, but all of them willing to fight and slay with the fury that was theirs. One, an officer in their ranks, had been the first to follow me. At the sight of the lighted castle he roared a barbaric oath.

"Lights!" he exclaimed, his black features agleam with the joy of impending battle. "By the Beauty of Tara, lights! Then at least there are some humans on this hoary, jagged world!"

"Suppose your men discover they are more than humans?" I asked him. "Will they flinch and run from the ghostly and the unknown?"

The Black drew himself erect as though he faced a thousand. "We are soldiers of Tara, white man!" he answered proudly.

Across the plain we started at a fast run—the five hundred Raiders at our heels. Ahead the howls of the pack were increasing. Despite their recent drugged condition, it had in no way harmed the stability of the Blacks, and they were able to keep the rapid pace I set. We had come within hailing distance of the warriors before the cave, when suddenly the wild howls ceased, and then from the gloom beyond there thundered the deafening clatter of twenty thousand hoofs in a mad charge, rattling out loudly on the petrified plain, and every instant coming closer.

For a moment I was unable to understand its meaning, though always it drew nearer, that deafening wild clatter. But then as thousands of fiery eyes cut through the gloom toward us, and winged forms appeared above them, screaming fierce commands, I grasped its awful significance and set myself to meet it.

The cloven-hoofed Wolves of Worra were advancing to the attack, led by nine vile women who had been dead a million years!

Chapter XII
The Nine Terrible Sisters

Three hundred yards could not have separated us from the charging pack as we dashed up to the warriors of Shebak to add our strength to theirs. Never before had they seen a Black Raider, or the ebon ones beheld the likes of such as they; but at least they both were human, and by common consent united against that bestial horde.

In the few seconds that were left to us, I made a mad effort to form the men into protective squares.

"Back to back! Back to back!" I shouted. "Form squares and protect yourself on all sides!" Then that black pack was upon us, and with a crash we met them.

A great brute dashed toward me, and with a leap sprang for my throat. But those white teeth never found my flesh or came within a foot of their target, for even as his jaws flew open a vicious whir of my longsword sent his black head flying from his body, and dropped the carcass to roll limp and lifeless in a pool of crimson at my feet.

The next instant my shortsword plunged into the breast of a second.

From all sides arose the hideous din that announced the beginning of that terrible battle. Howls of triumph, shrieks of agony, the crashing of clubs on bestial skulls, the horrible gasps of throat-torn humans. And resounding high above all else arose the wild screams of the Vampire-Women.

Standing beside me and swinging his bludgeon in crushing blows was Shebak. The valor and fury of the little men surprised even themselves. It was as though the pent-up anger of generations was being vented in this wild hour. The Black Raiders, of course, fought with the skill and bravery expected of them.

Foremost of our dangers was the Vampire-Women. Flittering back and forth, just above our heads, were the Nine Terrible Sisters. Each carried a long stone bludgeon, and time after time one of them would swoop down on some unwary warrior, and in passing over bring down the weapon in the resounding whack that would crack his skull like a nut-shell. In the eery light of a dozen torches they appeared as flittering spirits of evil.

For my own part, my two dripping blades were taking a frightful toll in the black pack leaping and snarling around me. On Earth I had hunted the wolves that roamed the dead sea bottoms or dwelt in the ruins of long-dead cities, though never had they been the size of these great brutes, or possessed the ferocity of the cloven-hoofed ones. Several times I slashed upward at the hovering forms above me, but I was never quite able to touch those black daughters, though it was evident they feared death by their screams of terror as my blood-stained steel whirred past them.

It was evident, too, that I had been pointed out to them, for several of the horrid things were continually fluttering above me, waiting for some unguarded instant when their stone bludgeons could crash against my head.

An hour passed. At that first onset we had been forced to give ground to the weight and number of our foes, but once we had accustomed ourselves to the manner of their attack that advance was halted, with the line of battle wavering back and forth. Though a hundred men were now down, and there was scarcely one who did not bleed from a score of wounds, at least ten times that number of dead wolves were scattered around us, and I began to be aware of a growing advantage.

Time passed. I had just beheaded an agile brute which had been evading my blade for some minutes, when a series of cries arose above the din at the far end of the line. Hurrying through the struggling ranks I was soon beside a Black officer who pointed to the gloom behind us.

"Look, white man!" he exclaimed, and I raised my eyes to behold that which dashed away my new-found hopes like a life-giving cup to a dying man, for there, charging over the plains to our rear came a second pack of giant wolves, equally as large as the first—led by two of the Terrible Sisters who floated just before them!

A chill came over me at that moment. Could it be possible that those nine black fiends did indeed possess superhuman powers? That they could continue to bring forth endless thousands of wolves till they had slain the entire lot of us? Shebak and many of his warriors had warned that such would be the case. But I would not believe it, and throwing back my shoulders turned to the officer beside me.

"Order half your men to turn and meet the charge!" I told him, then hurriedly retracing my steps; "Every other man turn and face the rear!" I shouted. "Every other man face the rear!" And the warriors were quick to obey and cleared a path to let me through.

It was Shebak himself who brought about my capture. As I hurried along the lines I beheld the old chief down on one knee, and battling desperately against three fiery-eyed killers. Already they had dragged him some distance from his men. With a shout of encouragement I leaped forward to whirl my blade in the slash that freed him of one of them while his bludgeon found the head of the second, and the other, glad to escape, leaped away snarling.

Only for a moment did I forget the danger overhead, but it was enough. There came a sudden flurry of wings, a warning scream from Shebak. Then a hideous red flashed before me and all went black.

When I opened my eyes I was tied to a stone altar that rose in the center of an enormous room of mighty, age-blackened walls and pillars, which towered to a lofty ceiling.

A score of flaming torches protruding from the bored holes in the pillars, lighted dimly with their dancing beams that massive, hoary hall, which thousands of centuries had gashed and seared with the ugly marks of time. The air was heavy with the dank smell of decay. Great clouds of cobwebs hung everywhere, and from countless niches in the towering walls came the grin of human skulls.

A large, door-like opening in the wall to the left showed a vast expanse of silent heavens and a glorious starlit night.

It needed no two guesses to realize I was a prisoner in the castle of the Nine Terrible Sisters.

I was later to learn that it was indeed one of the Vampire-Women who had felled me, then with another swooped low and grasping my unconscious body carried me off to the Castle in the Clouds, after which they returned to the battle. At that moment, of course, I was unaware of all this, although I was painfully conscious of the tightness of my bonds and the throbbing pain in my head.

For several hours I lay there struggling with my bonds, while all around me the grave-like stillness of that great room was broken only by the sputtering torches. Slowly, slowly my thongs were giving; one strand parted, then another, though I knew it would be hours before I could hope to be free. I realized, also, that the battle must now be drawing to an end, if indeed it was not already over, and with the thought of that second pack vivid before me I dreaded to visualize its probable outcome.

Time passed and the stars waned as the eastern skies grew brighter. The first evidence of dawn was streaking the heavens when a loud flapping of wings suddenly sounded, and the next moment, one by one the Nine Terrible Sisters came flying through the opening to the left and into the room—their eyes wide and maniacal, their bludgeons dripping crimson—great blotches of that same bright red staining their naked breasts and bodies.

"Hurry, Sisters!" warned one. "Hurry, Sisters—dawn is breaking!"

And indeed they were Nine Terrible Sisters. Nine black daughters, each a good six feet, with their long hair streaming behind them, who laughed wildly as they flapped around me, then rose to the tops of the towering pillars and the ceiling above, where each disposed of her bludgeon and obtained the small golden cup whose use was so soon to be apparent.

Then they settled lightly to the floor in a half-circle, a few feet from me, and one of their number—a veritable giantess, blood-smeared and wicked—came forward with a long, bejeweled knife. She looked upon me with a gloating, indescribable hatred, while those behind her sang a loud, barbaric chant.

"Rash mortal!" hissed the giantess. "Who are you who would defy us? May the maggots claim your foul carcass, and the memory of your Ancestors be cursed!"

"Hurry, Sisters!" came again the warning, "Hurry, Sisters—dawn is breaking!"

"Not till we have slain this carrion!" cried the terrible thing above me. "Not till we have sated our thirsts with the blood of the rash fool who dared to pit himself against us!"

All this while the chant of the others was growing louder, faster. And then they began to circle the altar in a wild, barbaric dance.

"Dance, Sisters, dance!" screamed the giantess with arms aloft and head thrown back, and her long dark hair fell to the floor.

"Dance to Capara's gods of evil, who send us victims that our years may be endless! Dance that we may forever guard the secret of the Black Tower, and protect the glorious Tara against the terrible ruin that would be hers were it known! Dance, Sisters, dance!" she screeched. "Dance to victory, vice and vengeance!"

Around the tiny altar whirled the nine Sisters. Higher, higher rose their chanting, wilder, faster became the dance, as the daughters of a million years gave themselves to mad abandon, and with wild shrieks strained their lithe bodies in terrible postures.

But all this while that dull red in the eastern sky was changing to a brighter hue, a clear and fiery brilliance, whose first warm rays would be upon us in a very few minutes. Yet on and on the dancers raced, while the tall Sister above me slowly raised her knife on high. It was the one that had already warned them who first realized their danger, and gave the scream that brought the Vampire Women to a halt.

"Dawn!" she cried. "Dawn!" And as the others looked wildly around them, "Run, my sisters! Run—run quickly! Run—don't let the sun's rays strike you!"

In an instant panic reigned. With loud screams the Sisters turned and fled for the dark opening at the far end of the room, screeching at the top of their voices, and pushing and falling against one another in their maniacal terror. Even the giantess who had stood above me joined in that mad rush. She had been last to leave, and for a moment halted as though to retrace her steps and bury her knife into my heart. But as the others disappeared and the first sun-rays crept up to the window she gave a loud scream, and dropping her knife fled madly for the opening.

At the same moment I gave that powerful wrench which snapped the bonds that held me, and brought me to an upright position on that hoary, blood-stained altar.

But I knew the course that was open to me, and wresting a torch from a niche I picked up the fallen knife and started in pursuit of the Vampire-Women. The dark opening at the far end of the room proved to be the entrance to a subterranean passage, and a moment later I was running down a flight of winding, age-old stone steps, that led deeper and deeper as a dampness arose to tell of the great distance below the surface.

They ended at last in the gloomy, vault-like room my torch revealed, from which several passages led off into pitch darkness. For a moment I halted, uncertain as to which I should take, but there was no need to tread an unknown way, for suddenly a distant thud reached me through the gloom of the one to my left—a noise like that of a heavy lid falling into place.

In an instant I was hurrying down its inky blackness till I came to the rotting wooden door that shrieked so loudly and dismally as I pushed it aside.

It was a far-reaching, low-ceiled dungeon into which I entered, covered with a damp sand, its rocky sides dripping moisture, and reeking with the terrible odor of the grave. Small, furry things scurried just beyond the torchlight. But there was no need to continue my searching, for there on either side of that gloomy dungeon and down its long length were nine huge coffins. Nine great, age-blackened, stone sarcophagi, covered with the dust of countless centuries, and I knew well whom they contained.

All around me was that stifling odor and the mournful silence of the tomb.

For a long while I stood there in that dripping dungeon, a half-mile below the tips of the Castle in the Clouds, wondering at the terrible tales that dreary place could tell, and steadying myself for the ordeal that lay ahead. Then at last on tiptoe, gingerly, I approached the nearest coffin, my jeweled knife upheld and ready, my heart pounding but resolute.

I will not dwell on the happenings of the next few minutes, for they were not pleasant. I remembered the words of Shebak that said cold steel buried deep in their hearts could alone bring eternal sleep to the Vampire-Women, and the blade I held was long and keen. True, the forms before me were feminine, but I did not think of them as women, or other than long-dead things that never should have been.

Suffice to say I was presently retracing my steps to the distant world above. When I had first entered that vault my knife was clean and sparkling. When I left, its blade was swimming in a foul and putrid crimson, and nine loud screams, the last it would know, had been shrieked in that awful dungeon. But never again would the Terrible Sisters sally forth at sundown, or leave the graves they had first known, a million years ago.

And so at last I came again to the great hall and the sunlight above; and all the world seemed bright and clean, and that distant pit but a memory.

The opening on the left led to a lofty balcony that gave a view to the tiny petrified world so far below. In the clear morning light of that high atmosphere its black, jagged landscape could be seen for miles. Far away were the three small hills that marked the entrance of Shebak's cave, and I was about to leave the balcony and begin a descent to the distant plains below, when my eyes fell on the massive structure that rose through the roof above, and towered on into the very clouds, that huge, mysterious edifice, whose sleek ebon sides glowed brightly in the morning sun, and of which I had heard so much—the Black Tower!

This then was the mighty tower which held the great secret that would bring destruction to Capara were it known—the mighty age-old structure in which the great god, Time himself, was said to be a prisoner! The two small windows at its top were the only means of entrance. Only for a moment did I stand there, hesitant. Then with a curiosity and a rashness that must have been akin to madness, I slipped the jeweled knife into my belt, and began a careful ascent to the lofty heights above.

To scale from the balcony to the roof was a simple matter. It was not till I had arrived at the base of the tower that the difficulty of an ascent was realized. The weird formation of the structure made climbing almost an impossible task. Projecting cylindrical stones, six inches in diameter, surrounded the edifice in a series of bands, which, alas! appeared only at five-foot intervals.

However, the protruding stones did give a fairly good handhold, and for the first sixty feet of the climb I encountered no great difficulty. The air was clear, and the brilliant morning sun helped to illuminate the structure. Slowly I would pull myself upward, then swinging one leg on to the projecting stones, would reach for the series above, and in like manner ascend to the upper tier.

Forty feet from the summit the protruding stones suddenly lessened from six to three inches, with the series increasing to some six and a half feet apart. Frantic straining could but encircle three fingers on the protruding stubs. An inch one way or the other meant destruction. So small was my grip a cough could have dislodged me. Then by some fiendish fate that would choose this moment of all others, a wind rose above the lofty Castle in the Clouds, to sweep past me in choppy, swishing gusts.

I glanced down. The tower protruded through the very edge of the roof, and a fall would mean to miss the castle completely and be dashed on the plain, five thousand feet below!

I had discarded my sandals to grasp the little stones better, and now as my toes strained frantically to cling to them, I flattened my body against the cold structure, to rise jerkily and swing my arms to the protruding rocks above. Again and again I was successful, and clinging desperately, could see the window-ledge and safety but a scant six feet above.

Slowly I rose for the last effort. A gust of wind sought to dislodge me, but ever I came nearer to my goal. Now my hand crept overhead for the friendly ledge. A prayer came to my lips as its hard outlines brushed my fingers.

I had made it! I was safe!

And then my toes suddenly weakened from the strain, and I toppled backward to the awful depths below!

Chapter XIII
What I Found in the Black Tower

If there is a cruel fate that suddenly spins us from good fortune, there must surely be another that just as quickly hurries to our aid.

As I toppled backward from the tower I had already given myself up as dead; yet six feet only did I fall. Six feet, and then my outflung hands grasped the very stones my toes had slipped from. For a moment I hung there, swaying, as the cold sweat broke from my body. Vaguely I wondered if this seemingly miraculous escape was but the brief delirium preceding death, and if in another moment I would crash upon the plain below.

At length, however, I pulled myself upward. Once more I must attempt to reach that window; indeed I had no other choice. Already my arms were so spent as to make retreat impossible. No, I could never hope to reach the distant tower base. There was but one alternative—success or death!

For the last time I put my feet on the protruding stones as I rose to my full height. Now I stood upright, my hand creeping slowly for the window-ledge above.

Flattened against the side of the tower I could hear the whistling of an oncoming gust of wind.

My body swerved at the impact, then started to sway.

With a maniacal strength I sought to cling to those small, four-inch projections, my toes pushing forward till the blood gashed from the tender skin. Not for long could they stand that awful strain. The strong winds were forcing me back as my grip grew weaker, and I was giddy and nearly senseless.

Then with a dread, sickening sensation, I could feel my right foot slowly slipping from the tiny edge it held. It was the end! I felt it! I knew it! Three seconds more and I would go toppling to that awful void below! One second more and—

And then my reaching hand found a hold on the window-ledge above.

Far below me lay the Moon of Madness. Even the roof at the tower's base was distant and dim. It seemed incredible that I had made that perilous climb, and now had the well-guarded secret of the tower before me. For a moment I paused to rest and listen, then, tensing my muscles for the final effort, pushed myself upward and my eyes topped the ledge.

It was a small room of hoary black stone into which I looked, that same aged petrification as the ebon tower to which I clung. In truth, I was to learn later that the tower was indeed but the highest mountain peak on the Moon of Madness, that shot up through the very center of the castle and continued on to its lofty height, and in its uppermost part this room had been chiseled, with its needle-like tip for the roof overhead.

The only furniture consisted of the great, throne-like chair that faced me, all black stone as was the thick pedestal that rose before it, on which glowed and sparkled a golden, crystal-like ball, the size of a man's head.

But what had at once caught my eye was the huge, statue-like figure which sat so majestically upon that age-old throne—a figure apparently carved from the black rock of the mighty seat itself, as also seemed the flowing robes that adorned his massive seven-foot frame, and the two large hands that held a weighty scepter in his lap. The great beard of that aged monarch, whitened by the snow of centuries and reaching to an amazing length, had grown around and around the throne upon which he sat, lost in deep revery, and buried in dreams.

And then as I raised myself cautiously through the window, the slight noise aroused the hoary monarch, and his heavy eyelids opened to turn upon me a proud questioning glance, weighty with ages. The next instant those eyes opened wide in amazement, though his statue-like features remained unmoved, nor did a single muscle flicker or quiver on his great frame. This made certain that which I had instantly suspected.

The giant was of such a hoary, unthinkable antiquity, and had so long occupied that great seat, that he himself had turned into age-blackened stone!

Then as I continued to stand and stare there came to me these words, although I heard no voice, nor did his lips betray the slightest movement.

"You—you are a human!" The amazement, the incredulity of the assertion, was almost unbelievable.

I nodded, looking intently at him.

"But how did you get here?" he went on. "Where are the Nine Sisters Tara left to guard me?"

"Dead. Dead in the death from which they will never rise again," and although I knew he understood me I could not hear my own voice. "Shebak's people first told me of this tower."

"Shebak's people?"

"The cave people," I answered. "The people who dwell in the tiny hand-made world beneath the three small hills, a score of miles from here."

He looked at me for a long, long moment.

"There were no such people, or any other in the beginning," he went on finally, "no such a thing as life or creation when Tara and I first floated through the endless wastes that were devoid of any planet, star or world, except this tiny, barren spot, that was the birthplace of us both. No; only I and the glorious beauty who floated at my side. Creation came eons later.

"I cannot understand how you were able to kill the Sisters in the first place, and now I do not know how, having escaped them, you were able to scale this peak and enter where no foot has trod for a hundred million years!"

115

"I was told that cold steel alone could bring death to the Sisters," I replied. "And perhaps it was good fortune that got me up this tower. But who are you," I asked him, "who talks of countless ages, and of things before creation?"

"I," he answered solemnly, "I am Time. With my birth all things began. Before me there was nothing.

"I am Time who started all, and Tara the Glorious, Queen of Capara, is my glittering, treacherous sister. We both came before the beginning, but you would not understand an explanation even if I attempted one, for its utter enormity is far beyond the grasp of a human mind. Suffice it to say that for many ages my sister and I floated through the lonely wastes of space—a space that had its own formation an instant after our birth.

"Eons passed; then came creation, first as a vast cloud of gas that filled all, or nearly all of space. The mutual attraction of the cloud's particles drew them together, so that the cloud condensed into a gigantic nebula. The nebula then condensed into suns, which by tidal attraction and numerous collisions flung through the great void the boiling matter that formed and cooled into the millions of worlds and stars that now whirl through space.

"Then in time to the countless worlds there came the creature, man—man in many shapes and colors, together with the beasts he either conquered or was conquered by; but all this while that great ambition had grown within the beauteous Tara: to destroy me and to reign supreme down through the endless ages. And then at last, with the aid of the Four Black Winds, her wicked purpose was realized, and I was banished to this lonely tower, a hundred million years ago!

"Through the ages I have been a prisoner here without hope of succor, for my tongue was severed and my great frame paralyzed, so I could neither call for aid nor flee. And the Ball of Life was set before me to prolong my terrible imprisonment, for as long as its warm rays continue to touch me I cannot die."

And his eyes signaled to the golden, crystal-like ball that flashed and sparkled on the pedestal before him.

"But if you have no tongue how can you talk to me?" I asked.

"I have spoken no word to you, nor you to me. If you will notice, my lips are not moving. You are but getting my thought-waves, and I yours."

This then accounted for that noiseless conversation. For a moment we stared at each other, an awed silence on my part as my amazed senses sought to realize the utter enormity of what my eyes saw. Then the hoary giant went on:

"Now I understand your presence here. It took me some moments to decipher your thoughts. You come from one of the many worlds the cohorts of Tara have conquered. I can also see you are a great warrior, and though several Blacks have fallen before your blade, your heart still cries for vengeance."

"It is all I live for," I answered. "The poisonous gases of the Black Raiders killed every living human on my planet, and I will never rest until I have destroyed the last one of them."

"Good! Then listen and I will give you that chance," was his reply. "But we must be brief, for at any minute Tara, though she be on Capara, a hundred thousand miles away, may sense your presence, and by her great mental power cut off all thought communication between us. Heed me well then.

"The globe you see before you is indeed the Ball of Life, the Ball from which emerged all notions of creation, the very golden globe from which I myself once sprung. The other—there are only two—gave birth to Tara and now hangs in the canopy above her throne, where its warm rays continue to preserve her blinding beauty. But the dazzling Queen keeps a hundred thousand miles between them, for she well knows what would happen if they ever came together—destruction!

"Ah, and such a hideous destruction, for once those two globes met they would radiate the terrible heat that within twenty pulses of the human heart would turn Capara and this tiny moon into a bubbling, molten mass."

Those age-old eyes were looking into mine with a fierce intensity.

"And that same destruction can be brought about and by yourself if your heart is strong. The ring you see around my finger possesses a strange power. Were it to touch the Ball of Life above the throne of Tara it would start the great magnetism that in ten days' time would draw this tiny moon across the void and to Capara, where the globes would meet to radiate the awful heat that would mean the destruction of both planets.

"Haste then while we can still commune. Take this ring and hurry back to the cave people, for I see before you the great adventure that will take you to Capara. There you must manage to steal into the throne room, and touch the ring against the Ball of Life. Ten days later this tiny moon will be drawn across space to Capara. Of course, it will mean our own deaths as well as the others, but your purpose shall have been accomplished, and I will gain my so long, long sought revenge."

To hesitate against the will of this commanding giant was unthinkable, and the mission he had outlined was one I readily welcomed. In an instant I had stepped forward, and removing the heavy crystal-like ring from his age-old stone finger, slipped it onto my own. Then I stepped back to learn my next immediate move.

"Now hurry, warrior. Descend the tower at once and return to the cave people. Haste, then, for I see—"

And then our communication ended with the same suddenness a string is snapped asunder. One instant the giant's thoughts came clearly to me, the next I could make out nothing. But I recalled his warning and intuitively knew that though she was on a different planet, the great Queen Tara, of whose beauty and power I had heard so much, had sensed my presence in this tower of Time, and by her own thought-waves had cut off our communication.

That alone told of the giant mentality of the Queen of the Stars who ruled in her distant palace of gold. It was useless to hope for any further information from the stone giant before me. I would have given much to know what it was that he had seen, but that I must hasten at once to the cave people was all I had been able to learn.

The eyes of the great god were looking down at me in an agonizing, beseeching manner, but no further message came to me, though one needed only to look at those eyes to realize the terrible mental struggle that was being waged in the brain of that massive stone head as he sought to convey some warning or advice to me. But evidently the mind of the distant Queen was even stronger than his own. I realized also that everything depended on my immediate judgment.

But what to do? The wind without had been gradually rising till it was now whistling around the tower with the fury of a tempest. To attempt to descend in that raging storm would be madness. I would be swept from the projecting stones and dashed to my death before I had descended my own length.

And yet I must do something, and at once. The eyes of Time were looking at me hopefully, imploringly. Wildly my eyes swept around that barren room for some other exit, but there was none. And then as I stood there, puzzled and desperate, there flashed to me that one way which showed how it could be done, a way so fantastic, so incredible, that it must have been akin to madness.

But yet it was a way!

I have mentioned the huge beard of the giant god. It descended from his great chin in a thick, snow-white mass, and falling to the floor wound around and around his stone throne. In that age-old mass of hair I saw my escape. In a minute I was beside it, unwinding its great length. The next I had stepped to the window, watching the huge mass fall and unfold to the void below, dropping,

dropping till its far end just brushed the roof a hundred feet beneath me.

I turned for one last look at Time while around the tower the wind whistled wildly, and though that hoary god could neither speak nor register emotion, those two dark eyes showed their approval of my act.

Then with a shout of farewell and a wave of my hand, I pulled myself upward and through the window; then lowering myself to arm's length from the sill, I grasped Time's great beard and began my descent to the roof below.

It is needless to mention that nightmarish descent, as swinging wildly and pendulum-like in that raging tornado, I worked my slow way down that most fantastic of all ladders. Sometimes the wind would come in great gusts that swung me a score of feet on either side of the tower. Sometimes it would abate for an instant that would send me crashing against the hard sides of the edifice, bruised and only half conscious. But the beard I clung to had been strengthened by the ages, and the purpose of my struggle was a just and worthy one; and at length I had traversed the long beard of Time, and felt my feet touch the roof a hundred feet below the tower's top.

From there I made my way to the great altar chamber, and from there to the courtyard below. Here I found the narrow pathway that led down through the mountain. Along this I hurried, and two hours later found myself on the black, desolate plain, with the Castle in the Clouds high on the peak above. By now the storm had abated.

Then without a backward glance at the mighty fortress or the lofty tower above it, I set off at a rapid trot toward the cave of Shebak, twenty long miles away.

Chapter XIV
Invaders from the Outside

It was late that afternoon when I arrived before the cave in the center of the three hills, but long before I reached it I had seen the grisly evidence that told the outcome of the battle.

Strewn all around the plain in the awkwardness of death were the mangled forms of men and wolves—most of the former so mutilated and devoured as to make identity impossible. On the far side of the hills and toward the valley lay a long line of fifty or more dead Raiders and a hundred wolves—proof that at the last moment the Blacks had broken into a retreat for the safety of their ship, but had been pulled down one by one by their relentless pursuers.

Nowhere was there a sign of life, and over all lay the silence of the tomb. Evidently, having gained their costly victory, the black pack had returned to their inner world, via the volcano's trail.

The entrance just before the cave was piled high with bodies, among which I recognized the torn form of old Shebak. Of course for every fallen man there were at least three wolves, and I knew the old chief had more than done his bit in contributing to the fatalities among the latter. Gingerly I stepped among the fallen, and forced my way through the entrance.

Sickened with horror and the dread of what I so shortly expected to find, I made my way down the shaft till I came upon the tiny man-made world and the village at its base—strewn with bodies and swimming in blood. If anything, the havoc here was even more horrible than that on the plains above. This, of course, could be accounted for by the fact that there had been naught but women and children in the village, with only a dozen of the oldest warriors to oppose the snarling pack.

And then in Shebak's hut I found her. On the floor lay four feminine forms, torn and mangled beyond recognition; but one was slender, taller, and more shapely than the rest. For a moment I hoped against hope, but when I made out the golden hair and the broken red feather protruding from the band around her head, I knew that never again could there be hope for the lovely Vonna, Princess of Penelope.

I will not attempt to describe my feelings at that moment—the numbness that seemed to claim my brain, or the realization of what the golden girl had come to mean to me. Vonna was dead. Vonna was dead! I felt that the essential me had likewise perished.

Of Abel there was no sign.

How long I remained in the village of Shebak I do not know, but it must have been a long time, for when I again emerged from the shaft, darkness had long fallen, and the stars were twinkling overhead. In silence I made my lonely way across the face of that dead world, to the nearby valley and the sturdy ship, where a merciful slumber came at last to banish sorrow temporarily.

For the next few days I was alone on that jagged world of stone, wandering aimlessly over its dreary plains by day and returning to the ship at night. As the flyer had been well provisioned I had no immediate worry, but I could not erase from my memory what was expected of me by the hoary god in the Black Tower. Nor had the terrible fate of Vonna decreased my hatred of the Black Raiders, and the desire for their doom. To execute that destruction I vowed to dedicate my life.

Again and again I would look at the heavy crystal-like ring encircling my finger, wondering how I could ever hope to gain the throne room of Capara and bring doom to that great planet. As the days passed, it preyed more and more upon my mind, and I had about determined to return to the Black Tower and try a further communication with the great god, Time, when there happened that which changed everything, and brought me to Capara in a strange and unexpected manner.

$\mathfrak{I}$ was in the sleeping-quarters one morning, making ready for a return to the tower on the morrow, when suddenly without the slightest warning a huge, arrow-like projectile came plunging through the side of the ship a dozen feet to the right of me. The crash had scarcely died away when a second tore through the exit chamber at the far end of the spaceship, leaving two huge gaping holes, as the great flyer shook with the force of the impact, and continuing on to smash against the cliffs.

At the same moment loud shouts reached me, and I made my way through the wreckage to halt in wonderment at the entrance door.

Overhead the sky was black with spaceships. As far as the eye could see there was an endless flow of oncoming gigantic flyers, and many of them had probably already settled on the plains beyond the cliffs. An awful assurance, that titanic display of power— an irresistible force that could sweep down all before it. And yet it was plain they were not Black Raiders, as there was something decidedly different about the construction of their ships, and the shining, fiery red hue of the strange metal that covered those thousands of giant craft.

Even as I watched, a black blur shot from the bow of one of them, and another arrow-like projectile burst through the ship beside me to complete its ruin. The next moment a dozen almost naked barbarians, wild and fierce-looking in loincloths and horned helmets, came streaming from the nearby pass, waving their longswords and shouting; and scarcely had I time to unsheathe my own weapons till they were upon me.

So sudden and unexpected had all this come upon me that I had no time to plan any defense, or a way to meet that wild attack. But whatever else was lacking, my strength and fighting-spirit most certainly were not, and springing forward to meet them I lashed out with my two keen blades in the furious exchange that plunged cold steel into two of their number at the very onset, and dropped them, bleeding and dying, as the others came to a wide-eyed halt. Then with shouts of rage they threw themselves upon me.

Did this, then, mean the end? Was I to go down before these strange warriors before I had accomplished the great mission which Time had given me, and the death of Vonna, my sire and my planet to go unavenged? It seemed almost incredible that one man could hope to hold off those wild killers—ten hardy red-skinned fighters of a standard six-foot height. But my years of training had been many, and my urge to live a great one; so setting my teeth, I fought as I never dreamed a human could fight.

My whirring blades wove a net of death around me, parrying a hundred stabs and cuts, then shooting out for a death thrust.

A third man went down, writhing. The others pressed me closer, and in the face of that sea of steel I was forced to give ground. The fight grew grimmer, more deadly. A wicked cut just missed my head—a knife-thrust I barely parried. And then my trained eyes saw an opening, and a fourth red man dropped, screaming at my feet.

On we struggled. Each instant death came closer. The clashing of steel on steel rang out and the warriors fought like fiends, but despite those glittering blades and lightning-like exchanges, by some miracle I was still untouched, and the next moment there occurred the happening which halted that uneven struggle, and led to a startling finish.

It came from an unexpected quarter. I had just disarmed a big fellow who had given me a desperate struggle, and the others, glad for a respite, stepped back for a breathing-spell. But surprise and respect showed on their faces, and then the one I had disarmed spoke.

"White man," he said, "you fight with the strength of ten. Were you not an ally of the Black Raiders it would be an honor to have you in our ranks."

"I am no ally of the Black Raiders," I answered. "They are my enemies, every one of them."

"Then how does it come you are in a ship of theirs, and where are the others?"

I answered him in a few sentences, wondering if all this was but a ruse to catch me off my guard. But the big fellow, who was evidently one of authority among them, seemed sincere enough.

"If this be true, it is something that should reach the ears of Jo-Mar," he answered when I had finished. "Put up your weapons, then, and I will take you to him." Then as I hesitated, "You may trust me," he added. "We of the Fire World do not stoop to petty tricks and treacheries."

I looked at him for an instant. It did not seem plausible that they would so easily overlook the havoc my blades had caused, but there was a truthful ring in the man's voice, and his gaze was steady. I sheathed my swords and followed him, while behind us came the others—two of them assisting one of my victims who had been painfully, but not fatally, wounded. The other three had been killed outright, and these were left where they lay. Evidently life was held cheaply among the newcomers.

Presently we emerged from the pass to the plains beyond. Out here was that mighty assembly of ships and soldiers that stretched away for miles. Swarms of fiery red-skinned warriors were hurrying to and from the vast number of spaceships in seemingly endless thousands. I was later to learn that this strange horde of Fire People numbered some five million fighting men, with each of their twenty-five hundred ships carrying two thousand warriors. Among these we made our way, my white skin an outstanding contrast to the bright hue of those around me.

As we hurried along, the man beside me, Varno he said his name was, kept up a continuous flow of explanations. I was later to become quite fond of this friendly fellow, who had seemingly already forgotten that our blades had crossed but a few minutes ago. He could not forget the manner of my fighting, however, nor cease to marvel at how I was able to hold off so many of them single-handed.

He said they were invaders from the outside—people who came from a sun so distant, so far beyond all other heavenly bodies, that no star or planet was visible from their fiery world. How they managed to live on a flaming sun he did not make quite clear, seemingly taking it for granted that I would understand; though he did mention briefly the bright red metal that covered their ships, and said that it entirely covered the many great cities on their distant world, adding that it was immune to any heat or fire.

But it seemed that for many ages the kings and sages of the Fire People had surmised the existence of other worlds than theirs, and had sent out spaceships that had returned to tell that there were many planets and stars, but that all had been conquered and were subject to the Black Raiders, a mighty horde of cruel tyrants who lived on a distant world. And so the king of the Fire People had sent out this great fleet to conquer the Black Raiders, so that the other worlds might again know freedom. Chance had brought them to this tiny moon for a final brief stop-off, before continuing on to Capara.

"And long has that journey taken us, from our distant sun to here," concluded Varno. "Some ten years, as you know time. We stopped at several of the worlds for brief rests, of course, as well as to replenish our supplies, and so were able to learn the language of the Raiders, which is, in turn, the enforced tongue of all the worlds they have conquered."

As he spoke we stopped before a spaceship, large even when compared to the other mighty metal monsters around it. Numerous guards and officials were hurrying to and from its many doors with handfuls of reports and other papers. This then was the quarters of Jo-Mar, commander of the fleet. Varno spoke a few words to a guard, and the man saluted, then turned and entered the ship.

"I have asked for an audience with the commander, that I may explain your presence," said Varno. "Unless I am greatly mistaken, Jo-Mar will welcome your being among us."

As we were awaiting the return of the guard, Varno explained briefly about the arrow-like projectiles that had been shot through the ship. It appeared, in truth, that they were just that—giant arrows of a hard, black metal, each weighing the poundage of ten heavy men—shot with terrific force from huge steel bows in the bow of each ship, which were drawn back and set by cranks. They were used only in destroying hostile fleets and cities. In land battles the red men fought with the longsword and shortsword each warrior wore.

"And Jo-Mar," I asked.

"He is the commander. Our great king put him in charge of the fleet with orders that he was to crush the Black Raiders, and give each star and planet back to their own, for ours is a just and good king. Ten long years have we been in crossing that awful void between our world and here. And then when we have vanquished them, it will be another ten before we can return to the huge metal-covered cities of our world that protect us from its terrible fires and flames."

All around us was the rising din of that vast host, whose many ships stretched away for miles. A great army, to be sure, five million men in fact, and yet I knew it was like tossing a pebble to down a mountain to expect them to destroy the invincible might of Capara. Never having seen the strength of the Black Raiders, they could not know their unbelievable power, or realize that the latter could readily bring a hundred ships and a thousand warriors against every one of theirs. The Blacks would but play with, then destroy them. And yet I could not bring myself to tell this to Varno, who had such implicit faith in his own.

Presently the guard we awaited reappeared. "The commander

will see you now," he said to Varno; "you and this strange warrior. Follow me."

Into the great ship we followed our guide, passing through several long chambers, where serious-faced men, evidently leading generals and officers, sat around tables littered with drawings and plans, hardly mindful of our presence, for that long-awaited battle was now almost upon them.

At length we halted before a small door. The warrior pulled it aside and we entered. Around the walls hung numerous charts and drawings of various stars and planets. The only occupant was the large stout red man who sat before a table strewn with papers.

Jo-Mar, the commander, wore the same scanty apparel of the others, soft sandals and loincloth, as well as a longsword and shortsword. Varno saluted him, then told briefly of me, after which the commander turned toward me.

"It is a marvel that you are alive, white man," he said, not unkindly. "As we descended to this tiny world, I noticed your ship, and thinking it contained Black Raiders, ordered it fired upon by my bowmen. Your escape was indeed miraculous, but then, from what Varno tells me, your swordsmanship is likewise amazing. We owe you a debt for having so nearly taken your life, and let me be the first to admit it."

As he spoke the old chieftain drew his shortsword and handed it, hilt foremost, to me. This was their way of acknowledging a wrong. I half guessed as much, as my returning of the blade to its scabbard was the gesture that released him from any obligations, and the one expected of me.

For half an hour I talked with Jo-Mar, the commander of the Red fleet, he asking many questions of my own distant world, and seemingly interested in everything I had to say concerning either myself or it. They were a just and likable race, the Fire People, and I dreaded to think of their certain destruction in the coming battle. Moreover, the present confidence of the Red men would make that defeat the more bitter. Plainly any suggestion of caution would be unwelcome, and yet I could not let them run headlong to their fate without at least a warning.

"It is strange you have not already met the fleet of the Raiders," I said presently. "After all, you are now but a hundred thousand miles from Capara."

"Their scout ships have probably already seen us," answered Jo-Mar, "and perhaps their fleets as well. But our vast numbers doubtless caused them to turn and flee. After all," he said smilingly, "we do have twenty-five hundred ships, and some five million men. Then again there are our great one-ton arrows we shoot for such a distance."

I knew I risked his displeasure as I leaned forward in my chair and said:

"It will be as nothing against the fleets of the Black Raiders, as nothing against the unthinkable power and numbers the all-conquering Tara can send against you. It was the great distance of your world from any other that protected you from them, or else you would know all this. They have great guns in their ships that hurl giant missiles and explosives of terrible force, a hundred times farther than your stoutest bows can hurl an arrow. They have strange green rays that hold one paralyzed for indefinite periods. They have a hundred ships and a thousand men for every one of yours. No, Jo-Mar; be not deceived by your strength and numbers, and I would not be a friend if I did not tell you. A battle with the Black Raiders can mean but one thing—your own swift and certain destruction!"

Then before he could answer I went on: "But there is a way," I told him, "a way that victory can be yours without drawing a sword or losing a man; a way that you may stay safely aloft in space, and behold that triumph; a way I cannot divulge, for it is a sworn secret."

"And—and I?" he asked after a pause, his eyes fixed steadily on me.

"Get me to Capara," I answered. "Arrange to have me transported, secretly and at night, to that great world. But help me to get into the throne room of Queen Tara, and I promise you on the honor of my fathers, that within ten days I will bring around the death of every Black Raider, and reduce that mighty planet to a bubbling, molten mass!"

Chapter XV
Billions of Miles Beyond the Sun

As I finished speaking there was silence, while the eyes of the others looked at mine. What their thoughts were I could not guess, though it did come to me that they might think I was a secret ally of the Raiders, trying to discourage their advance and return to Capara to report my findings.

And then Jo-Mar cleared his throat to speak, but the words were never uttered. Even as he attempted it he stopped, straightened, then stood up, motionless. At the same instant there came a confused murmuring above the general din without. The next, and feet came flying down the passage, and a man burst frantically into the room.

"A fleet, Commander! A fleet!" he cried. He stood there, panting and unable to find his words, while several officers appeared in the doorway behind him. Then he broke out again: "A fleet twice, three—yes, five times the size of ours! Far out in space, but bearing swiftly down upon us! It's the Black Raiders!"

In an instant all was confusion. The staff in the doorway burst into a flow of words all at the same time. The messenger sank panting to the floor. From without loud cries told that the news had reached the warriors. Only Jo-Mar retained his presence of mind. In an instant the old commander showed his mettle.

"Places!" he roared, and in the immediate quiet that followed: "We will meet and repel the attack, using the tactics planned a thousand times. Order all ships to rise at once and follow us." He wheeled to an officer. "We will take the lead and be in the foremost place of danger, where all leaders should be. Further, as every instant counts, I suggest we act immediately."

The firm voice of the commander did much to reassure his staff, and a moment later they were all hurrying about their various duties; nor was it much later till the great flagship was rising into the void, while behind it in that long, long line streamed the others.

Following Varno, who was in charge of the bow crew, we passed through the sleeping-quarters, the storerooms, the pilot-room, to enter finally the large, all-metal compartment in the bow of the ship. Against one wall, in tiers of five, the huge arrows were piled. There were six such tiers, and a dozen men who stood beside the giant steel bow, built on a solid platform rising from the floor. The heavy chain which pulled it back was worked by two large cranks, and then the arrow put into place, after which a lever released it.

A thick glass window ran around the room. Through this we could see the ground drop back. For a moment I had a glimpse of that ugly, jagged plain, and its volcano-studded surface, and from far away that last view of the distant Castle in the Clouds. And then that little world of stone fell away, with only the blue void stretching ahead and five million men behind.

For an hour the fleet plunged steadily onward. Several times small spaceships whizzed past us at terrific speed to join the mighty host in our rear. These were the scout ships that had been sent on ahead of the fleet, and their speedy return well told that some hostile fleet was coming toward us.

Jo-Mar and several of his staff had joined us, and with eyes strained on the window, stood looking into the void ahead. At a word from the commander the heavy chain of the giant bow was cranked back and locked, and with six warriors straining hard, a great arrow was lifted from the racks and set into place. The long, cone-shaped bow of the ship had a thick metal covering that could be raised back from the inside, and formed the barrel-like opening through which the giant shaft could plunge.

"The commander will direct the fight from here," whispered Varno. "The others have been instructed to follow and fight like us. That is why only the best pilots man this, our flagship. Under the guidance of Jo-Mar it will circle and maneuver till we encompass the Blacks—the Circle of Death we call it. It may be a hundred or a thousand miles in circumference, but by maneuvering swiftly around the foe there is less chance of our being hit, and they present a solid target."

The enormity of it was breathtaking. Here I was far out in the trackless void, billions of miles beyond the sun, an ally of a mighty host that had crossed another unbelievable stretch of space which hid their distant world! And coming to meet us was an all-conquering fleet so large as almost to dwarf the imagination! Dimly I realized that twenty million men might soon clash in that battle of space which might stretch away for ten thousand miles, with the giant sun a mighty light to illuminate it all. Gods of my fathers, what a spectacle for an all-seeing eye!

Presently gasps and exclamations arose from the watchers at the window. At the same instant I knew the cause of their excitement. Away and away stretched the vast void, but just at the limits of the eye range countless tiny dots were appearing. Steadily they hardened, grew larger and larger as their speed and ours shot us toward each other—a massive black fleet of giant spaceships—fearless—powerful—conquering!

One of the watchers gave a cry of dismay, with extended arm pointing before him. "There are thousands of them! Thousands!" he exclaimed, as the great warships came nearer, and as far as the eye could see they continued to stream forward. "They will crash us head on."

Jo-Mar silenced him with a glance. "Instruct the pilot to fly straight ahead, and at the last moment rise and pass above them. The others will follow in the move that may mean the beginning of our circle."

By this time the Raiders had drawn closer. Why they had not already begun to fire I could not understand. No sign of life or a cannon showed, but this was to be expected of course, as the great guns were hidden by a similar cone-like tip in the prow of each ship that was drawn back like ours. They were almost upon us now. Another moment and we would crash into their leading ships. Jo-Mar wheeled, shouted the signal that flew back the lid and released our first one-ton arrow—and then all hell broke loose!

Out from the bows of a thousand ships, like a single shot burst smoke and flame, a mighty, thundering fusillade that tore its way through a hundred Red ships and brought instant death to thousands. Then, as though foreseeing our intentions, the Black fleet swerved sharply to the left to prevent our rising above them, and in passing sent volley after volley of their enormous shells crashing into the navy of the Fire People.

There was no denying the bravery of the Black Raiders. Tearing alongside of their foes, as they wrought their frightful havoc, they were as indifferent to the arrows of the Red fleet as a hunter to a falling leaf. Not that they were immune to or safe from death and injury. Hundreds of the giant shafts were constantly shooting through the void, and though misses were frequent, many of them found their target, and tore their way through the metal ships as though they had been paper.

But they could not compete with the fury of the Black volleys, as rising and diving the Raiders shot from all positions. And on they came, seemingly endless thousands of spaceships, not a third of which were used or needed, and whose appearance was solely to impress and discourage their foes.

The unexpected maneuvers of the Blacks prevented any attempt at forming a circle and surrounding them, though Jo-Mar had made several attempts which were always met and blocked. Then circling to the left in a great loop, he sought to halt the onslaught temporarily and meet the enemy anew. But there was no evading the wily Blacks, as flitting on all sides they made the circle with us, and kept up their terrific and tireless cannonade.

It must have been clear, even to the old commander himself,

what the inevitable outcome would be; yet on he ordered that futile fight, while all around him the great Red fleet was being blown asunder—strewing the void with the fragments and warriors who would forever float in the cold wastes of space.

Working madly with the perspiring bow crew, I helped to put the great arrows in place, and turn the huge cranks that drew back the chain. Varno, who aimed and released the shafts, proved himself a splendid archer, and nearly all his arrows found a target in the Black ships shooting around us. And yet it was a feeble retort to that murderous onslaught of the Raiders.

Everywhere was the blinding smoke of thousands of cannon. Through it shot and flitted the gigantic outlines of spaceships—sometimes Red, but mostly Black. Yet it was that same smoke-fog which helped prolong the battle, for the Blacks had to pause occasionally till it lifted for fear of hitting their own. Giant arrows were constantly shooting through the whiteness. Often great space-flyers crashed together head on, rending, then crumbling, to pitch their screaming cargoes out into the void.

Two hours passed—two hours such as no pen could describe, which witnessed the annihilation of the Red fleet. At first I could not understand why it was, with all the destruction and bursting shells, that we had not been hit. Then as the battle went on and those thousands of Red ships continued to be blown asunder on all sides of us, I suddenly knew the reason of that seeming invulnerability. The Blacks had recognized ours as the flagship which would contain the leaders of the fleet, and were sparing it for the sole purpose of capture.

Evidently Jo-Mar realized this also, for presently he made his way through the perspiring men to where I and several others were pulling back the huge chain to release another of the rapidly diminishing arrows.

The old commander was disheveled, his eyes wide and glazed.

"The words you said just before the battle—that you could destroy Capara if we got you there—were they true?" he asked in a rasping tone.

I nodded, wondering why he should refer to it at this late hour.

"Then by the gods we will get you there!" exclaimed Jo-Mar grimly. "Another twenty minutes will see the end of the fleet. Too late to hope for victory, but not too late for vengeance. If I can help to bring around the ruin of the Raiders, then at least I can die happy. We will get you to Capara, white man. We will get you to Capara," and his voice shook with a fierce determination.

He turned and roared an order to the pilot room. "Full speed ahead! Full speed ahead! Capara is our destination! Not even death must stop us!"

"But the fleet, Commander," asked one of his staff. "That means we leave our warriors to their doom."

"Well do I know that," answered the other, "and in my heart I will die the death of each a hundred times. But this white man says he has a secret that means the destruction of Capara if we can but reach it, and fantastic as it may seem, I believe him. To stay here means but to share the fate of our warriors, nor can we hope to change it. A swift flight to Capara may at least avenge them, after which we can return again to perish with our own."

By now the battle had divided into a series of smaller combats, with several of the Black destroyers encircling each of the hundred or so remaining Red ships—the greater part of the Black fleet having retreated for some thousand miles to permit maneuvering. There they had formed the great circle which completely encompassed the fighters. To break through that circle and reach Capara was our problem. True, we were leaving brave men to their fate, but we could not help them, and as Jo-Mar had said, there was at least a chance we might avenge them.

Through the smoke and flame our great destroyer tore its way, now swerving sharply to one side to escape the bow of a spaceship, now dropping or rising sharply to avoid crashing into another; halting occasionally to release a well-aimed arrow.

Several times the Black ships sought to cut across our path and halt us, and once a huge destroyer nearly did jam us, head on. But we continued on and dove and rose till at last we were free of them, then shot out of that world of smoke to learn our efforts were in vain.

As we plunged out into the sunlight a gasp escaped our lips, for scarcely a thousand feet below were the well-kept fields of a little satellite—the Moon of Lost Souls—the terrible moon of exile from which I had escaped but fourteen days before. We had thought ourselves still far out in space. Evidently we had covered an incredible distance in the looping and maneuvers of that mighty battle, but the gun smoke of the Blacks had obliterated our surroundings. Fifty thousand miles away massive Capara covered half the heavens. Just before us were the three great circles of Black spaceships that must have totaled a good five thousand.

Even as we shot out before them a roar of flame burst from the guns of several of the nearest of them, and three huge shells tore through our ship, bringing death to many of its inmates, and a moment later the destroyer was falling, screeching hideously as it plunged swiftly downward, and drowning the frightened screams of the survivors, to come to a stop with that deafening roar as we crashed on the Moon of Lost Souls.

A good half of the crew were killed in the fall itself, and the three shells fired by the Blacks must have claimed nearly as many more. I had been flung clean across the room, to fall against the warriors already thrown there. With the others I went down in a screaming, writhing pile of humanity, and was among the few who slowly rose in all parts of the ship as loud shouts sounded and strong blows were rained upon the doors. But I doubt if there could have been more than twenty of us who came to our feet, dazed and bleeding, and turned weakly to meet the attack as the doors burst open, and a shouting swarm of Black Raiders streamed through the doorway. For despite the speed of our descent, several spaceships of the foe had just as swiftly followed, to come lightly to the ground beside us and disgorge their savage crews.

There was no fight. In the first place there could be no fight— they simply submerged us with their numbers, raining a volley of blows on our heads and bodies with the flat of their swords till we were nearly senseless. Then with powerful black hands clutching us on all sides, we lone survivors of that once great army of millions were hustled through the broken ship and into the opening.

Out here the world was alive with hostile warriors, and the heavens black with the fleets of the conquering Raiders, for I was to learn later that the Blacks, long aware of the oncoming Fire People, had a second fleet, equally as large as the one which destroyed us, waiting in reserve on the Moon of Lost Souls. Loud laughs and taunts greeted our approach as our captors cleared the way through the swarming thousands and toward the huge prison ship that would be our temporary jail till our fates were decided.

Sickened, tired, my head and body aching from the blows they had received, I was hardly conscious of where I was or whither I was going. Into the bare prison ship we twenty battered survivors were hustled, the wrist bands that held our arms above our head snapped shut, securing us to the walls. Then with a final taunt of impending death our captors departed, and we were alone.

For a while there was silence on the part of that sorrowful company, with no sound coming to us other than the faint din without. Never had I known a feeling of such utter despair. The words of the Blacks had told we would all soon know a terrible death, but I did not greatly mind, nor did it seem to matter.

My own world had been destroyed. Vonna was dead, Abel was no more. I felt, perhaps, that it would be just as well if I soon perished also.

And then the fighting-spirit of my fighting ancestors suddenly rose within me. My jaws tightened. Die? No; I had a mission to perform! I must first bring death to Capara and avenge my own world. At least I would not die without a struggle. If I must die, I preferred dying while making some effort to escape death, and I began to tense my muscles and test the strength of the metal bands that held my wrists. My efforts aroused old Jo-Mar beside me, who had been among the survivors, and he turned a battered, blood-smeared face to mine, that made a ghastly attempt at a smile.

"A terrible end, Earthman. A terrible end for all of us," he said. "For ten long years of your time have we journeyed across the great void, only to suffer defeat and come to this." His tired eyes traveled to the others.

"But all is not lost," I told him. "Perhaps there is still an escape for us."

"An escape? Not unless we can sprout wings and melt these bands with our thoughts. No, my boy, it is needless to delude ourselves. There can be no escape for us now, but for me it is not so bad. I am an old man and have had my years. My regret is for you young men who still have your youth."

A sudden hurrying of footsteps without silenced him. The next moment there came a harsh blare of a hundred trumpets in barbaric salute. Then the door was flung back, and following an officer who held a scroll-like parchment there entered a powerful, commanding black figure of fifty years or so, clothed in trappings of glittering diamonds whose flashing radiance was dazzling. There was something sinister, something terrible about this mighty Black; and then as his cruel, merciless gaze swept up and down the line of captives and his thin, half-parted lips revealed a row of teeth that shone like the fangs of a beast, his identity was revealed by the officer who was with him.

"Another victory to your long and unbroken string, O Great

One. A worthy triumph, this one, and all Capara has gone mad with joy, and will welcome you with the reception due a conqueror. And these, noble Metak, are your captives."

This then was Metak!—Metak who had brought about the death of my own planet; Metak, champion swordsman of the Blacks; Metak, who for some strange reason had exiled me to the Moon of Lost Souls; Metak the man whose son I had killed but some fourteen days ago.

And now I was a captive of Metak!

Chapter XVI
The Golden City

The grim features of Metak remained unmoved as his gaze traveled over the captives before him; then his lower lip dropped in a sneer.

"A grimy-looking lot of diseased dogs," he said. "And it was with such as these that they hoped to overcome us."

He gave a harsh laugh and strode to the far end of the line to begin his inspection, while behind him came the officer with ready pen and parchment. Four burly guards appeared and took places behind the writer.

"This one," said Metak, looking at the first captive. "I doubt if he knows how to hold a blade, but he might afford some amusement strapped on the horns of a wild taggot. Mark him for the arena then," and the officer scribbled a brief entry while the Black commander stepped to the next.

"And this one—bah!" exclaimed Metak. "A weak louse at best, and now hopelessly wounded. Dispatch him!" he snapped to the guards, and one of them stepped forward and drove his shortsword into the breast of the luckless captive, after which the twist bands were released and the limp Red man dragged from the ship by his heels.

"And you," went on Metak to the next. "An ugly brute but still able to work. He remains here on the farms."

Again the officer scribbled an entry; then down the line went Metak deciding the fate of the others. Most were sentenced to the arena, several to the farms, and one other badly wounded captive was dispatched. At length the Black came to Jo-Mar, who stood beside me.

"You?" he began questioningly, for the proud features of the old commander, though battered and bleeding, stamped him as one of authority.

"I am Jo-Mar," answered the old chief, and his gaze met the others unwaveringly. "I was the commander of the Red fleet my king sent to destroy you, and can only say how much I grieve that I was unable to carry out my monarch's wishes."

"Ha—the commander!" cried Metak, and his face lit. "Now we can indeed have a triumphal procession! So it was you who led these misguided fools against us. Ah, old man, the years may have whitened your head but they certainly did not bring wisdom to it. Perhaps as you are being dragged behind my chariot you will have ample time to regret your folly."

As he spoke another Black entered the doorway—one I immediately recognized, for it was the Kamma who had witnessed the duel when I killed Magog, then later escaped his bonds and raised the alarm that had nearly captured Vonna, Abel and me, when we fled from the Moon of Lost Souls. He had eyes only for Metak as he hurried forward,

"A great victory, worthy Metak," he greeted. "All Capara awaits your return with cheering billions and waving banners and rose-covered streets for your conquering footsteps. May mine be the honored ship that bears you to Capara—"

"Later, later, after I have dealt with these fools," broke in Metak, his eyes still on his captives. "And you," he said as he stepped toward me. "You will be—by the Beauty of Tara, you're a white man!" he exclaimed. "A white man! But how—"

There came a gasp behind him, then the Kamma roared: "Blood of a Thousand Devils! It's he! The Earthman you sentenced here who escaped! The one who killed Magog—Magog your son!"

"What!"

Metak's scream was hardly human, as his hand flew to his sword. Out shot a shining blade, and it would have surely been plunged into my eyes had not the Kamma sprung forward and seized his arm.

"Wait, Worthy One!" cried the Kamma. "You dare not kill him. The great queen herself has posted a reward of a million daggots for the capture of this rash fool who escaped from the Moon of Lost Souls, but he must not be harmed, for she would question him. It is a royal command!"

"But it was he who killed Magog!" shouted Metak, and the Black seemed to have suddenly gone berserk. "Swine! Beast! Dog!" he screamed, and drawing back his powerful fist, sent it crashing once, twice, four times into my unprotected face with the terrible force that turned my features to crimson, and I felt a warm trickle run down my chin.

But it in no way cowed my spirit, and looking into that furious face, I spoke with a fierce determination. "For what you have just done to me, some day I will kill you!" I said in a low tone.

"Then why not try it now—duel with me!" he cried. "I will have you released and given a sword."

"Nothing would please me better!" I shouted.

The eyes of Metak were terrible to behold. The mouth too had curled, revealing those beast-white teeth. The cruel face showed maniacal fury, then with a great effort, he controlled himself; the upper lip dropped, the firm jaw straightened, the eyes lost that mad gleam. When again he spoke it was with a deathly calmness.

"Everything between you and me will be settled, all in good time, and in a manner that I promise will be most gratifying to the winner.

"So you are Jan—Prince Jan of the Bardonians," the calm voice went on in mock politeness. "For long have I heard of you; you and your redoubtable sire; have heard of your city, your tribe, and their so many wonderful qualities and virtues. And now, your highness, may I be permitted to welcome you in a manner truly becoming to your race and world?" And with that the Black brute spat full in my face, then turned to the officer behind him.

"The rest of these carrion are to be chained and sent to the arena, after first being marched in the procession. Double chains on the old chief and the Earthman, and see that the latter two are put directly behind my chariot."

Then with the others clanking behind him, Metak the commander strode from the room, and we heard the loud cheers from without as the thousands acclaimed him.

The hours crept by and the night passed slowly. None bothered to bring us either food or drink, and consequently we suffered considerably from thirst. This was bad enough for any of us, but for the more seriously wounded it amounted to torture. Morning came and the forenoon was half spent when a dozen Black warriors entered the ship in a half-drunken condition, waving half-filled wine bottles amid shouts and laughter. At the sight of our helplessness they laughed the louder. Already had begun the celebration and festivities that were to make this a gala day in the history of Capara.

A few minutes later we were rising into the void toward the great mother planet, fifty thousand miles away.

From what I could make out we were being taken to Manator, the mighty golden city that was the capital of Capara, to march in the triumphal procession which heralded the opening of the Great Games. The Great Games would last for ten days, during which the thousands of captives from the thousands of planets would slash and slaughter one another in the arena for the amusement of the conquerors by day, and be the victims for their tortures and witness their terrible depravities by night, as the power-drunk Blacks gave themselves to the unprintable orgies that marked a Caparian holiday!

An hour later we were landing on that great world of ten billion people. Through the porthole beside me I had had occasional glimpses of its vast seas and mountains, growing larger and larger as our terrific speed shot us across the void. Then came landscapes of eery and exotic beauty—high peaks, mountains, and tumbling waterfalls, vast green plains and lovely valleys, studded occasionally with great cities of weird and wonderful construction.

And then from afar that blinding luminosity which at first seemed a great sea of gold; then, as we drew closer, gigantic structures took form, and a few minutes later we came down before the mighty walls of that mighty golden city—mighty, mighty Manator.

Gods of my fathers, what a city! A glittering city of solid gold whose indescribable, colossal enormity may be dimly visualized in the realization that it marked the looted wealth of ten thousand planets, and the labors of ten billion captives, over a span of ten million years; a city whose great buildings, whose countless minarets, domes and spires, all gold and dazzling in the sunlight, rose to such incredible heights they seemed to brush the very sky, stretching away to be lost to sight in all directions; a gigantic city of lofty landing-towers, crossed and recrossed by the thousands of elevated thoroughfares, glittering and golden, that continued on for miles—thousands of feet above the glass-enclosed pavements below.

The crossroads of space; the capital of the planets; the treasury of the worlds! The mighty golden metropolis supreme, where dwelt the glorious Tara, Queen of the Stars! Again do I say of Manator—gods of my fathers, what a city!

And along those higher thoroughfares, as well as the ones below, the millions were swarming, either on foot or in the countless chariots drawn by prancing kangs, similar to the ones I had known on my own distant world. Shooting across the skies from building to building were the flying forms of hundreds of Tors, serving as both winged mounts and messengers to the Blacks who rode them. The heavens were alive with flag-draped ships, and from every spire, turret and housetop streamed fluttering pennants and banners; for this day the conquerors celebrated Metak's triumph, and the beginning of the Great Games that started on the morrow.

Just before the mighty walls we landed, colossal barriers that towered upward for a thousand feet, on whose broad top an endless stream of chariots was hurrying. Nearby was the ship which had brought Metak from the Moon of Lost Souls.

An hour passed; then Black warriors entered the ship with heavy shackles, and the arms of each captive were secured. Stout leather collars were then placed around our necks and locked, after which a heavy slave-chain was run through the ring of each collar, leaving some three feet of slack between each two captives; nor was it much later till we were ordered out into the opening, toward the great gate that was slowly receding to unfold the wonders within.

With a thousand or so other captives—hairy, beast-like men who had attempted a revolt on one of the distant planets conquered by the Raiders—we were herded toward the golden chariot of Metak, and the links of the slave-chain were snapped to the ring in its floor.

Then with a hundred slave-girls leading the way with agile dancing as they strewed our path with roses, and the wild crashing of timbrels accompanying their steps, the long march that marked the triumph of Metak was begun through the wide streets of Manator's shouting millions.

Along boulevards where wine flowed like water, we, the captives of Metak, were hurried, through streets lined with the drunken rabble and lower orders of the city, as well as the countless slaves who were allowed a certain freedom. From the spacious galleries of the towering buildings the more elite and wealthy looked on in a less boisterous manner, though they too were loud in their cheering.

It was now that I had my first look at the women of Capara—tall, shapely Black women, whose scanty, jewel-encrusted trappings revealed their shapely bodies. Beautiful? Yes, no doubt, but in a languid, voluptuous manner; sloe-eyed daughters of luxury, who lived only for pleasure. At the sight of us they laughed loudly. I was later to see much of these dark beauties, and witness their wild carousals.

Through the golden streets of Manator the procession wove its slow way, and the heavens rang with the loud cheers of the Blacks, and rose petals fell like fluttering snowflakes. Metak stood erect in his chariot, his harsh features showing his love of applause. Frequently he would turn to send his long lash cracking around us fettered captives. This always added to the plaudits and the din, and increased the loud shouting of his name.

At long last, in the very heart of the city, we came upon the lake—a sky-blue, artificial lake, five miles square and cool and lovely, that flashed and sparkled in the sunlight; and rising up in its center, its lofty turret, domes and spires towering to the sky, was the supreme wonder of this world of many wonders—the gigantic golden palace that was the castle of Queen Tara, a weird and indescribable structure, of breath-taking enormity.

But we only skirted the shores for a few streets; then our winding way took us from the blue lake and back once more into the densely packed streets. Then at sundown the procession ended at the great amphitheater where we would battle on the morrow. Here we were lodged in the dank cells beneath it in pairs, fed, then left alone.

Jo-Mar the commander had been placed in the same cell with me, nor were we long in learning the reason. Shortly after nightfall the jailer and several guards came and led us to a large room at the end of the cell row, where several large tubs provided the means for a bath. Here we washed, then were given new trappings—splendid jewel-encrusted harness and soft-skinned sandals—after which we were taken to an office-like chamber, where several officers awaited us.

"These are the ones," said the jailer. "The old fool who led the

147

Red fleet against us, and the Earthman."

"Good," said one; then to us: "You two are to be taken to the castle. The glorious queen wishes to see and question you at once."

Several of the others secured our hands behind us; then the speaker went on:

"So you are the Earthman," he added to me. "Your daring and the manner of your swordsmanship has reached us even here. It is a pity we will not be able to see you battle in the arena and display your skill. Unless I am mistaken, within an hour that handsome head of yours will have been lopped from your husky frame, and left as a toothsome dainty for the scavengers beyond the hills."

Without the amphitheater awaited several Tors. Upon the backs of two of these Jo-Mar and I were hoisted. The officers mounted the others. Then, spreading their great wings, the bird-men rose into the air, the ground receding rapidly, and the glittering city sparkled below, then out over the waters of the lake to the great outline of lights that was the colossal castle of Tara, to land lightly in the huge courtyard that swarmed with warriors and officials.

Our coming was expected. Quickly we were ushered within, and down great halls of towering pillars and barbaric splendor, and through huge rooms and chambers till we came to the enormous folding-doors, before which a hundred warriors stood guard with gleaming swords.

Suddenly from beyond the doors came the thunderous boom of a great gong.

"The Queen will see you now," said the officer turning to us, "You first, old man. Speak only if she questions you, and be precise in your answers. Above all do not anger or in any way disagree with her. Ten thousand deaths could not be so disastrous. There, I have warned you. Come!"

With two guards on either side of him, the old chieftain was hurried toward the opening doors, which just as speedily closed again. Jo-Mar had turned to flash a brave farewell, but when the doors reopened, some ten minutes later, and the old man was led past us, he did not look at me again, nor would he ever look at another, for Jo-Mar had been blinded.

"The judgment of Tara is swift," commented the officer beside me. Then as the gong thundered again: "Your turn now, Earthman."

And with a Black warrior clutching me on either side, I was hurried through the great doors and to the mighty throne room beyond, to be judged by that famous beauty who controlled all life and destiny—Tara the Glorious, Queen of the Stars, Ruler of Space and of Planets!

Chapter XVII
Tara, Queen of the Stars

We entered a throne room of dream-like enormity. Monstrous golden pillars towered to a golden ceiling, carved as were the colossal walls with the countless hieroglyphics and paintings that had occupied thousands of hands for thousands of years, and strewn with huge clusters of priceless gems. Great glass-encased beams of light ran the entire length of the prodigious structure. Colored windows flung open to the two moons, and their lights reflected dazzlingly on the glittering floor we trod, for its long, broad length was one vast sweep of sparkling diamonds.

That enormous throne room was not unguarded. On either side a thousand warriors, each armed with a two-handed broadsword, kept silent watch. So straight and rigid were their postures they might have passed for rows of ebon statues. Through those silent ranks of soldiery we made our way, to halt at length before the mighty jeweled throne that rose before us.

And then I raised my eyes to behold, at last, Tara the Glorious!

Upon the jeweled throne before me sat a woman beautiful beyond compare, a dazzling Queen whose snow-white body appeared as a pearl wrought by god-like hands. The glittering, tight-clinging, gold-like tissue, that fell from her slender waist to her instep, made no pretense at concealing that wondrous form.

Her beauty—but how can one describe that which transcends description? Mere words are a mockery when applied to that glittering goddess who came before creation.

I could speak of dark eyes and long lashes, and delicately arched brows of a midnight hue. I could tell of red lips and snow-white teeth, and breath-taking features as though chiseled from pearl, or that wondrous, wavy black hair, that tumbled to her shoulders in lustrous splendor. But so far beyond all earthly conception was that blinding beauty before me, that for a wild instant I half suspected it was some ethereal vision I beheld.

"To your knees, dog, to your knees!" whispered one of my captors as they both sank to their knees; then as their bent heads touched the jeweled floor, he cried: "O Greatest of Queens! O Ruler of Space and of Planets, we again ask your infallible judgment in passing sentence on a captive. This is the Earthman who escaped from the Prison Farms to the forbidden Moon of Madness, and was later captured when we destroyed the Red fleet."

There was silence as those wondrous dark eyes went to mine, and though her dazzling features were as immobile as an ivory mask, I felt my very soul had been laid bare and read in that brief scrutiny. Then she spoke, and her voice was as vibrant as the tones of a crystal bell.

"Do you hold life so lightly, Earthman? Is it such an indifference to the mysteries of the unknown that caused you to welcome death and flee to the forbidden Moon of Madness—a direct disobedience of my orders?"

To attempt to cope with that brilliant beauty in a battle of wits was useless. She would but play with me. And knowing this, I decided on stolid silence and stared straight ahead. But she had no intention of allowing that liberty, for presently there came a silvery:

"Tara has ways of forcing a stubborn tongue."

"Perhaps it was a love of freedom," I broke out, forgetting my intended silence; "freedom, to a life of slavery in the service of domineering, brutal Blacks; a desire, maybe, to question the authority of one who has such unquestioned authority over man and the worlds around him!"

A startled gasp arose from the assembly of officials and warriors behind me, for never before in the long annals of time had one dared to speak to Tara in such a manner. The two on either side of me, still prostrate on the floor, evidently thought I had followed their example. At my words they looked upward, and seeing me still standing, sprang to their feet as though to drag me to my knees. From behind came a hurrying of footsteps.

But the eyes of Tara halted them in a twinkling.

"Desist! Do not touch him," went on that wonderful voice, and in the immediate silence that followed: "Truly it is different to see a man of spirit before me, especially one who stands in the shadows of a terrible death. Lies and deceit are the general rule, when they are not so terrorized as to be speechless with fear.

"But about yourself, Earthman. You know, of course, that you have earned a hideous death at the hands of my torturers—made but the more certain by the manner of your present conduct."

"I expected as much," I answered.

She watched me for a moment; then the faintest suggestion of a smile played at the corners of her lovely mouth as she said:

"That little world you come from, the Earth—tell me of it."

"There is very little to be told, I fear, that you do not already know. Vast sweeps of moss-covered desolation that once were great oceans, studded with the occasional piles of crumbling grandeur that were the cities of the ancients, are all that remains of a ravaged planet that has known a thousand invasions from the stars—except, perhaps, the bleaching bones of the tribes and beasts that fell before the Vapors of Vengeance, when the Black fleet released the terrible gasses that killed all life upon my world."

"And you?" she asked.

"I am Jan of the Bardonians," I answered, "prince of a tribe who dwelt in the ruins of the Purple City."

The Queen of the Stars gave a slight start.

"A prince!" she exclaimed. "A prince! La, then it is your royal heritage that gives you such a fearless carriage. A prince indeed!"

Tara the Glorious gave the musical laugh that sounded like the tinkling of far-away chimes.

"Ah, Prince Jan, it would indeed be strange if one monarch did not accord another certain prerogatives. I will therefore waive the death sentence that should be passed upon you. The slaying of Metak's son can also be forgotten. You will be allowed to fight in the arena and display the great swordsmanship of which I have heard, and should you manage to be the final victor I will grant the three wishes that can be claimed by a survivor of the Great Games."

That was all. At a gesture from the beauteous one the guards again led me through the ranks of black soldiery. My stay before the glittering Queen could not have been more than three minutes, but during that brief interval I had had time to observe the large golden ball that hung from the silken canopy just above the throne—an exact counterpart of the one I had beheld in the Black Tower.

This, then, was my goal. If I could steal into the throne room unobserved and touch the crystal ring on my finger against the glittering ball, I would have accomplished the mission Time had given me—the starting of the great magnetism that in ten days would draw the tiny Moon of Madness across the void to Capara, where the powerful attraction of the two Balls of Life would unite them to radiate the terrible heat that would mean the destruction of both planets.

It would take a miracle to get me by the guards, I knew, and yet it seemed that the impossible had just happened; for scarcely had the great doors of the throne room closed behind us when the guard beside me spoke:

"By the blood of my ancestors. Earthman, it was a miracle!" he exclaimed. "For years have I served at the court of the Queen and taken ten thousand captives before her, but never have I known her to grant mercy, or act as she did tonight."

"She laughed!" ejaculated the other. "She smiled first; then she laughed. The Queen has lightly dismissed the charges against this barbarian, and will allow him to fight in the arena. It's incredible!"

This he said to several Black officers who had gathered around us.

These in turn were voicing their own surprise when one said: "Look! Here comes Vaxarus to bid for the lovely princess the fleet recently captured." And I turned with the others to behold the tiny phrenologist who had brought about my capture by the Black Raiders when the fleet had first landed on my own world.

"The little runt owns half the wealth of Capara," murmured one. "And though the women of his harem number hundreds, his riches enable him to purchase from the Queen any new beauty her fleets capture."

"Sh!" cautioned another. "It would go hard with you if he heard, for he stands high in the favor of the Queen, and has brought many to their ruin."

By this time the little phrenologist was almost upon us, his disproportionately large head turning from one to another, his beady eyes narrowing to mere slits.

"Come to bargain for another beauty, Vaxarus?" said one coldly. "Afraid that if you wait till they are put on the auction block some other might be before you?"

The gaze of the dwarf went to the speaker. "It would be wiser if you kept your hatred for me better hidden, Notan," he snapped. "Several others, if they could now speak, would likewise advise you." And then his eyes fell upon me.

"Beauty of Tara," exclaimed Vaxarus, "it's the Earthman! The fellow who killed the four guards and whom I later captured with my paralyzing-wand. Oh, you recognize me, do you, barbarian? Remember the tortures of the green beam when it held you so helpless, perhaps? But what is he doing here?" he asked the others.

Several of them explained.

"He came from the forbidden Moon of Madness and the Queen has waived the death sentence?" he asked. "The punishment for the

154

slaying of Metak's son has likewise been dismissed?" Then as the others nodded: "But why?" he demanded.

"The gods alone know," said an officer. "Perhaps the glorious Queen desires to see his strength displayed in the arena."

Vaxarus looked at me steadily for a moment. "Yes," he answered at length, "it must be that. It—it must be that," he added slowly.

With two guards hurrying me through the numerous halls and rooms—my arms still bound behind me—we came at last to the courtyard without. There several Tors were waiting to fly us to the great city of lights that sparkled across the water. The outlines of thousands of spaceships glittered in the heavens above, some floating idly, others moving slowly across the sky.

"The incoming ships outnumber the stars," said one guard to the other as they lifted me upon the back of a Tor. "They convey the millions from all parts of the planet who have come for the Great Games. Every inn and hostel is packed, and the great streets swarm with those awaiting the trumpets that will announce the opening of the arena gates at dawn."

"I hear they will be the greatest in the history of Capara," said the other, "and that the slaughter for the ten days should number a good twenty thousand humans alone, as well as countless beasts."

"At least that," replied the first. "They say that for the supreme attraction on the final day Queen Tara plans to throw a hundred of the shaggy beast-men of Yat into the arena with a thousand maidens captured from the temples of some distant star."

When I had been finally returned to my cell beneath the amphitheater it was well past midnight, but sleep did not at first come to me. It was a narrow, stone-floored little cell, damp, and the walls for some feet overhead so moist and slimy that it was evident it was well below the surface.

A single, slanting hole, high up near the ceiling, was the only aperture for light or air. Through it I could see one bright star, and the sight filled me with hope; for it was the sun of my own world, the planet Earth, billions of miles away.

And I remember as I looked at it on that long-gone night, that it seemed to strengthen me for the ordeals ahead. My own people were gone, the golden girl dead, and the horrors of the arena awaited me on the morrow. But I somehow felt that I could win over all, and despite the dangers, gain access to the throne room and avenge my world. For a long hour I stood there, watching the star so far away in the great void above me.

And then at last I threw myself, full length, on the stone floor, and slept the sound slumber of a healthy fighting-man.

Chapter XVIII
The Great Games

At dawn the blare of a thousand trumpets heralded the opening of the Great Games—the last that mightiest of planets, Capara, was destined to know.

An hour later the guards came to escort the twenty imprisoned Red men, together with myself, to one of the huge, cave-like rooms encircling the arena, whose barred far end led to the sands without. Through these we were able to obtain a view of a good two-thirds of the mighty amphitheater, as well as the numerous surrounding cage-like rooms that held the many strange men and savage beasts we would so soon be battling.

Even at that early hour the crowds were beginning to pour through the numerous gateways; so by high noon a million people were assembled within the great amphitheater.

At its far end, beneath a brilliant-hued canopy was the luxurious box reserved for the Queen, surrounded by three ranks of soldiery.

At length came the great golden spaceship that conveyed Tara from her castle to the arena, nor was it much later till the Glorious One had tossed the slender wand onto the sands that signified the opening of the Great Games, amid the thunderous cheers of her worshipping subjects.

The first day was taken up almost entirely with the various ceremonies and drills performed by the leading regiments of Capara's imperial army; though just at dusk two giant beasts from a distant star—tanodons, they were called—were turned loose and made the air tremble with their roars as they tore each other to pieces.

On the second day the games commenced in earnest—they lasted from noon till dusk—beginning with two frail twenty-foot giants from a world of mist battling a repulsive, balloon-shaped thing, that seemed all eyes and tentacles, which finally ended in the death of both men and beast amid the wild roars of the great assembly.

Then followed a series of seemingly endless duels and struggles, men against beasts, men against men; sometimes evenly divided, again one side outnumbering the other. Then numerous battles between giant beasts whose savagery was awe-inspiring, as with hideous roars they slashed and tore, and left great pieces of quivering flesh on the blood-stained sands.

It was late that afternoon before we were called upon. Then the guards came and threw open the barred doors leading to the arena, and amid loud shouts and falling lashes we were driven into the glare of the open, and each given a longsword.

I cast a look around me. For a brief space there was the surrounding sand, then the wall that encircled it and protected the watchers above—a veritable sea of faces. At the far end of the arena the glorious Tara sat beneath the waving fans of perspiring slaves, surrounded by the boxes of her leading warriors and nobles.

I caught a glimpse of Metak in a box to the right of the Queen, and beside him a lovely white woman of a matured, dignified beauty, whom I knew to be one of my own world; his wife, no doubt, but this was not unusual, as many of the Blacks mated with their captives, especially if the latter were of high or regal station. But I felt a contempt for the Earthwoman who would voluntarily surrender herself to the destroyers of her planet.

I had not long to view my surroundings, for coming through a large gate to the left were twenty yellow men, each armed with a long spear and mounted upon a kang—our foes. The next moment they sighted us, and with loud shouts to their chargers thundered down upon us.

A bloody battle followed, while the surrounding horde laughed and roared their approval, a battle where quarter was neither asked nor expected, and ended only when the last of the yellow men lay lifeless on the sands, and I and the four remaining Red warriors

158

were returned to our quarters.

At sundown the games were halted for the day, and we prisoners were returned to our individual tiny cells beneath the arena, fed, then left alone to await another day of slaughter.

On the third day I fought twice in the arena, and did likewise on the fourth—always against some warrior who had previously distinguished himself. But ever I proved more than a match for my opponents, so that at last the cry, "Bring on the Earthman!" was frequently roared by the howling thousands.

Then on the fifth day, at the order of the Queen, I fought directly before her box. This time my opponent was a powerful Blue man of Rana, who had previously mowed down all before him, and who extended me to the fullest. For ten long minutes our blades clashed and crossed, with the advantage alternately wavering from one to the other. But at length, amid the deafening roars, I penetrated his guard, and caught a glimpse of the glorious Tara leaning forward, her wondrous face lit with wild joy as my blade tore through the Blue man's heart.

I could fill a volume in telling of the Great Games alone; of the countless duels and miniature battles between strange warriors; of shrieking girls tied to the horns of great bull-like creatures that had been tortured to a frenzy, then turned loose; of brave men being pulled asunder by lumbering pairs of ponderous pandons, as well as a thousand other terrible deaths and tortures.

And then that one night when the games lasted much longer than usual, and finally ended with a great glass floor being laid on the sands, after which the arena was flooded, and the two huge boats constructed for the purpose were floated in, to wage the fierce naval battle that terminated in the burning of both ships and the destruction of their crews.

At nights I would lie in my tiny cell looking up at the slanting hole near the celling, through which I could get the occasional glimpse of the brilliant fireworks shooting from the gardens of the

Black nobles, as the conquerors gave themselves to wild carousals.

ine days passed. Fourteen times I had fought in the arena. One by one I had seen it claim my Red companions, as well as thousands of other captives. One by one the various warriors from the various worlds had gone down to their death, so that on the dusk of the ninth day there remained only myself and a huge Blue warrior of Rana whom I would meet on the morrow to decide the final survivor of the Great Games.

That night a visitor came to my dank little cell below the arena, as I lay on the tiny cot watching a patch of starlit sky that showed through the slanting hole near the ceiling. The intrusion itself was unusual. Excepting my jailer and the officers who had escorted me to the castle of Tara, the first night of my imprisonment, none had entered this cheerless cell. So it was with some surprise that I raised my head as the door grated and swung back to behold an old acquaintance, and one of riches and importance—Vaxarus the royal phrenologist.

Standing in the doorway the little dwarf regarded me intently, his abnormally large head huge and grotesque in the torchlight.

"Perhaps you can guess why I am here," he said at last.

I shook my head. "You are the phrenologist," I answered.

The jailer behind him carried a torch. The tiny Black ordered him to thrust it into a niche above the door, then leave us; after which Vaxarus turned to me.

"Hardly a fitting place for a prince, Earthman," he began, indicating the damp stone walls around us. "The jailers of Tara show no favoritism to her captives."

"They would be showing a trait alien to any Caparian if they did," I answered. "Clemency and justice are words that have no meaning to a Black Raider."

The little phrenologist gave a throaty chuckle. "By that I take it a change would not be unwelcome to you."

160

I made no answer, but raising myself to a sitting position watched him steadily. It was not the purpose of seeing me that had prompted this visit, and I knew it. Perhaps it was my silence that encouraged him to go on.

"And you can have that change, have it with such quickness that by this time tomorrow you may wallow in luxury and riches.

"Tomorrow you will again fight in the arena, Earthman," he went on, his voice lowering slightly. "Tomorrow you will kill the Blue warrior of Rana and be proclaimed the winner of the Great Games."

"Suppose the Blue warrior of Rana kills me?" I put in.

The phrenologist smiled thinly. "You will win," he answered. "I have seen a million warriors and have yet to behold the one who could stand before you. Yes; you will win, and that means you will be given the three wishes granted to a survivor. It is of that which I would talk. I want one of these wishes for myself."

"For you?"

Vaxarus nodded. "I suppose it does seem strange that the richest man in Capara should come to a captive for help—especially one that he himself helped to capture. But for once I find myself in a position where neither riches nor my high standing can avail. You recall some nine nights ago when I met you in the castle of the Queen, and one of the guards mentioned I had come to buy a princess the fleets of Tara recently captured?"

I nodded.

"Well, that was true; I did. I have seen the lovely princess and would add her to my harem. But the Queen thinks I already have too many royal daughters, and would not grant her to me. Instead she prefers to have two young nobles—sons of illustrious families and men who have bid for her—fight for the right to possess the princess on the arena sands tomorrow."

The eyes of Vaxarus narrowed to mere slits.

"But tomorrow when you slay the Blue man, Tara will grant you

161

three wishes. Now if you would but ask her for me—"

So that was it. His riches unable to purchase another royal beauty for his harem, the cunning Black had come to ask that I request it. Luckily I remembered his powers as a phrenologist, and strove to keep my mind a blank as I answered blandly:

"But why should I? How could a request like that help me?"

"In more ways than one, Earthman," answered Vaxarus slowly, and his eyes never left mine. "Your other two wishes will doubtless be a demand for your freedom and riches. The latter will, of course, be granted to a reasonable extent. But you can never hope to know great wealth as the nobles of Capara know it. Now with me behind you all that can be different, and Vaxarus never forgets a favor.

"Yes, with me and the good wishes of the Queen you should go far. And you surely have won the esteem of Tara. It is the talk of the city how the fearless fighting of the Earthman thrills and pleases the Glorious One."

"This princess," I asked after a pause; "how will I know her?"

"Quite easily," answered Vaxarus, his face lighting. "She will be sitting in the same box with the Queen upon the morrow. You will be sure to recognize her by the golden fetters encircling her wrists. It is the plan of Tara to have the two nobles battle for her immediately after you fight the Blue man. Both men of importance, it will be a unique duel. I will be sitting in the box to the left of the Queen; so after you have slain the Blue man—"

The phrenologist then went on to tell how, after I had slain the Blue man (he evidently believed there could be but one outcome to the struggle) I was to kneel before the box of the Queen and receive the royal congratulation, after which I was to request, along with my asking for freedom and riches, that her loyal servant, Vaxarus, be permitted to take for his own the captured princess—the tiny Black going to great lengths in explaining how I would never regret such a favor, and could be able to count upon him as my staunchest friend in the future.

ometime later he took his departure.

Although I made no promise, I had vaguely hinted I might remember him on the morrow, and the Black seemed satisfied with this. Of course, I had no intention of helping him or any other Caparian. I lived only for revenge now. Were I able to win over the Blue warrior I would ask only my freedom, then in some way strive to gain entrance into the throne room of Tara and start the great magnetism that would bring around the destruction of her planet.

But I felt all this would be better were it not known by Vaxarus.

His mention of the captured princess had again brought to mind the lovely golden girl who had been the princess of Penelope, the blue-eyed Vonna whose slender body lay cold in death, along with the hundreds of others in the little village of that tiny buried world beneath the petrified Moon of Madness—indirectly another victim of the cursed Black Raiders. I blessed the hour that would see their doom.

Of course, I realized the hideous horror and destruction that hour would bring about, and in imagination could see the frantic Black billions as the two worlds drew closer, wide-eyed in terror, their mouths contorted, gnawing at their hands and gibbering in an insanity of fear. Then at the end of the tenth day the two worlds would crash, and within twenty beats of a human heart both be reduced to a bubbling, molten mass.

True, I would die along with the rest, but revenge would be complete, and the other worlds forever freed of their cruel Black masters.

It was quite late before I lay down on my cot, but even then I was not to know sleep long. It seemed I had scarcely closed my eyes before I was awakened to find a gag thrust in my mouth, while four muffled figures were busy securing my arms and legs.

Before I was fully myself or could begin to struggle my hands had been tied behind me, my feet trussed up to meet them, I had been lifted from my cot and was being carried down the dark passage to the steps that led upward to the arena sands.

Up these I was carried, then out onto the arena and a glorious starlit night. No words had been spoken by the men, each of whom wore a black silken mask that hid his features. Now on reaching the sands one of them whistled softly, and the next moment six Tors winged downward from above and landed lightly beside us.

At a word from my captors two of the Tors picked me up, while the four men mounted the backs of the others. Then spreading their great wings the bird-men rose into the night, and we were mounting upward. Higher we rose, till below were the glittering, far-flung outlines of the golden city; then out over the lake and above the mighty castle of Tara, and the cool night wind whistled in our ears.

Presently we began to descend at the far end of the lake—the more lowly part of the city, to land lightly on a deserted pier, behind which rows of gloomy freight sheds stood out against the blackness of the night. Before us the dark waters rolled and splashed.

Nearby was a small, one-story building, from whose single window came a feeble light. To this I was carried; then stepping up to the door one of the men rapped twice—a pause, then three more sharp knocks. A moment later the door was opened from the inside. I was lifted through, and thrown on the hard floor of the interior.

The little room was feebly lighted by the glare of a single torch. Seated at a table in its center were four men talking in low tones.

The sound of my intrusion caused them to turn, and as the eyes of one of them fell full upon me I recognized the grim, terrible features of Capara's champion swordsman and my foremost enemy—Metak, the Black commander.

Chapter XIX
In the Silent Watches of the Night

As the eyes of the Black commander fell upon me they flashed a light of triumph.

"Ah, your highness, this is indeed a pleasure," he sneered, rising and coming forward. "So fate has seen fit to cross our paths again, eh?" Then with a laugh, "I welcome you," he taunted. And drawing back his sandaled foot he kicked me heavily in the side.

Metak turned to the four masked men. "Everything came off as planned?" he asked.

"Precisely, your excellency," answered one.

"You were seen by no one?"

"By no one," said the other. "The jailer, of course, knows all, but he has been heavily bribed, and can be trusted. In the morning he will say when he went to the Earthman's cell the door was open, the prisoner gone, and that is all he knows. Evidence will point to a well-planned escape and—"

"The Tors that brought you here," interrupted Metak; "where are they?"

"Just without, awaiting their pay. Each was promised ten daggots for his service and silence."

"Silence, bah!" exclaimed Metak. "A sword-thrust is the only guarantee of permanent silence, and that is what we want. Why, if those cowardly Tors were as much as suspected they would scream all they knew even before they were sent to the torture chamber."

The eyes of the other widened. "You mean—"

"Of course. Take them inside the sheds on a pretense of payment, then use your swords."

The other gave a short laugh, spoke a few unintelligible words to the others, and then the four masked warriors departed. Metak turned to the three seated men at the table.

"You will come with me, Shovan," he said to one, and then as the man arose, Metak glared at the others.

"It is needless for me to tell what would happen to all of us if this fellow escapes—a drop into the Pit of Blackness at best. Guard him well, therefore, till my return tomorrow night. Then we will know just how much he has been missed, and how we can best dispose of him. Till then I leave him in your care with a final word of caution—the fiend has the strength of a pandon."

The door closed behind them, and I heard their retreating footsteps.

From where I lay I cast a look around me. It was evidently some shack or toolshed. The walls were bare, the ceiling low, with no other furniture except the few chairs and the table. From without came the splashing of the lake waves against the wharf. To the left, a small door, slightly ajar, showed the black entrance of an unlit room.

For some time the two men left to guard me sat at the table, occasionally looking in my direction, and more frequently helping themselves to generous portions from the large wine bottle before them. When it had finally been consumed it was tossed into the corner, while from the nearby room one of the men brought forth a second.

Midnight passed, and the torch sputtered and burned low. By this time the two men had drunk themselves into a stupor, and sat motionless with their heads and arms on the table.

Again and again I threw myself against the bonds that held me, but they were many and strong. I felt a wave of madness sweep over me as my efforts met with failure. Here I lay like some bound beast awaiting the butchers on the morrow, unable to help myself. If only I could get near those ropes with my teeth there might still be a chance that—I suddenly became conscious of light footsteps without.

166

Amid the splashing of the waves and the snores of the men I could hear them—light, quick-moving footsteps, now on the wood of the wharf, now on the patch of gravel just before the door, occasionally pausing, then drawing nearer. At the door they stopped again for a moment, as though the newcomer wished to make sure all was still within, while I raised my head and waited. Then the door was slowly opened, and the night air came whistling into the room.

The next moment a slender yellow girl, wide-eyed in excitement, glided through the opening and closed the door noiselessly behind her.

She immediately saw the sleeping men at the table before her. In the flickering torchlight she stood watching them, panting; then her wandering gaze fell upon me and a glad light leaped to her eyes.

Cautiously she came forward and knelt beside me.

"Sh!" she cautioned. "I come to save you, Earthman." While she spoke I could feel her working at my bonds. Occasionally the cold steel of a knife touched my flesh. A moment later I was free.

"Come!" she whispered.

Scarce daring to breathe we began a careful tiptoe toward the doorway, the girl leading me by a hand's width. The breathing of the two at the table rose and fell. The lapping of the waves drowned our almost noiseless advance, yet even then would come the occasional squeaky tread that might well awaken a light sleeper. The girl flashed a look from the warriors to me that said, "Will we make it?" plainer than words.

We were at the door now. Another five seconds and we would be safe—and then the guard nearest to us moved and murmured sleepily.

With a noiseless spring I landed on my toes beside him. For a long, nerve-racking moment I waited with ready hands but an inch above his throat. Then the fellow gave a sigh as though in the throes of some bad dream. His eyes partly opened, his shoulders raised slightly. Then he slumped forward once more, and a moment later there came the sound of his regular breathing.

The next instant we were beyond the door. Out here all was still and calm, for the great city of Manator slept. To the right the waves splashed against the pier. Two miles across the water the colossal castle of Tara was a gleam of lights. Overhead a million glittering stars shone.

We hurried on past several sheds and storehouses, to halt at last in the shadows of a great structure. I looked at the yellow girl for a moment before I spoke.

"I cannot understand it," I said at length. "Who are you? How did you know I was a prisoner there, and why did you save me?"

"Because I have seen you fight in the arena, Earthman, and if ever a warrior lived who could best Metak it is you. Because in his heart I know the tyrant Metak fears you, and dreads lest on the morrow you ask to meet him in combat."

"You know Metak?"

She gave a bitter laugh.

"It would be strange if I did not. For the last six years, ever since the Black Raiders captured me on my planet of Lahara, I have been forced to slave along with the many others in the great castle of Metak. There I serve both him and the lovely white woman who was once a queen of your own world, the planet Earth. She is gentle and kind, but he is a devil. Often have I heard her crying, and always is she sad-eyed and longing for her loved ones, for she was stolen from the Earth, long years ago. Metak won her in battle in the arena, and Queen Tara compelled her to marry him."

"But about myself?" I asked.

"It is simple. Early this evening I was doing some duties near the great hedges at the far end of the garden. As I was well within their shadows it is not strange that I was not seen by Metak and the others when they planned to have you taken from your cell to the shack on the pier. So tonight I waited till the castle slept, then stole from my quarters and came here. I was terribly frightened."

"You are a very brave girl," I answered. "And you did all this for me—a stranger." She drew herself up proudly.

"I would not be a true daughter of Lahara if I did not try to save the one man who can best Metak, the destroyer of my world."

As she spoke I had been looking out over the water to the mighty outline of lights some two miles away—the castle of Tara—gradually realizing that this was that opportune time for which I had been waiting. The hour was late, vigilance lax, and most of the guards and warriors sure to be sleeping.

I turned to the girl. "It is a great debt I owe you for what you have done, but now you can do no more. Give me your knife, then, and return to your quarters," and I reached for the knife she carried.

"And you?" she asked.

"I shall be safe," I assured her, "and seek only to avenge myself upon the Blacks. Hasten back to your quarters, then, for if you are found it will undo all you have accomplished this night."

She nodded. "I go, Earthman, and will pray that on the morrow you will challenge the Black tyrant, and pass your sword through his heart."

Then she was gone, and securing the knife to my belt I turned to the task before me.

Grasping the edge of the pier I lowered myself to arm's length, then slipped noiselessly into the water. The next moment I was making steadily toward those glittering lights across the lake, and the cool water eddied and gurgled in my wake. With only my leather trappings around me my arms and legs were free, and the gap between me and the pier grew ever wider.

With long, powerful strokes I swam steadily ahead. Several small boats were at rest upon the water, and a golden twinkle glimmered from two of them, but I was careful to stay clear of them, and used the safe and silent strokes that made my passing noiseless. I saw no one, though several times great spaceships passed far above me; and once from the now distant shore came that drawn-out cry that might have been some terrible laugh or scream. But the mighty golden castle loomed up ever larger before me, and at last my feet touched the sandy bottom of the beach.

Silently I waded through the surf to the shore. It was a dark, lonely part of the beach—the great castle of Tara rose from a man-made island, in the heart of a man-made lake some five miles square—and no challenge from a guard or sentry came to halt me. Just ahead a steep bluff rose up for a score of feet. But the protruding weeds and shrubs made it not difficult to scale, and presently I was raising my head cautiously above its edge.

It was evidently the rear of the castle that I had come upon, and the stone-flagged courtyard before me no doubt led to the great kitchens. Several small fires flickered and flamed, around which a half-hundred slaves and servants were sleeping and perhaps again that number slumbered just within the huge doorway that showed black and sinister beyond the firelight.

Of course where I lay there was no immediate danger of detection; yet to remain there forever would gain me nothing. In the castle beyond was what I had come for, and it was to that mighty structure I would go. I caught a glimpse of thick foliage at its corner, growing up along its side. This was enough to decide my immediate movements; so with a prayer on my lips I rose quietly to my feet and sped swiftly across the courtyard with the stealth of a disembodied spirit.

In the shadows of the foliage I threw a glance back at the slumbering figures, but they were still motionless and silent. The stout vines before me that had grown along the walls of the great castle for centuries provided an excellent ladder. Cautiously and slowly I rose up that leafy frame, as a false step or a crackling might prove my undoing. But a kind fate was surely with me that night, and presently I was swinging from the vines into a window— evidently the spacious sleeping-quarters of some noble.

All this had been done with the utmost stealth, but I now felt haste was also necessary, as the hours were flying by and I had yet to reach the silken canopy above the great throne and touch the Ball of Life ere the coming dawn brought the awakening of the thousands of guards.

At the far end of the room was a doorway which opened to—I reasoned—a corridor that in turn led to a stairway and the great chambers and mighty throne room below. That was my goal, and with the unthinking rashness so typical of me, I acted. Quickly I tiptoed across the room, past the sleeping figure on the bed, found the handle, drew back the door—and there was a giant Black guard with uplifted longsword dashing toward me!

As my eyes fell upon the glittering blade of the huge Black, my right hand flew to the knife at my belt, while a quick leap sent me flying backward into the darkness of the room.

Inwardly I cursed the stupidity that had caused me to forgo caution and march into the corridor with the assurance of a commanding officer. Even were I able to escape his sword and subdue the Black, the din of the struggle would be sure to rouse the attention that would be my ruin. With the speed of thought I whipped my knife from my belt—and then I stopped.

The Black warrior had not moved! His sword was in the same position, his face still showed the same hate and cruelty as when I had first seen it. Even the uplifted foot, ready for the spring that would send him crashing into me, was motionless. Then I suddenly realized the posture of this weird sentinel would be the same in an hour, or a year hence, as it had been for centuries past.

My foe was a mummy!

A sigh escaped my lips as I lowered my knife. I had heard that certain Black warriors who had distinguished themselves in battle were preserved in the great castle of Tara, but I had never seen them. In the semi-darkness of the corridor I examined my gruesome find. Dust lay thick on its arms and legs, the lips and face had shriveled with time. The leather helmet crumbled as I touched it, and the entire form threatened to collapse. Yet I could not but admire the work of the ancient taxidermist who had strengthened this warrior for the ages. Even the hair of the hands and fingers showed plainly on one who might have lived ten thousand years ago.

Out here the corridor led down a long passage to come at length upon a great hall, in the center of which, surrounded by a small railing, was a huge circular opening of such enormous size that an ordinary house might have been dropped through it.

But no sentry or warrior guarded the pass, as constant ages of security had lulled the vigilance of the Blacks.

With ready dagger I crept forward; though to tell the truth my silence could be attributed to awe rather than fear. The unbelievable grandeur, the strange hieroglyphics and paintings that adorned the towering walls and pillars around me, must have taken centuries in their formation. At last I reached the railing that ran around me, I leaned forward and looked down, into the great throne room forty feet below.

Yes; it was indeed the mighty throne room of the glittering Queen of the Stars—that colossal hall of gold and diamonds, whose erection had drained the treasuries of a score of worlds, glowing and flashing in the moonlight that poured through its open windows. And rising up in its very center was the great jeweled throne of Tara, and above it the silken canopy that contained the Ball of Life.

This then was my goal, but how to reach it? For a moment I was puzzled; then my eyes caught that which showed how it could be done. Adorning the wall beside me were three slender but strong leather hangings, each some ten feet long. It was but the work of a moment to tie them into one long strip, and secure one end to the railing.

The next instant I was making a silent hand-over-hand descent to its thirty-foot end; then I released my hold to drop the last ten feet, and land lightly on my toes on the jeweled floored throne room.

In that death-like silence I looked around at the gigantic pillars and mighty walls that towered on all sides of me. Here was the colossal Hall of Destiny, the hall of dream-like vastness, where the fates of the planets were decreed and decided; the jeweled hall of a billion years, whose continuance and power were said to be eternal—now silent and lonely, for who would dare steal into the throne room of Tara?

And just before me, glowing in a flood of moonlight that poured through the open windows, was the jewel-encrusted throne of the Queen of the Stars, and above it the silken canopy from which was suspended the golden Ball of Life.

And there I stood, alone in the silence of that vast throne room, recalling the words of the great god Time, as I drew his huge crystal-like ring from my finger. Chaos—the destruction of billions would follow.

But it came to me also who had destroyed my own world, and the terrible fate of dear Vonna.

And then I stepped quickly forward, mounted the three steps to the throne, and raising my arms touched the crystal ring of Time against the glowing warmth that was the golden Ball of Life—to tense to rigidity the next instant as the sound of approaching footsteps reached me. Footsteps of marching men—the guards!

But at last I had accomplished the great mission, and even were I to be taken, the planet of Capara was doomed!

Yet I had no desire to be captured, and my eyes swept around for some concealment. It might have been fate that sent them to the great hanging, which in turn led to the discovery of the secret door, for I was to learn later that for centuries none but the Queen had known of its existence. Yes; it might have been fate, or it might have been luck, but whatever it was my eyes beheld a huge tapestry hanging on the far wall. This seemed the ideal place for concealment, and I sped across the room, slid behind it, to touch with my back the little button that swung open the small door behind me.

Into this I stepped and closed it noiselessly, just as the great throne room doors were thrown open and a hundred guards came marching into the room, to take their pre-dawn stations in all parts of the huge hall.

It was a narrow, musty passage in which I found myself, with the utter blackness of the tomb. No eye could have begun to penetrate that stygian gloom. Cautiously I moved forward with outstretched hand till I touched a wall, then hugging its side began a slow advance ahead. The thick layers of dust on the floor and walls gave evidence that this lonely vault had long gone untrodden, perhaps for centuries.

For several hundred yards I continued along the passage that led ever upward; then my progress was suddenly halted by a heavy wooden door, barred upon the side of my approach.

Carefully I ran my hands around that unseen barrier. Along the tops of the bars were deep layers of dust—further proof that the passage had long gone unused. As I pushed the door aside it shrieked out loudly in dismal protest against this unaccustomed disturbance. For a moment I paused to listen, fearful that it might have caused some alarm. But presently, as I heard nothing, I continued my advance.

And then as I groped along in that tomb-silenced blackness I thought I detected a cool draft of fresh air blowing steadily toward me.

With increasing hopes I continued along that upward path, till at the end of fifteen minutes I came to three stone steps that led upward to another door, which might in turn lead to freedom beyond, or else discovery.

For a moment I halted, then quietly pushing it back, stepped into the spacious room beyond.

Though it was not yet dawn, the room was brilliantly lighted. A huge chamber of startling magnificence whose floors, walls and ceilings were a solid mass of diamonds, it was evidently the luxurious sleeping-quarters of some great noble. The air was heavy with a sweet perfume. In its center rose a huge bed, completely covered with a thin, gold-like tissue. To the left two large glass doors were flung open to the silent night, and a lofty balcony.

Then as I continued to stand and stare, there came the faintest rustling of silken sheets within the bed that told the awakening of its occupant. Then again that wonderful voice I had heard once before—soft, calm and musical.

"Who is there?" it asked. "Who is there?"

There was a pause while I froze to rigidity; then it came again, still soft and lovely, but more demanding.

"Who is there? Who is there? Answer me!"

But I could think of no answer, or whither I might flee, as once more sounded the faintest rustling of silken sheets. Then the gold-like tissue around the bed was suddenly parted, and from it stepped that dazzling long-limbed beauty who had known countless ages before creation.

Tara the Glorious—Queen of the Stars!

Chapter XX
The Magic Mirror

𝔉or what seemed an eternity I stood there, watching her slow advance as that wondrous beauty came toward me, her wavy black hair tumbling to her shoulders, the sheer sleeping-robe making no pretense of concealing her white body.

Just before me she stopped; then her dark eyes widened in surprise.

"You!" she exclaimed. "The Earthman!"

Then, as I nodded: "But how does it come you are here?" she asked. "How were you able to escape from your cell and come here? True, I meant to have you transferred to the castle tomorrow, but now you have made that transfer needless. How did you do it—and why?" she insisted.

"It is always possible for a determined man to find what he wants," I answered, watching her tensely.

Tara the Glorious gave a slight start.

"I have it!" she exclaimed, her dark eyes lighting with a sudden joy. "You were looking for me! You were searching for me!"

The Queen of the Stars gave that silvery laugh which seemed to come from a million miles away.

"La, then it is no dream. I fall to sleep with the memory of you the last thing in my mind, then wake to find the mighty barbarian prince has escaped his prison, swum the Blue Lake, eluded my guards—killed several of them perhaps, then comes to my very bedroom to claim me for his captive!"

Tara the Glorious sank to the great couch beside her. "Was there ever such a man?" she exclaimed.

"But you need not remain standing, Prince Jan," she went on, pointing to a chair. "Do sit down and tell me about your many adventures this night—how your great muscles enabled you to escape from the pits beneath the arena, swim the Blue Lake, as well as all the other exploits that must go with it."

As she ceased speaking a low growl suddenly sounded from the far corner, and a large cat-like animal arose from where it had evidently been sleeping—a huge four-footed beast with a great head and a thick mane that I had noticed invariably sprawled at the feet of the beauteous one in the royal box at the Great Games. It had lain at the foot of her throne, too, the night I had been summoned to the throne room—the royal pet, as I was to learn later.

Tara wheeled.

"Down, Ranga!" she ordered, and as the great beast slunk back into the corner: "My most faithful guard," she smiled, turning to me. "Strangely enough it has descended from a species of animal that once roamed your own planet, the Earth—an animal the ancients of your world called a lion. But come, Prince Jan, rest yourself."

A thousand thoughts raced through my mind as I did her bidding. Seated on a golden chair I watched that brilliant beauty. Did she really know what had brought me to her castle? Was she fully aware of what had happened in the throne room, and was now but playing with me—leading me on?

"I am a poor narrator of events," I answered. "I prefer to perform, rather than talk them."

She nodded.

"Ah, I know that well. Fourteen times I have seen your flashing steel drip crimson in the arena, and I know. Yes; you fight with the strength of ten, Prince Jan, and I thrill as I watch you.

"And tomorrow," she went on, "I will watch you again. Tomorrow I will see you slay the Blue men as the thousands cheer, then watch as you come before me to claim the three wishes allotted to a survivor of the Great Games. I wonder what those three wishes will be?"

"Only tomorrow can tell, Queen Tara," I answered. "But surely I must go; I rob you of your sleep."

"No," she put in hastily, one perfect hand half raised in protest. "Stay. I am the Queen, my word supreme, my actions infallible and beyond censure. No, Prince Jan; stay and talk to me this lonely hour, while the rest of the world sleeps."

And she nestled deeper into the silken cushions of the couch, smiling, her tumbling black hair wavy and lustrous, the low V-shaped neck of her filmy sleeping-garment revealing perfect white shoulders.

"Suppose we talk of your world, your Majesty," I ventured; "of your armies, the stars and planets they have conquered."

That dazzling smile deepened.

"Always the warrior, thinking ever of battle and bloodshed. Perhaps I should put you in command of one of my fleets so that desire might be sated, for often my space-fleets have conquered as many as twenty worlds during their journeys far out in the trackless void.

"That of course was many years ago, before my power had begun to assert itself. Only rarely now do they come upon some star that has not already been conquered, and mostly they are occupied in collecting the ransoms I demand and in subduing the endless uprising; though occasionally some ship, traveling on and on through the limitless wastes, comes upon a strange star, which is soon conquered and subdued, or, if it is without wealth or fine slaves, destroyed."

"And tributes and treasures continue to come to Capara?" I asked.

"Endlessly," she answered. "My great treasure castles at the bottom of the North Sea—Capara's mightiest ocean—groan with riches. My jewel vaults in the hallowed mountain of Zoranda threaten to burst that great mount asunder if they are increased. And yet each day the treasure-ships bring added riches and ransom, or else the news that some planet's wealth is exhausted and it is unable to pay; in which case my royal seal sends one of the fleets with the Vapors of Vengeance to destroy that unfortunate world."

And her ivory fingers toyed with the large signet ring she wore.

"Victories, always victories," I mused. "But was no world ever able to beat off your warriors and destroy their ships?" I asked.

"Yes, several of them. But I always sent other ships, then others, with their millions of fighting-men, till at last the worlds screamed for peace; which I sometimes granted and sometimes did not, but in all cases exacted a frightful vengeance.

"I recall once when we destroyed the rat-men of Pambra—tall, white-skinned men of your own size, and human in every respect except for their hideous, rodent-like heads. Well, I had dispatched a fleet to conquer this Pambra—a star the ancients of your world called Venus—but it did not return. I then consulted my Magic Mirror, and was surprised to learn that the great mental powers of the rat-men had advanced them far in the field of hypnotism—so far that they had been able to waft my warriors into a trance-like condition, and were forcing them to toil in their fields as beasts of burden.

"I was amused, and secretly applauded their wisdom and strategy, but, of course, I had to destroy them. Yet as their world was rich in gold and jewels, as well as their great fields of agriculture, I did not wish the Vapors of Vengeance turned upon it, as that powerful red gas tarnishes all gold and jewels it touches."

"And so?" I put in unthinkingly.

"And so I knew there could be but one way," she went on, "—mental surrender. I had my scientists concoct a blue, fog-like vapor, that would neither tarnish nor kill, but all who breathed of its sweet aroma were doomed to an instant and permanent insanity, as it robbed the brain cells of their power.

"Thus I was able to conquer Pambra, for, staying aloft and encircling that planet, the fleet released the blue vapors from the tail of each ship. Then, after allowing time for the gasses to disperse, they landed. A few of the rat-men—now hopeless idiots—were returned to Capara for the experimental tables of my scientists; the rest destroyed. I then had a million conquered subjects—green people from a far-away star—migrated to Pambra in spaceships, to till its great fields and extract its great wealth; and today that world numbers some two billion submissive and dutiful subjects.

"But come, we will talk no more of me or my world—let us hear of yours; that bright green star you call the Earth."

"I am afraid there is little I can tell that you do not already know," I admitted. "For hundreds and hundreds of miles the dreary plains of my world stretch away to show only the occasional ruined cities of the ancients; then dreary moss-covered wastes that were once the bottoms of mighty oceans, for today there are no great bodies of water—only the occasional small lake and stream."

"Yes, I know," she answered nodding. "And yet it was once a great world of thundering cities and hurrying billions."

"But how could you know that?" I asked.

The royal beauty gave a little gurgle of pleasure, enjoying my visible surprise.

"I surprise you, Prince Jan? Ah, but I know the history of the green star as well as I know this room—as well as I do the history of all the worlds my fleets have conquered.

"Come, I will show you."

Tara the Glorious rose to her tall, lovely height, with the grace of a falling leaf. To the corner of the room near the balcony she led me. Here a strange, screen-like mirror, some four feet square, composed of some sparkling material that shimmered and glittered, was supported by two side posts. We paused before it.

"Behold," said Tara, and there was a sudden solemnity in her voice. "One of my greatest treasures, composed of the star dust of distant worlds—the Magic Mirror!"

I looked at it with interest, for I realized by her tone that it was something of importance. "But what purpose does it serve?" I asked.

"It is a mirror that reflects thought," she answered, "as well as to recall from the centuries, even from the beginning of time, any scene or occurrence that might have happened on the various worlds. See, I stand before it thus and think of your world, desiring to witness the most important events that have occurred on it since it began. Watch carefully!"

𝕱or a moment there was nothing, and then that glittering screen suddenly came to life, presenting a series of pictures so startlingly realistic one felt they might talk to the characters in them. First I saw a great bubbling ball that filled nearly all the screen.

"Your world at its beginning," whispered the wondrous beauty beside me.

Then slowly that great globe ceased bubbling and grew hard. Of course, as the Queen explained, what happened on the screen in minutes had in reality taken centuries. Gradually there appeared great seas; then eons later (though on the screen it was but minutes) came land, vegetation, then life—weird beasts of mammoth size which crashed through leafy jungles and roamed great plains, then shaggy men with clothes of skin and knotted bludgeons, who hunted or were hunted by them, to give way in time to men of more human appearance.

Then came small dwellings, then larger ones, then great crowds of humans laboring on huge stone structures.

"The Egyptians," came the soft voice of Tara. "An ancient race of your world building the pyramids."

Then came pictures of wars—wars by land and wars by sea. We saw great armies march to battle. We saw thousands trampled down and overridden by great chariots and mailed horsemen, while the air was black with shooting arrows. We saw huge ships at sea meet and crash head on, then great flames rise and envelop them, while their struggling crews were swept to the waves, blood-smeared and screaming.

Then slowly civilization rose, and the screen showed great cities that grew larger and larger with the passing ages. Strange quadrupeds had appeared too; they seemed the universal mounts of those ancient days, as the fleet kangs had been to my own, for they carried the warriors to battle and drew their heavy carts and wagons.

Then suddenly they disappeared, to be replaced by countless tiny black cars that hurried along at an amazing speed without any visible means of movement, while the heavens were black with little flying-ships, for by now the world had grown to a great populace, and its cities were huge and many.

"Observe closely," whispered Tara. "It is your world at the height of its power."

And indeed it was a wonderful world, and I thrilled to think that my planet had once known such greatness; a great world of mighty cities and broad highways that stretched on and on, while in its vast seas huge ships plowed steadily through the waves to distant shores with cargoes and their thousands of passengers, and all were prosperous and happy.

And then came destruction—another war, but this time one more terrible than all the others, a hideous struggle that seemed to be a war of the races, for we could see the yellow hordes struggling against the others, and smoke and flame was everywhere, and great cities crumbled and fell; till finally the world was covered with charred, smoking ruins, and most of its inhabitants lay dead.

Century followed century, but never again did the world know its former splendor; for all the arts seemed lost, and its people content to remain idle and dwell in the charred ruins of their ancestors. Then came invasions from the skies, then other invasions, then others—each more terrible than the last—while the world slowly dwindled in numbers and intellect, and its vast seas gradually dried up; till at last there remained but the few shallow lakes and streams, the great moss-covered wastes, dreary landscapes and the primitive tribes I had known.

And then came those final scenes that showed the ships of the Black Raiders encircling the Earth as they released the Vapors of Vengeance; and the few remaining tribes clutched at their throats, then died, and every animal staggered and fell, and the birds dropped lifeless to the ground, and only bleaching bones remained when the red gases at last lifted, to show the dismal and final ending of the green star.

And then the scene grew hazy and died away, and Tara turned, smiling, to show that all was over.

I turned to the beauteous one beside me. "My world," I said, "and every living thing upon it died. They are all dead."

She nodded, a half-smile in her dark eyes. "They had no wealth, nothing I wished, and they were unable to defend themselves. They met the fate that must ever overtake the weak—destruction."

"Was it necessary to kill them because they had no wealth?" I went on, my voice rising with my mounting anger.

Those magnificent white shoulders shrugged slightly. "Ah, Prince Jan, need we discuss such matters?" she asked.

"Suppose one mightier than yourself—"

"There is none mightier than Tara. There can be none mightier. And even if there were, the Great Secret of the Bells would have her. No; with the warm rays of the Ball of Life upon her, Tara will go on and on throughout eternity—always the Beautiful, always the Glorious.

"But come, I will show you the history of other worlds; of the red star your ancestors knew as Mars, and the ringed planet that is no more, as well as many others whose pasts are both interesting and instructive."

And seated before the Magic Mirror with the Queen of the Stars beside me, I watched for hours while the histories of the different worlds were shown on that glittering screen. And all the while I sat there the soft, musical voice of Tara interpreted the various scenes for me.

A golden dawn was stealing across the sky when we finally rose.

"Come," said the royal beauty, and taking my hand she led me out on the lofty balcony, her delicate sleeping-robe fluttering in that early breeze.

Out here the world was awakening to a new day.

Far below us the blue waters shimmered and sparkled, while across the lake the first rays of the rising sun were falling on the great golden city with a dazzling brilliance that was blinding.

And standing beside me on the lofty balcony was Tara the Glorious, breath-takingly beautiful in that early light. For long the wondrous Queen of the Stars looked at her sparkling capital, with its mighty elevated thoroughfares that stretched on and on for miles, and its towering peaks and spires that seemed to brush the very sky; then at last she turned to me.

"Is it not wonderful, my great golden city?" she asked softly.

"It surpasses description," I admitted truthfully.

"You like it?" she asked, and as I nodded: "Then it is good," she went on. "It is very good, for I intend to have you remain here with me always."

"Have me remain here always!" I echoed, showing my surprise. "But why should you? How could my future be of any possible interest to your Majesty?"

The dark eyes of Tara went to mine. "Oh Jan, Jan!" she cried. "How can you be so blind? Has not my every word, my every look been an open invitation to you? Why do you think I allowed you to go unpunished when you were brought before my throne? Why have I always had two hidden archers waiting with ready arrows when you fought in the arena—ready to drive their shafts into the heart of your foe should he prove more than a match for you? Why have I allowed you to stay in this room where no man has ever trod, and talked to you through the long hours—and was happy? Why, Jan, why?"

She came closer, her breast rising and falling, her dark eyes wide, her magnificent body trembling.

"Because at last there has come to me one who knows not fear. Because at last there has come to me one to whom I would give my throne, my life, and myself. Because at last, after countless centuries of waiting, love wild and burning has come to Tara the Glorious!"

The next instant her white arms were drawing my face toward hers.

"Kiss me, Jan! Kiss and love me!" she panted, and those blood-red lips rose up to mine.

Chapter XXI
I Find One Who Was Lost

es, I, Jan, prince of the green planet, Earth, in the year 1,001,940, stood on that lofty balcony of the golden palace of Tara, which rose up in the center of the Blue Lake in the heart of the mighty golden city of Manator, on that distant world, Capara; while with her shapely white arms around my neck the glorious Queen of the Stars pleaded for my love.

But those red lips never found mine, nor had I time to make any response, for at that same instant, from across the lake, arose the harsh blare of a thousand trumpets that announced a new dawn and the last day of the Great Games; while from the far end of the room the huge doors were suddenly flung open as a score of slave-girls—the hand-maids of the Queen—entered the great suite to awaken, bathe and array their royal mistress.

Tara had stiffened as the blare of the trumpets reached us, though her arms still remained around my neck. Then as her hand-maids entered she turned to them, then back to me—the slave-girls staring at me in wide-eyed amazement.

"A new day, Jan—it has interrupted us," she whispered. "But there will be others, many others, and nothing will interrupt us— nor will any of the wishes you may publicly ask me this day be denied," and her white hands slid down my arms to gently squeeze my wrists.

"My King to be!" she murmured; then turning to her slave-girls she issued rapid orders.

A few minutes later, at the orders of the Queen, I had been quartered in the great left wing of the palace—a huge suite of breath-taking magnificence that overlooked the Blue Lake. Here I bathed in a scented pool, ate of the rarest foods and donned the harness that was a solid mass of glittering diamonds which Tara had sent to me.

Then, at my own request, I was returned to my cell beneath the arena to await my coming battle with the Blue man. At the command of Tara three Black officers had accompanied me; but I could not help wondering how soon all this would change when the Moon of Madness began its wild plunge toward Capara. Tara, I knew, would instantly guess who had caused the catastrophe, and I had heard enough of the terrible tortures inflicted on those who displeased the Queen to know what a death I might expect.

Of course the love declaration of the Queen of the Stars had come as my greatest surprise, but it was a passion I could never reciprocate. I knew now that my heart lay in that far-off buried village on the weird Moon of Madness, where the body of the lovely golden girl lay cold in death.

An hour passed. From without came the din of the thousands pouring into the arena. I had kept the manner of my escape from the cell on the previous night a mystery, and of course my jailer had wisely maintained silence. Yet it was a keen source of mystery to the Black officers beside me, and at last I heard one say:

"The escape was amazing, the first as long as I can remember. And perhaps we never will know just how it was done, as the Earthman will not tell. Yes; it is a mystery as great as the secret of the Temple of the Bells," he turned, smilingly to me.

I had been paying little attention to the chattering trio, but at the last words of the Black I picked up my ears. "The secret of the Temple of the Bells." Only last night I had heard Tara use them. I had not delved into their meaning, though her tone, as well as that of the Black, told that it must be something momentous. Casually I turned to the officer beside me.

"This Secret of the Bells," I asked him. "What does it mean? I have heard it mentioned several times since coming to Capara."

"It would be strange if you did not," he answered with a laugh as the others nodded, "as it is Capara's greatest and most honorable defense.

"Ages ago," he explained, "many ages ago indeed, for our world was then young and war and conquest were unknown, our beauteous queen sought only to protect her planet, and so ordered the great labor that took a million men a century as they dug the great shaft that penetrated down and down into the very heart of our world. And there, a thousand miles below the surface, was constructed a huge chamber that might well hold a small city.

"And in that chamber, at the Queen's commands, were put thousands upon thousands of tons of explosives of undreamed-of power, so constructed that they would last throughout eternity, and could be instantly discharged by the breaking of the delicate glass vial that sealed the huge doors of the chamber. A thin glass vial so delicate that it could be snapped asunder by a loud vibration and—"

"And that will ever save Capara from the heel of a conqueror," put in another, "for hung along that mighty thousand-mile shaft, at regular intervals, are ten great bells, each weighing many tons. When the first bell on the surface is rung, its booming echo will vibrate along the silent corridor to the next bell, a hundred miles below, where the sound will snap the tiny glass vial above the second. This will release the force that will ring the second bell, whose sound in turn will continue along to the third.

"And so on and on till the ten bells have been rung, and their vibrations have reached the delicate vial that seals those distant doors, to break it with their loud din and cause the hideous explosion that will blast Capara to a hundred trillion atoms!"

"But better that than have our beloved planet fall before a conqueror," put in the first. "Though now we are so powerful there is no need to fear anything."

"But the Great Secret?" I asked.

"Where the great shaft begins," he answered. "Where hangs the first of the great bells. A tiny temple is said to be built above it—

the Temple of the Bells—but as to its exact location only Tara knows, the glorious Queen and the four warriors who each year stand guard there."

"Could they not tell?"

"They are never given the chance, even if they would. Once each year the Queen sends four of her hardiest warriors to guard the temple, while those who served the previous year are publicly executed so that no loose tongue may tell the Great Secret. Nor does that stop the volunteers. To serve the Queen and guard the bells for one year, then meet public execution, is considered one of the greatest of all honors, and one for which all warriors strive."

"Suppose one did manage to ring the first bell?" I asked after a pause. "How long before the vibrations would ring down through the great shaft to the center of your world and explode Capara?"

"The matter of an hour," answered my informer. "The bells are a hundred miles apart, but the shaft is so constructed that it takes some six minutes for vibration to reach from bell to bell, making one hour in all. But that of course will never happen, for now we are the conquerors of ten thousand planets and—"

It was the sudden entrance of two Black officials that stopped him, officials whose duty it was to escort me to the arena. I rose and followed them. "By royal command you are to fight directly before the throne of her Majesty," said one as we hurried along.

At the huge barred door leading to the arena we halted while that stout barrier was pushed aside. Here I was given a jeweled longsword; then, with the good wishes of the others in my ears, I stepped out onto the arena sands and into the dazzling sunlight, where half a million kill-crazed Blacks roared and shouted for blood.

Directly before me was the royal box of Tara, and beneath the waving fans of her slaves sat that wondrous beauty who ruled the stars. Her dark eyes were smiling upon me, one ivory hand half raised in greeting. At her feet sprawled the huge black lion that was her constant guard.

In the box to the left the grim Metak glared at me. Beside him sat the lovely Earthwoman who was his wife, while from the box to the right of the Queen, the tiny Vaxarus half rose from his chair, gesticulating with his eyes toward the seat of Tara. Vaguely I remembered his words of last night that said the captive princess he wished for his own would be there in golden fetters.

And then, unthinkingly, I raised my eyes to find her, raised my eyes to the slender figure that stood beside the Queen—to behold Vonna!

Yes; there, scarcely ten feet above me and leaning forward, her blue eyes wide and staring into mine, her scanty jewel-encrusted trappings glittering in the sunlight, her wrists imprisoned by the huge fetters that encircled them, was the lovely golden-haired girl I could have sworn lay cold in death in the tiny buried world beneath the weird Moon of Madness at that very minute.

For an instant I stared in open-mouthed surprise, my mind numb with amazement. It was the quick look of warning from the blue eyes of Vonna that brought it back to rationality. Plainly there was something she feared I might or might not do; though whether it was to recognize her publicly before the others or not I could not tell. But the approach of the warrior who was my opponent prevented further speculation, and the next moment, amid the wild roars of the vast assembly, our blades crossed.

But whether the Blue man of Rana was a good swordsman or not I shall never know, for with the eyes of Vonna upon me I was no longer a man, but a veritable superman that nothing could withstand, and a moment later my sword had found his heart.

And then I wheeled again to the royal box, still unable to believe my eyes, to behold Vonna staring wildly at me, some frantic appeal in her eyes, while the glorious Tara arose and stepped forward till she was just above me. A short blare of trumpets brought an immediate silence; then the musical voice of the Queen of the Stars came to me.

"You, mighty warrior from a far-off world, have fought your way through the dangers of the Great Games. For ten days have we watched and thrilled at the strength of your sword-arm. And now I, Tara, Queen of the Stars, publicly proclaim you as the winner of the Great Games, and according to custom will grant you any three wishes you may desire. Ask, then, what you would of me."

And the beauteous one paused, smiling, to await my answer.

But all this must be unreal, I reasoned—some wild hallucination, perhaps. With my own eyes I had seen the mutilated body of the golden girl cold in death, and yet there she now stood beside the Queen, scarcely ten feet above me—the result of some dark act of necromancy, perhaps; but whatever it was, the princess of Penelope was before me, alive.

And I was to be allotted three wishes. Three wishes that I knew were a mockery, for but a few short days from now Capara was destined for that great catastrophe, and all upon it would know a terrible end. Of course at the time I touched the Ball of Life with the ring of Time I had not dreamed that Vonna still lived, and was a captive of the Queen. Had I known it, that very fact would have stayed my hand, for it doomed both captive and captor alike. But too late for that now.

And before me the beauteous Tara was awaiting my answer.

"Three wishes you have promised me, Queen Tara," I answered. "Three wishes that are the privilege of a survivor of the Great Games. Then I ask for the first one that mercy be granted," and I wheeled and gestured with my sword, "and that yon captive maids be allowed their freedom!" I cried.

A roar of protest arose from the surrounding thousands at my shouted words.

And just above me stood Tara the Glorious, a quizzical, half-

191

frowning smile on those wonderful features. For a long moment she stood thus in silent surprise, and then, suddenly, as though conscious for the first time of the wild turmoil around her, wheeled and flashed a glare at her subjects as she raised an ivory hand. Five hundred thousand voices stopped as though suddenly turned to stone—an instantaneous silence that told of their awe, and the absolute rule of the fearless beauty they served.

Then slowly, as though choosing her words with great care, there came her musical answer.

"Truly it is a strange request you ask of me, O Prince. It robs us of a riotous spectacle, and I hardly expected you would demand it. Yet as Tara has given you her promise, that promise shall be kept, and the captive girls will be freed, and allowed to return, unmolested, to the planet from which they were taken.

"But come," and that beauteous face lighted, "you have still two more wishes. What would you ask of me for the second?"

"Something for which I have long waited, O Queen," I answered, "and if my first wish robbed your subjects of a spectacle, the second should fully recompense for it, for I ask that I be allowed to meet, here and now in combat, the Commander of your fleets, and the man responsible for the death of my planet—Metak the Cruel, champion swordsman of Capara!"

Again a wild roar arose from the crowd, but this time it was one of joy, for it pitted their greatest swordsman against this rash fool who had challenged him. Hesitantly Tara gave her decision, though to do him justice, there was nothing backward or unwilling about Metak. With an agile leap he sprang completely over the railing, landing lightly in the arena, and advanced toward me drawing his longsword, with the loud cheers of his countrymen accompanying him.

Then, as was the custom when a battle between two distinguished swordsmen took place, a strong-voiced page stepped forward to acclaim us.

"By the royal sanction of Tara our champion meets this white man who has mowed down all before him. Once again Capara's greatest warrior will waive his rank to meet a captive in combat, as he has so many times, and always successfully, done in the past. And now," he wheeled to us, "by royal command I order the beginning of the duel of these two famed gladiators.

"Metak, our Commander!" And the thousands howled.

"And the other!" he cried. "Jan, Prince of the Bardonians, of the planet Earth!"

Above and just behind the ready Metak was the box in which sat his wife, the Earthwoman I have already mentioned. Often I had noticed her in my coming to and from the arena, and somehow I felt a strange attraction toward her—her mature, kind and lovely face, always sad and wistful—and could well imagine it was against her will that she sat there day after day. That she had guessed I was of her own world I could well believe, but never till now had my full identity been made known. She sat there calmly, expecting no doubt that another victim would soon be added to the long list of Metak.

Now it so happened that my gaze was toward her as the page cried my name. And then a strange thing occurred, for as she heard it she sprang to her feet screaming, an agonized horror on her face, to fall limply forward in a swoon.

And then the sword of my foe clashed against mine, and in an instant I knew why Metak was the champion of Capara.

Never in all my life have I known such swordsmanship. In a moment he had me entirely on the defense; then rushing me under a shower of cuts and thrusts almost too quick for the eye to follow, I was forced to give ground and back away, while the surrounding Blades screamed for their champion and shouted for my death.

But despite that rain of steel upon me I was as yet untouched and far from beaten, although I had parried some of those wicked thrusts by only the scantiest of margins. But I fought coolly and swiftly; then suddenly stopping my retreat I lunged ahead with the swift thrust that nearly got him, and halted his advance. This I followed up with another and another, and there we stood, each refusing to give an inch, fighting frantically as our blades clashed and slashed in that wild outburst of sword-play, the equal of which had never been witnessed upon that or any other planet.

I was fighting to avenge my world; Metak for his life and honor; and five minutes passed with naught to choose between our flying blades. But it must have come to the Black champion that he courted disaster in a long drawn-out battle, for I was not only much younger, but had a strength and endurance far superior even to his.

And knowing this he suddenly began again the rushing tactics that he had so nearly got me at the beginning of the fray.

But this time I was waiting and ready, and swaying slightly back as though a retreat was my intention, I lunged forward in the same movement with the lightning-like thrust that shot through his wonderful guard like an arrow, and drove my sword to the hilt in his breast.

Metak of Capara sank lifeless to the sands.

In the death-like hush that followed I turned again to the royal box as five hundred thousand pairs of eyes watched me; for the defeat of the hitherto unbeaten and supposedly invincible Metak had brought both silence and respect. Then looking straight into the dark eyes of the glorious Tara I spoke softly and slowly, and my gaze never left hers.

"And my third wish, O Queen, I now ask of you—a wish that will cause neither bloodshed nor sorrow, and one that can easily be granted by your Majesty, for I ask for my freedom and the hand of—"

"Yes, yes, Prince; speak quickly; the wish shall be granted," and Tara leaned forward, eager, expectant.

"I ask for the hand of the captive beside you—Vonna, the Golden, Princess of Penelope!"

Chapter XXII
Dungeons of Despair

"A hundred million deaths could not atone for what you have done! The destruction of ten thousand worlds is but a trifle in comparison! You have dared to spurn the love and hand of Tara for another, and for countless centuries and throughout eternity must your name and memory be cursed!"

So cried the beauteous Tara as her black eyes blazed with fury.

When I had made my request on the hot arena sands, the Queen of the Stars had gasped, gone white, then reeled as though struck by an unseen hand. Then she commanded her guards to seize me and I was beaten down beneath a hundred swords, and, fighting madly, bound hand and foot—hearing the screams of Vonna begging for my life as I was picked up, only half conscious, I was carried to the royal flyer which in turn conveyed me to the island castle of Tara. There I was carried to the great throne room, thrown on the jeweled floor before that mighty seat, then left alone.

For a long hour I lay there, wondering what I might expect and what had been done with Vonna. Then suddenly the hidden door I had discovered the previous night was rolled aside, and from it stepped that long-limbed beauty who was Tara the Glorious, to stride majestically toward me, her magnificent body like a shapely pearl, scantily hid by that tight-clinging gold-like tissue that fell from her waist to her instep, the diamond breast-plates blazing a barbaric splendor.

Standing above me she watched in silence, those black eyes flashing a wild fury.

"A mighty frame and powerful is Prince Jan," she said at last, "a body that rolls with rippling muscles and arms swollen with sinew. And yet how soon my torturers can change all that, and reduce to a whimpering, bloody mass the fearless Bardonian swordsman."

I made no reply, had not even deigned to look upon her after that first glance of recognition. This seemed to infuriate more than a direct reply.

"Speak!" she cried, "Find your tongue, or by the stars I will have my torturers find it with the plucking-tongs! Quickly! Who is she? Who is that pale creature you prefer to Tara?"

"She is the woman I love," I answered from where I lay, my eyes meeting hers. "She is the woman I will always love, and nothing that you or anyone else can do will ever change it."

Tara screamed a wild, "Stop! Stop, or I will have you torn to shreds! Stop or else—"

Then with a little sobbing cry, half anger, half sorrow, the Queen of the Stars sank to her knees beside me.

"No, no, Jan, you cannot," she moaned as her white arms raised my head, and those wondrous eyes, wet with tears, stared into mine. "You must love no other but me. For countless ages I have awaited your coming, and the hour when I might surrender myself to you. Ten thousand worlds I endow you with, my lover. The golden city of Manator is yours for the asking. Tara herself will fall to her knees and obey you without question. But love me, Jan. Only love and want me—me alone!" she cried.

And then with a wild outburst of passion she strained me fiercely to her, and her hot lips rained a hundred kisses on my brow, my eyes, my cheeks and mouth.

"Love me Jan! Love me!"

With a shudder of disgust I wrenched my bound form from her. This was no longer the cold, brilliant Queen of the Stars, but a panting, love-crazed creature, wild-eyed and flushed, who seemed oblivious to all else but her desires. The sudden effort tore me from her grasp, and raised me to a sitting position.

"Jan of the Bardonians does not desire you," I answered.

There came a gasp from Tara, followed by a long moment's silence as she stared at me in wide-eyed amazement. It was as though astonishment had temporarily paralyzed her. Then a look of shame crept over those exquisite features, a red flush mounted her cheeks. Slowly it must have come to her that she, Queen of the Stars and ruler of destiny, had been scorned by a captive!

Then with a scream, half maniacal, half bestial, she sprang to her feet, her facial muscles working horribly, her hands clenched into white fists which she raised above her head.

"Die!" she screeched. "Die, cursed spawn of a million hells, and the pale one perishes with you! Die while I shriek with laughter as I watch you both writhe in your death agonies!"

Leaping toward the huge gong beside her, Tara the Glorious sent the golden hammer that hung above it crashing into its glittering side with a roar that threw open the great throne room doors as a hundred ready guards came tearing to her aid.

"To the pits with this carrion!" she screamed as the furious guardsmen crowded around me. "To the pits! Take him to the deepest cell of the deepest dungeon, that he may not pollute my person with his gaze! Bind him with a score of chains and—"

"Queen Tara! Queen Tara! O, most Beauteous One—hear me!"

It was the loud shouting of a powerful voice that sounded even above the cries of the Queen. The next moment there came the sound of running footsteps. Then I was lifted to my feet by guards of Tara, to behold the tall and dignified old Black who came running, and stopped sharply before her, panting.

"What means this intrusion, Kovan?" screamed Tara, wheeling toward him. "Has the royal astronomer gone mad, that he would dare come before me like this, unheralded? By your ancestors there had better be a good cause for such an act if you would keep your eyes!"

The royal astronomer, who had been struggling for breath, broke out again:

"O glorious Queen, but hear me!" he cried. "But listen to the loyal Kovan as he tells that most terrible news. For the age-old prophecy is at hand at last, your Majesty, and the tiny Moon of Madness has begun a wild plunge toward Capara."

"What!"

"Yes, yes, O Beauteous One!" sobbed the royal astronomer. "Yes, yes, it is true! Through the great glass I have just now seen it! The Moon of Madness is being drawn toward Capara as though by supernatural means, and within ten days will crash upon and destroy our world!"

Tara the Glorious went white.

I doubt during that moment if any of the assembly so much as breathed. Of course the Queen must have instantly realized who had brought all this about, but she remained in a long and terrible silence, her white body tensed like some magnificent statue, and when last she did speak, her voice was so low as to be almost inaudible.

"Remove the prisoner to the dungeons. I will deal with him later."

Held in the hands of four stalwart Blacks, I was hustled down a seemingly endless corridor that finally terminated at the entrance of a subterranean passage. Here waited another Black with a bunch of keys protruding from his belt.

As we drew nearer the tall man smiled, and grabbing a lighted torch from its niche and motioning us to follow, led the way down a vast series of time-worn steps. We made our slow way ever farther into the earth. A cold dampness arose to tell us of our great distance below the surface.

At last we halted before a sturdy wooden door, held by massive iron bars upon the side of our approach. Stopping only to unlock and push it aside, we entered the long, low-ceilinged vault that was destined to be my prison.

It was a foul-smelling pit whose jagged ceiling was damp with moisture, and whose floor was a hard, black clay. Huge rings were set in the stone walls. To these were fastened heavy chains, and at the far end of several of the chains the attached forms of whitened skeletons lay gruesomely about. Nearby, with his back toward us, lay a shackled prisoner, evidently in sleep.

One of the skeletons the Blacks kicked aside. Then the huge padlock was opened, and the chain that had so recently held the bones of one long dead was clasped around my own ankle, after which the Blacks left, taking the light with them, and I was alone in the deep dungeons of the castle of Tara with the dried bones of dead men for my companions.

For an hour silence reigned, then from the blackness came a sudden gasp and an intake of breath, followed by the sounds of a moving body which informed me that the sleeper I had seen on entering the dungeon had awakened. A moment passed; then evidently he either sensed my presence or heard my breathing, for he called softly in a voice that was tantalizingly familiar.

"Who is there?" he asked shrilly.

"An Earthman," I answered softly. "Jan of the Bardonians. But who are you who speaks from the darkness and—" But before I could go further there came a high scream of joy and a wild flow of words that rang through the gloom.

"Prince Jan! Prince Jan—it is I! It is I!" cried the voice. "Abel—Abel who loves you!" And there came a series of thudding sounds I knew to be that of the poor fellow who was jumping up and down in his excitement and joy. Then the clanking of chains told me he was straining as far as possible toward me.

So this was Abel—frail, timid, faithful Abel, the bird-man, who had so worshiped my physical powers and in esteem held me away above all others. I believe that now he was almost glad to be here, for to be near and to serve me was ever his greatest joy. It was some minutes before his wild babbling would permit sane speech.

"But about yourself, Abel," I was asking presently. "How in the name of sanity is it that I find you here, and only a few hours ago saw Vonna in the royal box of the Queen, when with my own eyes I beheld her mangled form in Shebak's cave?"

"But it could not have been her, Prince Jan," he answered. "You see," he explained, "I was in the village with the princess while you and the others battled with the wolves on the plain before the cave. At last one of the warriors, wounded and exhausted, entered the cave for a respite. He said you had been carried off by the Vampire-Women, that the battle was lost, and that in a few minutes the wolves would come tearing down the shaft into the village.

"So, knowing this, I picked up the princess in my arms and flew up the shaft to the outside. Once there I rose up into the heavens and made for the ship that had brought us to the Moon of Madness. It was my plan to secrete the princess Vonna there while I went in search of you. But we never reached it, for just as I topped the peaks of the valley and was descending, a giant spaceship suddenly zoomed down from the sky. Its side door was flung open and we were drawn into it. It was one of the fleet of the Black Raiders looking for us. Then we were brought to Capara and the castle of the Queen, and I was sent to this dungeon where I have been ever since. I do not know what has become of the princess Vonna."

"But Vonna," I put in. "I saw her dead with my own eyes. The features were mangled beyond recognition, but I could make out the golden hair and the slender head-band with the long red feather around her head."

"Ah, Prince Jan, I think I can explain," answered Abel after a pause. "Just before we fled from the village several young girls clung around the princess and me, screaming with fright, for the terrible din of the battle above reached us plainly. One of the girls was tall and had golden hair. In an effort to soothe and console her, the princess Vonna removed and gave her the head-band. It must, therefore, have been that girl you saw dead."

This then accounted for what I had seen in the village of Shebak. The girl had not been Vonna. Vonna had been saved—but where was she now? Had the vengeance of Tara been turned upon her? I feared it. I had not seen her since I had been dragged from the arena, though I had heard her screams as she struggled to aid me, and could now, in imagination, picture her writhing under some terrible torture. With a groan I buried my head in my arms.

Twelve hours passed. During that time, as we spoke in low tones, I had told the bird-man of the coming disaster that would soon destroy Capara, but my companion did not seem to mind. Evidently Abel figured that so long as he was beside me no harm could befall him.

Then suddenly footsteps sounded, the door was pushed open, and with two plates in one hand and a torch in the other, the tall, evil-faced Black who was our jailer entered that dreary vault, his thin lips curled in a sneer at our helplessness.

"Still here?" he jeered, standing just above us as his torch crackled and spluttered. "Yes, I thought so. I figured that it would take more than your great thews, Earthman, to escape from the pits of Tara."

"Perhaps we are just as well off here as elsewhere," I answered. "Nine more days and every living thing on this world shall die. It will take more than the brilliance of your Queen to keep the Moon of Madness from crashing into Capara."

The Black gave a roar of laughter.

"That's what you think, you dull-witted fool," he taunted. "Oh, yes, we all know now that it was you who brought it around, and if you were to as much as show your nose in Manator you would be torn to shreds. But don't think for a minute that the coming crash will harm either the Queen or a single one of her subjects."

He threw the plates, clattering, to our feet.

"If you could but see the frantic construction that is going on in the world overhead, as, by the royal command of Tara, the people work madly day and night to build the needed ships. None sleep, and all the fleets have been recalled, for at dawn on the seventh day from now the golden spaceship of the Queen will rise into the air, followed by a million others, each containing the ten thousand souls that together will number the entire ten billion that is the populace of Capara."

He stepped back a pace, regarding me mockingly.

"And where do you think our beauteous queen is taking her people for this great migration? I could give you a hundred guesses, no doubt, and you would not be right in one of them. Well, I will tell you, rogue that you are, for it can help nor harm. It is to your own planet the Earth. Yes, the green star is where we are going, for the gasses that destroyed it have now long lifted and it will be safe. And we will take our great treasures with us, and colonize the Earth with a splendor that will outshine even the wonders of Capara. Yes, seven days from now we will all leave, and be a two-days' journey out in the void before the Moon of Madness strikes our world."

At the door the jailer paused for a final taunt.

"So, my would-be clever Earthman," he jeered, "as you eat your swill you will have time to reflect upon your own dismal failure, and the ultimate triumph of our brilliant and glorious queen."

Then he went out, closing the door behind him.

Six days passed—that is six days as I could best reckon time in that dreary vault of inky blackness. At intervals the jailer would come with food and drink. It was then that I would hear of the frantic building of the spaceships, and the haste and hurry of the outside world as they made ready for the great migration. Several times I asked what had been the fate of Vonna, but as my answer was always the same—a mocking laugh—I at last desisted.

I will not attempt to pen my feelings. Not only were the Black Raiders going to escape from the coming catastrophe, but they were going to migrate to my own world as well. That was the bitterest blow of all. As for Abel and myself, I felt that we would be left to perish in the chains that held us, once the Blacks had departed from their homeland.

And then late on the sixth night footsteps sounded, the dungeon door was thrown open, and followed by two guards whose lighted torches flamed and flickered, Tara the Glorious entered that dreary vault and was standing before me, wrapped in a long black cloak from neck to instep, tall and graceful, her face white and wondrous in the torchlight, the tiny diamonds sprinkled in her wavy black hair glittering like numerous water drops.

The Queen of the Stars wasted no time in greeting.

"Stay where you are," the words snapped out like a whip as I made a motion to rise to my feet. "Remain there wallowing in the filth as behoves you, for in the years to come you will know much of such misery—blinded!"

No love or kindness was evident now. Immobile as a mask of pearl were her exquisite features. Only those dark eyes seemed alive as they flashed like angry meteors.

"Yes, I am taking you with me in my own spaceship to the planet Earth, that you may be the ridicule of my court as you grope your way through the years as my captive, with the red collar of shame around your throat.

"Tomorrow night then my torturers will come to slay the birdman and to blind you. But before your eyes are lost to you forever there is one sight you must see—the marriage of the pale creature you love to the hideous black dwarf, Vaxarus. I myself shall perform the ceremony, and will arrange for you to see it. Then you are to be immediately blinded, so as to carry always in your memory the vision of your beloved being given to the arms of another."

At the doorway she paused.

"So resign yourself to the inevitable, Earthman. When next you hear footsteps it will announce my torturers coming to blind you!"

The hours passed slowly—five, ten, then twenty, while Abel and

I lay in the dungeons of Tara, waiting for the death and torture to come. Above us we knew the hurrying billions worked frantically for the great migration to the green star, but down here all was the stillness of the tomb, and as hour followed hour we began to believe that that great migration had already begun and we were alone on Capara. Then suddenly light footsteps sounded, the door was again pushed back, and a slender feminine figure entered.

I recognized her at once. She was the Earthwoman who had so strangely attracted me when I fought in the arena, the wife of the man I had recently killed—Metak. But in the name of sanity what could she be doing here?

She was quite alone, and she held a torch in her right hand. For a moment she stood still, peering fearfully into the silent gloom before her, and the traces of a once great beauty were still evident in her matured and dignified loveliness. Then her eyes suddenly fell upon me where I lay, besmeared with grime and staring at her. A gasp escaped her lips as our eyes met; then with a little sobbing cry she ran toward me, dropping the torch and sinking to her knees as she threw her arms around me and cried out the last words I ever expected to hear.

"Jan!" she cried. "My little baby! Oh, it is I, darling, it is I—your mother!"

Chapter XXIII
The Temple of the Bells

"My little boy, my dear little boy," sobbed my lovely mother, her eyes wide with love and alarm, her white hands brushing the grime from my hair and wounds, for the bruises from my struggle with the guards had been many. "Oh, what have they done to you—what have they done to you?" she wailed.

"Ah, but thank the Gods I have found you," she went on. "Even now I cannot believe it. It seems too good for one who for twenty-three long years, night after night, could but look at the distant green star and think of the husband and the little son lost to her there, when the Raiders came and stole me from your father's side and brought me to Capara, where the Queen forced me into the loveless marriage with Metak."

I cannot clearly remember what I said or did, other than for the first time in my life my eyes knew tears and speech was difficult as I felt again the love of those two arms that had so long been lost to me, and the sweet voice I had not heard since my cradle days.

Minutes passed, lost to us in the great joy of our reunion, but presently the thoughts of her own danger came to me.

"But Mother, you must not stay here," I said suddenly, realizing her peril. "I do not know how you possibly found me, but if you were ever discovered—"

My mother kissed me again with a happy smile. "What could they possibly do that would hurt me after the joy of finding my son? No, my boy, I do not fear them, or anything they could do now.

"But come, my son, you must escape, as we have much before us," and she reached for the small pouch at her waist. "In two hours it will be dawn and the great golden spaceship of Tara will rise into the void, followed by a million others, to begin the great migration to the Earth before the Moon of Madness falls upon Capara. It is you and I who will stop them, my son. It is you and I who will avenge your father and prevent them from ever bringing death and destruction to any world again."

"We still stop them!" I echoed. "But how, Mother?"

"By blowing Capara to a hundred trillion atoms before the spaceships have risen and put off for the Earth. By making use of the great secret I learned long ago from Metak, when one night in drunken braggadocio he told how he had learned from an ancient parchment the secret that was supposed to be known to none but Tara herself—where stands the tiny Temple of the Bells."

As she spoke I had been hurriedly unlocking the padlocks that held my chains with the key she had produced. Freed, I turned to release Abel.

"Hurry, my son," went on my mother. "I only learned of your whereabouts by heavy bribery, and at any moment we may be discovered by the guards. My spaceship lies now in the courtyard, beside the Queen's great golden flyer. We must reach it and make for Skull Mountain, a wild, towering peak, the highest on Capara; some two thousand miles directly to the north of us. It is on the top of this peak where stands the Temple of the Bells.

"Haste then, my son, for in their frantic excitement as they prepare for the great migration they will be blind to our departure, and at this moment Queen Tara is engaged in the throne room in some ceremony. We should have ample time to start the ringing of the first bell, then get well out into the void before Capara is blown asunder. Once in space we will make for our own world, Jan, for my ship is well provisioned and—oh!"

It was the frightened cry of my mother that caused me to wheel and learn its cause from where I knelt, freeing Abel from his shackles, to behold the huge Black jailer leaping upon me with uplifted dagger, his black features distorted with rage. Behind him I caught a glimpse of a second. Their entrance had been quite noiseless, and

I was doomed, despite the fact I was free of my chains, for I would be unable to rise and defend myself before that descending knife had plunged into my flesh.

It all happened in five seconds—five terrible, terrible seconds. I made a mad effort to scramble to my feet—the burly guard leaped forward, his long knife shot toward me—and then with a little cry my dear mother sprang between us, and her lovely white bosom received the keen blade meant for my own heart.

I killed the guards. Yes, with my naked hands I snapped the neck of the first, and seizing the wrist of the second stabbed him with his own dagger, all in a minute or so. Oh, vengeance was swift, to be sure, and in my wild rage I was a veritable maniac that nothing could withstand, but it could not save my lovely mother, who perished in my arms with a little sigh as she gasped my father's name.

Time passed. It might have been an instant, it might have been an age that I knelt there, with the slender form of my mother in my arms, my mind numb with sorrow. But at last I became conscious that Abel was shaking my shoulder and his shrill voice was in my ear.

"Please hear me, Prince Jan—please hear me," he was saying. "We must get out of here at once if we are to do what your mother planned. In an hour it will be dawn and the fleets will depart. Please do not stay here longer, Prince Jan. We have much to do."

I looked up at him. "Yes, Abel," I answered dully, "I will come— we have much to do."

Presently we were making a silent ascent up the great winding stairs to the world above, armed with the longswords and shortswords of the two guards I had killed, while behind us in the silent pits, my brave mother lay in that last terrible sleep from which there is no awakening.

Vaguely I recall Abel leading me up numerous long flights of stairs, and down seemingly endless corridors, several times pushing me into a side room while footsteps hurried past us, till at last we came out upon a little balcony to behold the great throne room of Tara sixty feet below us. Yet everything was quite a blur up till then, but suddenly I became cool and collected as the meaning of the ceremony taking place below became intelligible to me.

Though it was not yet dawn, that mighty room was brilliantly lighted. A hundred or more guards and nobles were assembled there, crowded around the great throne in its center. And upon that huge bejeweled seat sat Tara the Glorious, her golden wand extended above the heads of the two who knelt before her—Vonna and Vaxarus the dwarf. The hands of the golden girl had been tied behind her back, and a burly guard held her to her knees; but even from the lofty balcony I could see the struggling of her slender form as she fought against what they would do to her.

I quickly realized the meaning of it all. Vonna was being forced to marry the hideous little dwarf. Another moment and the wand of Tara would touch the head of both of them to conclude the ceremony. Another moment and she would belong to Vaxarus forever. There was but one chance, and with the quickness of thought I took it.

In a flash I wheeled to the bird-man, and whispered a score of words in his ear. Abel paled, but the loyal fellow never failed me. In an instant I was on his back, my right hand holding my gleaming longsword, my left hand free and ready. The next the bird-man had leaped lightly over the small railing before us, and with me securely straddling him shot down toward the assembly below with the speed of an arrow.

Straight toward the kneeling Vonna Abel winged at terrific speed, and then at that very last instant swerved and rose up slightly. But in passing, my left arm swung the slender princess up beside me, while my right sent my keen longsword whirring in a vicious slash. Then as the head of Vaxarus tumbled from his shoulders to the floor, and the astonished assembly gasped in open-mouthed horror, the great wings of the bird-man churned the air loudly, as with Vonna and me clinging to him he rose slowly above the heads of the others, and toward a tiny balcony at the far end of the room.

From below came a roar of voices as the others found their tongues, but it did not stop the struggling Abel in his slow, upward flight, and a moment later we were standing on a frail little balcony near the lofty ceiling that led to a narrow passage and a tiny porch without.

Toward this we hurried. Sixty feet below us I could hear the silvery voice of Tara screaming for our capture, and the wild patter of footsteps hurrying to obey her. But for a few minutes at least we were safe, and the lofty gallery we came out upon showed the great courtyard below, unguarded, for most of the warriors and guards were either in the throne room or elsewhere. And there, golden and gigantic, lay the great spaceship of Tara, and beside it was the smaller one that my mother had mentioned was her own.

Down to the doors of the latter I ordered Abel to fly us, then with two strokes of my shortsword cut the bonds of Vonna and motioned them both within.

"Hurry!" I cried, for there came a sound of running footsteps and the shouting of excited voices. "Hurry—we must get the ship aloft before they are upon us!"

And indeed there was cause for haste, for suddenly on all sides a wave of Black guards appeared from nowhere, running toward us and shouting. But we were well within the ship and had slammed shut its heavy doors before they were upon us, and the next moment we were rising above their heads and shooting northward, while our erstwhile captors howled and gesticulated below.

How we managed to get the ship aloft will ever remain a mystery, but desperation can bring around many seeming impossibilities, and with Abel beside me, instructing me in the use of the various gears and devices—his many years of captivity among the

Blacks had familiarized the bird-man with their usage—the great spaceship rose as lightly as if a seasoned pilot guided her course.

"Now on!" I cried. "On to the Temple of the Bells! Our one hope is to blow Capara asunder before the Blacks put off for my world, if we would cause their doom and avenge ten thousand planets!"

"But carefully, Prince Jan," cautioned Abel, moving the speed control a single notch. "We must stay at our slowest speed if we are to see and recognize Skull Mountain, for this is a spaceship and possesses terrific velocity. Even now we are traveling with the speed of an arrow."

And indeed we were. All around us the sky was lighted by the coming dawn. Through the lookout window we could see the many great cities just below us, intermingled with vast stretches of plains and sparkling rivers. The huge square of every metropolis was crowded with spaceships, and we could see the thousands of black dots hurrying into them. All over that great planet, in every city and village, the ships were making ready to take off, waiting only for the rising of the great golden ship of their Queen to announce the signal for their departure.

And in the spaceship of my mother I hurried toward Skull Mountain, to prevent their departure and to destroy them. As we shot along I told Vonna my plans.

Presently a towering, gigantic mountain showed directly ahead, and a moment later we were able to distinguish the tiny temple on its top. Just beside it we descended lightly; then cautioning Vonna and Abel to remain within I drew my two swords, flung back the heavy door and sprang into the open in almost frantic haste, for I feared that even now I might be too late.

It was indeed a tiny temple that stood upon that mighty mountain top, the highest mountain top on that great world. A tiny little temple which was scarcely more than a weirdly roofed structure, open on all sides, hung above an enormous black bell which stood on a stone platform. Just behind it was the beginning of the great shaft that legend said led down through the mountain and into the very heart of Capara, and the huge stores of high explosives hidden there.

On all four sides of that mighty mountaintop—a tiny flat top, but a hundred yards square—the earth fell away to the distant plains thousands of feet below.

But stretches around a tiny campfire directly before that gigantic bell was that which was of more immediate interest to me—four Black warriors, the guardians of the Bells!

Even as I appeared in the doorway of the ship one of them raised his head and saw me; and then as I dashed toward them he sprang up with the loud shouts that brought the others to their feet, drawing their weapons. But I was upon the first before he could fully unsheathe his own two blades, and my longsword found his heart even as he drew them. Then as the first rays of the rising sun shot up to tear the sky with flame, the weapons of the other three clashed against my own.

The warriors who guarded the Temple of the Bells had not been chosen at random. Each was a renowned fighter whose swordsmanship and bravery had made him eligible for that high office. But with such a wild fury, and so great a cause to fight for, in that supreme hour I was a veritable superman nothing could withstand. Steadily they were forced back as I drew ever nearer to the great bell.

On we fought. Our keen blades glittered, clashed and crossed. Of course the guards realized my intentions and screamed frantic orders to each other, but they were unable to stop me, or do other than give ground. Another moment and I would be beside the bell, and release the iron catch above it that would cause the booming roar which would shoot down the great shaft to the second bell, a hundred miles below.

Triumph seemed within my grasp—and then by some cruel fate

a lucky sweep of a warrior's blade sent my shortsword flying from my hand!

There came an exclamation of joy from the warriors. The trio ceased to retreat, then with shouts of triumph leaped forward, heartened by my misfortune and fighting like fiends. Six blades now fought against my one, as flitting like a silvery serpent my longsword caught or parried each savage slash and thrust. But not for long could I hold against that veritable rain of steel. Then a lightning-like thrust grazed my side. I was forced to give two paces; and the next instant with a shrill cry Abel dashed past me, and sought to beat one of my foes to the earth with a flurry of his great wings.

Poor, brave little bird-man, ready to die for me whom he loved! It was a noble but futile act. The brute before him but laughed at his efforts as he ran him through with his shortsword, then threw his dying, quivering body heavily to the ground.

A shout escaped me, a hoarse shout almost maniacal as I sprang forward, crazed with grief and anger. With one sweep of my sword I disarmed him of his weapons. Then lashing out in that wild, superhuman stroke, which caught the Black squarely in the center of his head, my blade slashed on through skull and trunk, and tore to the very middle of his body.

With cries of terror the others gave way before me, leaping backward. That little retreat was all I needed. In an instant I had sprung forward, releasing the iron catch and hearing the mighty roar of the bell that spelled Capara's doom. And the next instant I raised my eyes to behold the sight which announced my own. For coming swiftly out of the dawn in the east was the great golden spaceship of Tara the Glorious!

But I had no time either to watch its advance or flee from it, for the two guards had recovered from their panic and were leaping forward to attack. Once more our blades clashed. Vonna screamed for me to flee and pointed to the approaching ship. But the two be-

212

fore me fought bravely, and when at last I did dispatch one, the great ship had landed and its huge front door was swinging open, to discharge, as I supposed, a thousand warriors.

But no wild rush of armed soldiery came tearing through that portal, no shouting Blacks hurrying forward to aid the one I fought. No; it was a tall and long-limbed beauty who strode majestically through the open doorway, and she was quite alone—a glorious, black-haired Queen who had known ages before the dawning, and those wondrous dark eyes, wide and flashing, took in the situation at a glance, sweeping around that flat, lofty mountaintop, then returning to me again.

I was still engaged with the guard before me, but it was evident Tara realized that not for long could the Black withstand me. Already he was streaming blood from several serious wounds, and though fighting madly was being steadily forced back to the lofty peak's stone edge. Another moment and he would either be forced over it, or fall before my sword. And then the gaze of Tara fell upon the golden girl.

A wild joy leaped to that wonderful face, and running toward the slender Vonna she forced her to her knees, whipping out a long dagger and holding it above her heart, at the same instant my long-sword pierced the body of my foe. And then I sprang forward to aid the princess of Penelope, but the wild scream of Tara stopped me in my tracks.

"Back!" she cried, her black eyes blazing, her left hand holding the struggling Vonna with the ease one might a child—her shapely right hand raised and holding the long, jeweled dagger. "Back before my blade is buried in the body of this pale creature!"

I halted—there was nothing else I could do—for there was a wild light in those flashing eyes that was almost maniacal, and another step might send her long knife plunging downward.

"Oh, I knew I would find you here," she went on with a terrible calmness. "I knew it from the moment they told me they found the body of Metak's wife—your mother—in the dungeons. So she did know the secret then—where stood the Temple of the Bells. I often suspected as much.

"But she perished just the same, and so shall this pale one you love!" cried Tara. "For all your fighting ability, and for all you have accomplished, it will not save this woman, or make less terrible my vengeance on those whose doom I seek. Behold—she dies!"

And with a high wild scream, she drove her knife toward the breast of the kneeling, helpless Vonna!

But that long knife never touched the flesh of the golden girl, nor was the vengeance of Tara realized. Even as she spoke, I had become conscious of the moving form behind her—Abel the Tor, bleeding, dying, but yet alive. Slowly, painfully he was sneaking up behind the unsuspecting Queen. It was that which helped to hold me, as I hoped my presence would distract Tara from his advance.

And so it was that even as the sharp knife began its plunge downward, Abel seized her wrist and held it. Then mustering the last of his waning strength, the bird-man spread his great wings and rose slowly upward, his single white garment dripping blood, and the struggling, screaming Tara held firmly in his grasp.

Higher, higher into the blue the flapping bird-man mounted, as fighting madly the frantic queen sought to release herself.

And there we stood at the very edge of the mighty mountaintop, Vonna and I, staring like two wide-eyed statues at that weird, nightmarish scene—the shrieking queen, the great depths below, the loud and dismal flapping of the bird-man's massive wings. Even now I cannot recall it without a wild thrill shooting through me.

A hundred feet above our heads and out over the great void, Abel suddenly released his victim, as a gasp of horror escaped both Vonna and me. And then, screaming wildly, twisting and turning over and over, the white body of Tara the Glorious shot downward, just missing the edge of the jagged peak, to go falling, falling to the terrible depths, thousands of feet below. A high and silvery drawn-out scream stabbed up to us in a blood-chilling echo.

But she did not fall alone, however. Hardly had the beauteous Queen of the Stars plunged past to her destruction, before a shudder shook Abel's slender form. His great wings suddenly faltered and fell, as the last of his strength waned from him. And then in a terrible silence the limp form of the bird-man dropped in the wake of his screaming victim to the awful depths below.

Chapter XXIV
Back to Earth

Vonna was sobbing wildly, hysterically, when I reached her side. "Come!" I cried raising her to her feet. "Come quickly—we have not a moment to lose!" For out from the great shaft behind the temple had suddenly roared a metallic thunder that announced the echo of the second bell, a hundred miles below.

"In fifty minutes this planet will be blown to atoms, and if we are not far out in space by then, we shall perish with the rest!"

Together we hurried into the golden spaceship of Tara. It was well fueled, well provisioned, much faster than the other and just as easily piloted. I turned to its glittering controls, remembering the words of Abel which advised of their use. Once more luck was with us, and presently the huge flyer, well able to hold ten thousand in its mighty interior, was rising into the void, at first comparatively slowly but gradually increasing as Capara dropped away; then once beyond the pull of gravity and out into space I set the guiding needle toward the planet Earth, and pulling back the speed control to its final notch, I sent the great golden spaceship shooting toward my distant world with the speed of a falling star.

Through the lookout glass of the pilot room we could see mighty Capara fall away, vast cities, seas and plains growing smaller with each moment. And then its continents, appearing as massive black outlines on its huge expanse which covered half the heavens; then a third, then a fourth. And through that thick lookout glass we could also see the Moon of Madness, now but twenty thousand miles from Capara and swiftly coming closer. In two more days it should strike the mother planet in the hideous crash that would mean the destruction of both worlds, but long before that Capara would be no more.

"But Jan," Vonna asked as the great ship tore along, "will not the inhabitants of Capara follow in their spaceships and escape the explosion the same as we? They were supposed to leave at dawn."

"But not till Tara leads them," I answered, with hands on the control gear and looking through the glass before me. "The great migration was to begin with the rising of ten thousand ships from the golden city of Manator. Then from all parts of Capara and its other great cities the ships of the others would fall in line behind. But this huge ship of Tara's was supposed to lead them, and at this moment, back at her capital, her officers and generals are awaiting her return."

Moments passed, tense, anxious moments, as we drew swiftly away from Capara. Our terrific velocity shot us wildly along. Of course it would take some hundred and fifty long days during which we must remain within the ship as the golden flyer tore through the cold wastes of outer space. But I felt I had avenged my own world, and my eyes were fixed on Capara, for in a few minutes should occur the great explosion which meant the end of that planet.

And then there came that sudden scream from Vonna which broke upon my thoughts and wheeled me in my tracks. The eyes of the golden girl were staring into the room behind us, wide with horror and fear. In a twinkling my gaze followed hers to behold, the reason.

The pilot room in which we stood was a tiny one, compared to the other rooms of the great ship. A small and open frail door was all that separated us from the next, an enormous chamber. In the center of that chamber a long passage led on and on through the other rooms, to the far end of the ship. And walking slowly up the passage toward us was the huge beast I had seen several times before—Ranga, the great black lion that was the pet and guard of Tara!

In a flash I realized our helplessness. My own longsword, I had dropped when assisting Vonna to her feet. The golden girl, of course, was unarmed, and any weapons that might be in the ship were in the rooms beyond the lion. The great beast had already seen us, and its green eyes were gleaming wickedly. For a moment it stood watching us intently, lashing its black sides with an agile tail. Then that tail suddenly extended to its full length, quivering as though from excitement. The huge mouth opened to reveal long, white, cruel teeth.

And then with a deafening roar that echoed through the spaceship in a fearsome bellow, it charged straight down the passage and upon us with the speed of an arrow.

But at the same instant I sprang past the frail door and locked that little barrier behind me, temporarily protecting the girl. Then, weaponless, I wheeled to meet the charge of the huge beast, just as the great black lion rose upon its hind legs to grapple with me.

As the great cat reared up, its ears were glued against its head, and its green eyes glittered hate. It snarled and its foul breath shot into my face in nauseating waves. Then the great mouth flew wide to seize me, but it was instantly halted and blocked, as with an instinct quicker than any brain, I drove my right fist straight into its slavering jaws.

The next instant the huge teeth snapped shut upon my forearm like a trap, and we both went crashing to the floor.

Over we rolled, once, twice, then stopped with me on top. In a flash the mighty paws smashed against my naked side—for I wore only a loincloth and sandals—as it sought to rake my body with its claws. But luckily the attendants at Tara's court had kept those same claws well-trimmed and dulled, lest by some mishap they might scratch their royal mistress. And so, though they did manage to tear and lacerate me badly, I knew that for a time at least they could not kill.

My fist and arm still occupied the mighty jaws of the brute, gave it something to chew on. I knew that at all costs I must keep them there, despite the excruciating agony. Slowly I forced my fist farther and farther down that slimy throat.

But could I keep it there? At the onset I had blocked the huge jaws, but the torture was hideous.

The hind-quarters of the beast were thrashing wildly beneath me, and despite the trimmed and dulled claws they were still terrible weapons, for they ripped savage stroke after stroke that laid the flesh of my thighs, hips and sides open to the bone. Then as one hind claw sank deep into my thigh, and caught there for a second against the bone, I pinned the leg beneath me with a quick turn of my knee. The other paw still tore and gashed, but a few moments later I was able to pin it also.

Meanwhile the hideous growls never ceased for an instant, nor the black bulk its wild thrashing.

Everything within me cried out for relief from the terrible torture. But even then, from the depths of me, a stronger will asserted itself—the subconscious will to live. At first my defense had been that of a doomed and cornered creature: self-preservation. But now the fires of fury and hope of victory were rising steadily within me. I was no longer fighting to save my life. I was Jan of the Bardonians, defending my mate and destroying an enemy—a hideous, hideous enemy!

The lion coughed and gasped. I redoubled my efforts, stifling my screams with teeth that bit through bleeding lips. And then there came that last horrible crunching sound, a final, frantic heave from me, and the right front limb of the black lion snapped in my strong grasp, broken!

How much longer I could keep up that terrible struggle I did not know, but I began to be aware of a growing advantage. My efforts were telling. I knew by the lion's growing distress as it strangled and contorted its body in paroxysms of torture. Its hind-quarters lashed and lashed; its chest rolled beneath me. And then it choked again, and its breath came in harsh gasps of agony as it strove madly to disgorge the hand that stifled it.

Those green eyes that once flamed such a wild hatred were now dim and popping. The roars and snarls had died away to a horrible gasping sound. The tongue flopped out sidewise between its jaws as if paralyzed. And then as I saw it was weakening I shouted a loud, half-crazed laugh of joy, and pressed the offensive fiercely.

I raised my body up and beat it down again and again on the lion's gaunt torso. I raised a knee and hammered it down into the chest and vitals of the beast with all my strength, and heard the flesh and ribs give way. "I'll get you!" I snarled into that savage face. "I'll get you!"

More than a moment of this. To me it seemed an hour. And then with a final convulsive shudder, the body of the great black lion straightened out and went limp. The jaws relaxed slowly. The beast was dead!

And yet for several minutes I clung there, fighting against the descending blackness, before I dared loosen my hold on the four corners of the brute and slowly draw forth my mangled hand. It was a sickening sight, red, ragged, shapeless, and almost without feeling, for the nerves had been mutilated. Even if I could save it, it would be of little use to me henceforth, I knew.

Weakly I rolled off the black body and got to my feet. I made my way toward the little door. It swam before me, but I somehow managed to unlock and push it open, then sink to my knees on the floor of the tiny pilot room beyond.

I have a faint memory of Vonna running to my side and striving frantically to ease me. Of her dear voice in my ear crying again and again that she loved me. Then my dimming gaze went through the lookout window to the giant planet, Capara, now a hundred thousand miles away. And even as I watched, a gigantic cloud of flame and smoke shot up in its very center, tearing it asunder. And when the void had cleared again, the world of the Black Raiders was no more!

Then the black clouds rolled forward to claim me, and I lunged unconscious to the floor of the pilot room.

𝕴t was months later that we landed upon my own world, the green planet, Earth.

During that great journey it was the tender and tireless care of Vonna that slowly nursed me back to life and health. While that mighty ship shot on and on through the endless wastes of space, we came to realize that we had been meant only for each other, despite the fact our respective worlds were many millions of miles apart. And during the slow passing of the many, many hours, it was the golden girl who taught me to read and write, and so made this narrative possible.

And then one dusk that journey ended, and the great spaceship came to rest at last upon the Earth that was my home. But I did not possess sufficient skill to land the huge ship lightly, and though Vonna and I were both unhurt, its great bow crumpled with the force of the impact, and rendered it useless for further flight.

It was a wild and desolate spot upon which we landed, thousands of miles from my homeland, and near the edge of a mighty canyon—a colossal abyss that fell away for thousands of feet, and of such enormous size that the eye could not see its farthest side. Miles away and dimly in the north was the beginning of a dreary moss-covered waste that had once been the bottom of a great ocean. A cold, autumnal wind told of the oncoming winter.

That night while a million stars gleamed coldly overhead, Vonna and I stood on the rocky brink of the great canyon talking in low tones. Behind us lay the golden spaceship which had brought us across the great void—now crumpled and useless for further flight, but still a home and haven, and streaming a flood of light from its open doorway.

And we were alone! The only man, the only woman upon the planet Earth! I said as much to Vonna, said it in a tired, lifeless tone.

"But we can begin it anew, my Jan," answered Vonna softly. "Can start this world all over again, just you and I."

"Begin all over again, remake the world, you and I?" I gave a tired shrug, my right arm hanging limp and useless at my side.

"Yes, yes, beloved," she went on eagerly, her beautiful face glowing with earnestness. "We can start again like the first pair in the dim and distant dawning. We have our strength, our hopes, our love. The ship is well provisioned, and we can stay in it during the coming winter. And then in the spring when the snows have gone and the world returns to sunshine, we can begin preparing for a home"—her voice dropped low, and faltered—"and perhaps for the beginning of a new race, Jan, with you and me as its parents."

I turned to find the golden girl looking eagerly at me, her lovely face lit with that wonderful light that needs no interpretation. And my arms went out and around her and I nodded my assent. And then our lips met in that long, long kiss that made us one forever.

Far out in the mighty void a single star shot across the heavens—falling—falling— falling!

ALSO AVAILABLE

Want to get an e-book for free? *The Infernal Bargain and Other Stories* is available exclusively for DMR Books mailing list subscribers. Go to www.DMRBooks.com and get your copy now!

Lands of the Earthquake by Henry Kuttner/Under a Dim Blue Sun by Howie K. Bentley – The first split release from DMR Books in the tradition of the Ace Double series! *Lands of the Earthquake* is a classic science-fantasy adventure from the pulp era that has never been published in book form before. On the flip side you'll find a brand new sword-and-planet tale. A US soldier hijacks a Nazi spaceship and lands on a planet threatened by snake-men!

The Thief of Forthe and Other Stories by Clifford Ball – After the death of Robert E. Howard, Clifford Ball was the first writer to follow in his footsteps and pen sword and sorcery stories for *Weird Tales*. For the first time ever, all of Ball's stories are collected into one volume. A must-have for pulp historians and fans of fantasy, horror, and weird fiction!

The Sapphire Goddess: The Fantasies of Nictzin Dyalhis – At last, the stories of one of the most unusual writers of weird fiction are collected! This volume contains all of Nictzin Dyalhis' works of fantasy and science fiction, many of which have never before been reprinted. Those who love the wild imagination and masterful prose of authors such as Clark Ashton Smith and C.L. Moore are sure to enjoy this collection.

The Chronicles of Caylen-Tor by Byron A. Roberts – The Wolf-King of the north, Caylen-Tor, does battle with imperial armies and sorcerous serpent-men in three exciting novellas! Spectacular sword-and-sorcery by the lyricist of Bal-Sagoth.

The Road to Infinity by Gael DeRoane – Aran Dyfar's wanderlust leads him on a quest to discover the mythical Road to Infinity. Along the way he encounters friends, monsters, and wonders beyond imagination. A picaresque adventure sure to please fans of Jack Vance's *Dying Earth* and *Lyonesse* series.

Death Dealers & Diabolists – Eight action-packed tales of swords and sorcery! Includes stories by Keith Taylor (author of the *Bard* series) and Buzz Dixon (writer for *Thundarr the Barbarian, G.I. Joe* and *Transformers*).

Warlords, Warlocks & Witches – Eight more fantastic tales of action and adventure! Features stories by David C. Smith *(Red Sonja, Oron)* and Geoff Blackwell *(Swords of Steel)*.

Swords of Steel Omnibus – *Swords of Steel,* with its novel concept of fantasy stories written by members of heavy metal bands, was the most critically-acclaimed sword-and-sorcery anthology series of recent years. Now every story from all three volumes is packaged together! Features Howie Bentley (Cauldron Born), Byron Roberts (Bal-Sagoth), E.C. Hellwell (Manilla Road), Mike Scalzi (Slough Feg) and many more.

Wulfhere by A.B. Higginson – In the Dark Ages of England, king-doms were ready to be carved out by any with the ambition and might to do so. The mightiest ruler of all was Penda, Lord of Mercia, a man as strong as he was ruthless. He had no equal in martial prowess, excepting his son Wulfhere... Originally serialized in the pages of the legendary pulp magazine *Adventure,* DMR Books is proud to present the first-ever publication of this historical novel in book form.

Karnov, Phantom-Clad Rider of the Cosmic Ice by Matthew Knight, Howie K. Bentley and Byron A. Roberts – Returning from battle, the warrior Karnov discovers his family murdered and his home-land ravaged by vampyres. Aided by witchcraft and sorcerous al-lies, will Karnov's powers and burning lust for retribution be enough to avenge his loved ones, or will undead wraiths corrupt the earth forever? Classic horror film atmosphere meets pulp-style swashbuckling adventure in this action-packed epic.

Renegade Swords – This anthology contains eight fantastic tales, each of them obscure or overlooked in some way. Includes stories by Robert E. Howard, Clark Ashton Smith, Manly Wade Wellman, and more!

Swordsmen from the Stars by Poul Anderson – Three classic novel-las from the pages of *Planet Stories.* Heroic science fantasy at its best!

The Eye of Sounnu by Schuyler Hernstrom – This collection con-tains all of Hernstrom's critically acclaimed stories for *Cirsova Magazine,* as well as a few uncollected and unpublished tales. Running the gamut from sword-and-sorcery to sci-fi, these heroic adventure stories will satisfy fans of Robert E. Howard and Jack Vance!